SMOOTH

A Novel

By

Alexandra Y. Caluen

SMOOTH

Cover design by RK Young

Cover photo by Preillumination SeTh @7seth
unsplash.com

This is a work of fiction. The characters of The L.A. Stories, the main events, and many of the named businesses are fictional. The Underground Cabaret and its productions are the author's invention. Any resemblance to real persons is entirely coincidental.

SMOOTH

The playlist:

(Don't You) Feel My Leg
Big Bad Voodoo Daddy

Sway
Pussycat Dolls

Hollywood Nocturne
Brian Setzer Orchestra

Mambo Swing
Big Bad Voodoo Daddy

Love's Great Ocean
k.d. lang

Blue Angel
Squirrel Nut Zippers

Bring Me Sunshine
The Jive Aces

Smooth
Carlos Santana feat. Rob Thomas

SMOOTH

CHAPTER 1

March 2011

Vince Connor absently tapped a rhythm on his cocktail glass, watched the bartender mix other people's drinks while shooting the shit with the bar back, and figured neither of them guessed he could understand what they were saying in Spanish. He'd caught a reference to the fact that he was sitting there alone. His phone was on the bar as if he was expecting a call. When he felt a tap on his shoulder, he glanced to the side. "Good, you made it."

"Did you think I'd bail?" His friend Elliott slid onto the next barstool.

"That's kind of how things are going recently."

"The Lounge Lizard Life letting you down?" There was a hint of a snicker from Elliott.

Vince mentally rolled his eyes. "Don't get me started. So what's up?"

"I have a big favor to ask you."

"Let me guess. You want to start your own real-estate office."

"Um, no." Still with the snicker.

It was all Vince could do not to sigh. *Suck it up.* Put on his best sardonic face and tone, act like this inevitable and laudable progression was not a personal blow. "I was hoping it would be the easy one. So, you're moving in with Alicia."

Elliott blinked. "Damn, you're good."

"I am old and wise." Vince swallowed some of his cocktail while Elliott gave in to the snicker. "But also I

1

could kind of see that coming. You've been dating for what, six months? That's a record, right?"

"Yeah, uh. How'd you guess I'm moving to her place?" Vince just gave him a look; he'd seen the inside of Elliott's apartment. "Right, okay. The big day is the last Saturday of the month. Can you help us out? We're hiring movers for the big stuff, but I'd really appreciate having you there to supervise the movers at my old place while I'm at the receiving end to direct traffic."

Vince had been having a minor flashback to the last time Elliott moved. "Wow, no heavy lifting?"

"We're too old for that shit."

"That is a damn fact." Vince took another sip of his drink. "You want one of these?"

"Yeah, actually. Just one." They got the bartender's attention and pretty soon Elliott received his requested beer.

They reminisced for a while, then were quiet for a moment. The bartender came over, checked in with Vince, and got his signal that they were done. He looked over at Elliott. "How about the fish?"

"The fish are coming along for the ride. But I'm doing that separately, they can't just slosh around in the back of a truck."

"I get that. Anyway, let's get you on the schedule." Vince woke up his phone and pulled up his calendar. "Here you go, 'help Elliott move' and next day, 'conduct mourning rituals.'"

"Huh?"

Vince sat back, smiling ruefully. Maybe Elliott hadn't really thought this part of it through. "Dating is one thing, cohabiting is another. Alicia's not going to want you hanging around at bars with me. Probably not even the one night a week we've been managing lately."

"But we'll still get together. And there's the office." They both knew it wouldn't be the same.

After a quiet moment Vince straightened up, drained his glass, and gave Elliott another look. "Don't encourage her to set me up with people. Not everybody needs to be part of a couple."

"Alicia wants her friends to be happy. And she likes you." Elliott didn't actually know any women who didn't like Vince.

"At least tell her to pick girls who like to dance."

Elliott laughed at that. "Yeah, okay." They walked out together, Vince heading one way down the street to his car, and Elliott the other. It was a strange feeling. Not the going-separate-ways, but the knowledge that this was a permanent change. It might have been a normal part of growing up, of becoming an adult, but it still felt like losing something.

Kelli Lopez only had her phone out to turn it off, but it buzzed in her hand. Seeing a text message from Brent should have lifted her spirits. Instead she rolled her eyes and thought seriously about not responding. A voice from above said, "Trouble?"

Kelli glanced up at her salsa teacher and shrugged. "Guy I've been going out with. Wants to get together."

"And?"

Sandra's tone betrayed amusement. Kelli huffed out an irritated breath. "Tonight! He's all like hey got tickets to the game wanna go. We had this long-ass conversation about sports. Or more accurately he gave me this long-ass presentation about why sports are great while I tried not to order three more drinks." Sandra laughed. "Well, come on! It's on a weeknight, it's downtown, it's *tonight*. He knows I'm out here with you on Thursdays." Kelli wouldn't have said the performance class was the absolute best part of her week, but only because she didn't want to sound pathetic. She'd been out in L.A. for almost four years. If this was the best she could do, she might have to admit her mama was right, and it was time to move back to Baltimore. She texted back much more politely than she wanted to. *Sorry not tonight, out in Santa Monica for my class, talk to you soon.* Put the phone away, duty done. "So when do I get to see you and José dance again?"

"We're doing Salsa On Two at the Challenge in May. You'll have fun once the group is done. There's a ton of social stuff to do." Sandra put out a hand and pulled Kelli to her feet. "Come on and warm up."

At work the next day, Kelli was feeling good. Her feet were sore in that pleasant 'I got to dance a lot' way, her voice was a little bit husky from laughing and talking so loud – the other people in the class were so much like her, it was hilarious – and she had a lunch date with a new work contact. The worst thing about living in a big city, one far away from family, was meeting people. Work friends were good, but when you were in HR there was always that 'can I trust you' thing. Kelli understood it, didn't resent it, but regretted it. She liked the work. It would have been nice to have co-workers she could just hang out with. So she was excited about meeting Alicia. They'd spoken on the phone a bunch of times – Alicia worked with a firm of legal recruiters – but this would be the first face-to-face. And they weren't going to be talking about a candidate; this was a personal meet-up, so Kelli was watching the clock. When the time came, she hustled across Avenue of the Stars to the mall and made her way to the restaurant.

"Hi! You must be Kelli!"

Eye contact with the well-dressed Asian woman waiting by the host stand, a smile, offering a hand. "You must be Alicia."

"How's my last placement doing?"

"Oh, she's great. Everybody's happy. Uh, I hope she told you that too."

Alicia laughed. "Yes she did. Good. We're ready," she told the host, who was wearing a 'let's get you to a table' expression. "So tell me what brought you to L.A."

"Girl, please. We only have an hour." Kelli was grinning because Alicia's laugh was so just-right.

The morning after Elliot's move, Vince was in his apartment, sprawled on the couch, squinting in the light from an east-facing window and holding a heat pack to his shoulder. A cup of coffee was steaming on the end table next to his ringing phone. A glance over at the display told him it was his friend Vicky. He picked up and connected. "Hey chica. What's new?"

"You're not gonna believe what we just did."

"Were you naked?"

"Nooooooo, my God, it's always the same with you. We told our coach we want to dance at the Gay Games in 2014."

Vince blinked. "Whoa, that's different."

"He's been trying to get me and Sharon to compete pretty much from day one, but he kept trying to match

5

us with guys at the studio, you know?"

The offended tone almost made him laugh. "The nerve."

"Right? So we looked up same-sex ballroom and you know what, it's actually a sport in the Gay Games." Vicky sounded thrilled about this.

Vince was deeply confused about this. It seemed like a minute ago, Vicky was his girlfriend. Friend with benefits, at least. Now she was talking about the do what? "Hang on a sec. Processing. Need coffee." He put down the heat pack, picked up the coffee cup, took a long drink.

Vicky said, singsong, "I'm waaaaitinnng."

"Right, I'm back. I helped Elliott move yesterday and wracked my neck. He said 'no heavy lifting,' and he lied. I have to move slowly."

"Aw, poor baby. If you had a girlfriend she could massage it for you."

"Oh, eat me."

Vicky laughed heartlessly, then added, singsong, "Not any moooorre."

"Damn, you've gotten *mean* since you dumped me!"

She was still laughing. "You're right, I'm sorry. Come over for dinner tonight and I'll fix your neck."

"Sounds great. What can I bring?"

"A few good stories. We can handle the rest."

"What time?"

"Let's say seven."

"See you then." Vince disconnected, finished his coffee, thought about the relative utility of doing anything else, and turned on the TV.

That evening, he pulled up outside an apartment building in Santa Monica. Walked up to the gate, carrying a bottle of wine, and rang in at the keypad. Vicky answered on the intercom. "That you, Vince?"

Vince did his best Bela Lugosi Dracula impression. "Good *evening*." The gate buzzed and he went in. He was greeted at the apartment door by Vicky, nearly his height in her bare feet, her lively black hair waving loose down her back. "You look great," he said, handing over the bottle.

"You look broken," she said critically.

"'Help me, Obi-wan Kenobi, you're my only hope.'"

"Get in here."

The table was set for three. Vicky thanked Vince for the wine and he waved to Sharon, who was busy in the adjacent kitchen. "So is that actual cooking I see happening?"

Sharon waved back. "Yep. We had one of those epiphanies."

"Oh yeah?"

"Yeah, we figured out that we can do steaks at home for about a quarter the price of Ruth's Chris and they're just as damn good."

"What's the secret?"

The women answered in unison. "Butter!"

Vince laughed, then winced. Vicky finished opening the wine, set it aside to breathe, and motioned him to a chair. He sat down, slumping a little. She dug her hand into his hair and lifted, not as gently as he would have liked. "Ow!"

"Sit up straight."

"Jeez, okay, bossy." She did a quick exploratory

massage of his shoulders and neck, found the problem, then spent a few minutes working the strained muscle. He bitched and yelped, and then sighed with relief.

"You're such a baby," said Sharon.

"She's got strong hands."

"The better to spank me with." All three of them laughed.

"So I hear you gals are going for the gold." Vince could now turn his head without wincing, so he forgave Vicky for the hair thing. Should have gotten it cut, so she couldn't do that.

Sharon made a sound best described as a groan. "We're so screwed."

"It'll be fun!" Vicky was snickering.

"Can you imagine us in Cincinnati, or wherever the hell it is, with a convention center full of actual, you know, athletes? And we're not exactly rainbow poster girls."

"Our parents are still in denial," Vicky told Vince.

"Well, does this thing make you pass some sort of gayness test?"

"I don't think so. We've got a lot to learn about it."

"We don't even know yet if there are qualifying events beforehand, or if we just, you know, show up in all our rhinestones and shit and say Hi!" Sharon flailed a little in the kitchen.

"So do you both wear dresses, or what?"

"Another thing we don't know. Honestly, we may not even end up going, but having something to shoot for just seems like it'll make our dancing more fun."

"Steaks are coming out!" announced the chef. Vicky gave the salad a toss and took a seat. Vince poured the wine, then filched a piece of warm bread from the basket. Sharon carried out three sizzling steaks on a board, and plopped them on the plates with a pair of tongs. She was back a moment later with a bowl of roasted vegetables. The conversation languished for a few minutes.

Vince sat back after demolishing his steak. "You're right, it's just as damn good."

"Thanks," said Sharon. "Seriously, the hardest part was learning to wait till the broiler was completely hot."

"Well, I mean, when you're hungry, you're hungry."

She pointed her fork at him. "Exactly!"

"So back to this whole dance fever you've got going on." He and Vicky used to dance a lot, so this made him the tiniest bit jealous. "Are you just taking all those lessons, or are you social?"

"We've gone to Cicada a few times, the Mayan, Monsoon, the Granada, and a few ballroom things."

"I usually go to the ballroom things in drag," Vicky said.

Vince was mildly astonished. "For real?"

"Pretty much. I wear tuxedo pants and a shirt, pull my hair back in a ponytail and tone the makeup down."

"Not that she looks like a guy," Sharon assured him.

"Uh, that would be *hell* no."

The women laughed. Sharon added, "We get the side-eye a little bit, but honestly there's so many extra ladies at these things. I think the straight gals are glad we're doing our own thing."

"Guys don't ask you to dance?"

"Oh yeah."

"The way she looks, of course they ask her to dance."
Vicky brushed her fingers across Sharon's hand.

Vince noticed. *Be something other than pathetic now.*
"There are moments of movie star going on there."

"That's what I think."

Sharon was smiling. "Aw, you're sweet." To
Vicky she added, "We should invite him over more
often."

Vince made an expansive gesture. "Plentiful and
sincere compliments in exchange for steak and a neck
massage, sounds like a good deal to me." He turned to
survey Vicky again. "And of course you've got the
Mafia Princess thing going. Actually I bet you look
extremely hot in drag."

"Yes. Yes, she does."

Vicky studied Vince for a moment. He still had the
Latin Lover thing going, and she still appreciated it
even though she'd moved on. "You know, Vince, if you
went to these ballroom things you would be swarmed."

"Swarmed," Sharon agreed, nodding.

"Eh, I don't know."

"The way you look, and the way you dance? If you
ever get tired of bars, give us a call. We'll take you to
the friendliest places."

Vince fiddled with his glass for a moment, then
gave her a rueful look. "I think I may actually be tired
of bars."

"Say *what?!*" Vicky sat up straight.

"There must be a story here. And you owe us a
couple of stories, fine wine notwithstanding," Sharon
pointed out.

"You know, now that I think about it, maybe our
Vince was already a little bit over the tomcattin' last year.

10

Remember our first date at the beach?"

"Ooh yeah. The one we didn't even know was a date."

Vince laughed. "My little jealous fit. Yeah, getting possessive, that was a new thing."

"I got a kick out of that," Sharon said smugly.

"How so?"

"Because *I* was jealous of *you* all the time."

Vicky said, "Wow, this is good for my ego."

Vince couldn't help smiling. "Well, you're something special."

"Hey. Back off, barfly." Sharon brandished her steak knife, and they all laughed again.

"So, do tell." Vicky topped up the wineglasses, emptying the bottle.

He took a drink, composing himself. "Okay, well, here's the story of my terrible, horrible, no good, very bad New Year's Eve. I went to a big salsa and swing thing in Palm Springs. Always tons of single ladies, right? And I was flying solo, thanks to *you*," he said, glaring at Sharon, who laughed, "so hey. I called up to order my pass and the gal working the passes was someone I know from the Mayan, and she told me I could have a free pass if I worked as a dance host because they needed extra guys."

"All dance things everywhere need extra guys. Extra guys who can actually dance, that is," Vicky specified, and Sharon nodded agreement. They shared a glance that was eloquent of stomped toes.

"So of course, free pass, no problem, right? I upgraded my room. Anyway there I am, New Year's Eve, everyone is dressed up and the music is good and there's this one little catch. Dance hosts aren't

11

supposed to be drinking."

Sharon hooted. "Wow, that must have been painful."

Vince nodded. "I am stone cold sober in a big loud room full of increasingly drunk people."

"Ballroom people don't drink very much," Vicky noted.

"And I've been pawed and groped all night by barely-legal little cholas and lonely middle-aged divorcées."

"What you get for being so goddamned handsome," Sharon said unsympathetically.

"Thanks?"

"Quit telling him he's handsome." Sharon did a 'duh, he *is*' thing and Vicky laughed. "Well, in ballroom we do have some LMDs but not many cholas."

"You're making it sound better all the time."

"So I'm guessing you were pretty sick of everybody by the time the ball dropped."

"I couldn't wait to get out of there. That's the first New Year's Day I've woken up alone since I was, like, seventeen. As pathetic as it sounds, it *sucked*." Vince didn't want to say 'I felt old,' but that's how it had felt.

"Aw. Poor old Vince. And of course I called and woke you up with my tale of conquest," Vicky said. "Insult to injury. If I wasn't still so smug about it, I might feel guilty."

"At least *somebody* had a good time." Vince emptied his glass.

Sharon said, "Okay, that's one. And you're right, it's pathetic. Let me get the dessert while you work up

12

story number two." She quickly cleared the table.

"Need any help, sweetie?"

"Nah. You can load the dishwasher later."

"Deal."

Sharon brought out a lemon meringue tart from Michel Richard, sliced it neatly, and served.

"Oh awesome, I love that thing," Vince said, fork poised.

Sharon agreed. "It's the best thing, isn't it?" They took their first few bites in appreciative silence.

"Damn, that's good. Okay, so next story. I make the mistake of going out the Friday after Valentine's Day."

"Why is that a mistake?" Sharon said, mouth full of meringue.

"Because the bars are full of bitter women who expected some kind of proposal." Vicky and Sharon both laughed, no surprise there. "Anyway, so I'm up at this little joint that's got a tiny dance floor and I ask this cute girl to dance. And we dance, and it's cool. Then I ask if I can get her a drink."

"Aaaaaaannnd?" Sharon prodded as he paused.

"And she practically spits in my face, 'what kind of slimeball are you' and hauls outta there like I pulled her panties off or something." Vince shook himself, troubled by the memory.

Vicky was nonplussed. "Jeez, that's … weird."

"Totally weird."

"I mean, I danced with you. A *lot*. You were never anything but a perfect gentleman. Even when I was next best thing to shitfaced."

"Well, thanks. The mamacita trained me pretty well. But what the fuck, right?"

13

"She was tripping," Sharon said. "You're not creepy."

"Not at all. What a freak."

Appreciating their reaction, Vince went on. "Anyway, it kind of put me off my game. I'm standing there thinking 'what did I do,' you know?"

"Just … wow. I know women can be freaks, but that is some serious freak."

"Maybe she got roofied before," Sharon suggested.

Vicky was not cutting any slack. "Then why the hell hang out in bars?"

"That's what I thought, too," Vince said, "after I got over it. If it's not gonna be fun, what's the point?" He changed the subject then, and had his usual good time with his friends. But on his drive home he couldn't help thinking about the way things used to be. Wondering what was next. He would have copped to the fact that Vicky had been significant for him. Not the love of his life, but not just another girlfriend. He also knew Sharon was exactly right for Vicky in more than one way that he wasn't.

His old ways weren't quite no fun, but were definitely not as much fun anymore. Was he ready to settle down? Not quite. Not in the sense his mother would like. He didn't know what his other options might be. All he knew was, he was ready for something different.

CHAPTER 2

Kelli scrolled through her options on the dating site, thinking *ugh* most of the way through. It couldn't be her imagination, could it? Did she have a bad attitude? Were there really no single guys out there who were less than five years older than she was, but not five years *younger* than she was, who had decent jobs and decent manners and were ready for a committed relationship that did not involve instant marriage and babies?

It wasn't that she didn't want to get married or have kids. Those things were definitely on her wishlist. But not right this second, like these late-thirties and over-forty guys wanted. Plus, after getting burned once she was disinclined to see 'ready for commitment' as anything more than a tagline. "You are getting cynical," she told herself out loud. "And you're not old enough for that shit."

But it *wasn't* her imagination. The guys she'd been out with so far in L.A. might be committed … except it was, without exception, to their sports team of choice. Okay, sometimes to their jobs. Not one of them seemed to think that *her* job was important, or that she had a right to prioritize a date with a girlfriend. Not one of them seemed to agree that her performance class had as much value as their fantasy-sports night or gaming night or last-minute long weekend in Cabo.

She'd've liked a long weekend in Cabo. But she was not the girl who was going to call in sick to work on a Friday for a long weekend in Cabo. Especially not when the invitation came eighteen hours (or less) before some guy planned to catch a flight. "Fuck you," she told the site, dismissing the last ten notifications. Maybe a talk with Diana would be a better use of her time. *Who am I kidding, of course it would be.* Kelli tapped her nails on the table while she listened to the phone ring. Her sister connected, finally, after four rings. "Well?"

Kelli cracked up. "Well what?"

"What's going on?"

"Does something have to be going on?"

"You're calling at a time when you should be getting ready for a date, so yeah. Talk to me."

A happy sigh, getting comfortable in the corner of her couch, settling in for a chat. "Thank you. I'm feeling cynical and burned-out so I needed to be reminded that breaking up with Hunter was the right thing to do."

"Let's see." Some getting-comfortable sounds on the other end. "Your college boyfriend who proposed right on schedule and said you were The One, then managed to find something wrong with every possible wedding date and venue and thing, up to and including the flowers, cake, music, first-dance song, and reception menu? The one who somehow never managed to find the ring he said he was going to give you? Who stood you up for a venue tour and then let some tramp post a picture of them out on a harbor cruise? Whose name was God-help-us *Hunter*?"

Kelli managed to stop laughing long enough to gasp out "I know!!"

"Yeah, honey. Breaking up was the right thing to do."

"I just." Kelli sighed again, less happily. "I thought by the time I was thirty for sure. Five years to get over that idiot and try out a new city, fresh start, big pond with lots of fish in it. Now here I am officially launched on my fourth decade and *shit*."

Diana snorted out a laugh, trying to stifle it because all the rest of them got married before thirty. Nobody was exactly putting the pressure on (except their mother) but it was one of those Things. "I'm sorry baby. You're dating, though, right?" Kelli made a disgruntled sound that meant 'kind of.' Diana said something to someone else, probably her husband the doctor. Kelli thought dark and envious thoughts, waiting to hear what her big sister had to say next. "What's the common denominator?"

"Of the guys I should like and don't? Fucking sports. Why is it always fucking *sports*? This city has everything! There's plays and live music and clubs and, shit, I don't know. Kayaking in the marina, whatever. I'd rather go to Third Street Promenade and people-watch for six hours than sit through some goddamned basketball game. And don't say baseball," she added, because Diana's man bled Orioles orange. There was another stifled laugh, followed by a slightly-apologetic sound, at the Baltimore end. Kelli rolled her eyes as if Diana could see her. "I'm not giving up. But I'm over this online dating bullshit. I'm going to throw myself on the mercy of my friends, and their friends, and anyone else who asks. Find me a man. Preferably a man who can dance."

"And who doesn't give a shit about sports," Diana suggested.

"Please God. Tell me about your kid." That was always a great subject-changer. Kelli stared out the window, half-smiling while she listened to the latest about her nephew.

June 2011

Vince turned sideways to the bar, looking out over a packed club, unconsciously tapping on his cocktail glass in time with the thumping music. He watched the ebb and flow of people on the cramped dance floor, watched people dancing with drinks in hand, watched guys go back to groups of guys and girls go back to groups of girls. One young woman took a phone picture of herself and her friends. They all made the duck face. They were all cute. He couldn't have been less interested in them. He finished his cocktail and left, uncomfortably aware that this was really not his scene anymore.

As he walked out the back, Vince glanced at a small table between the restroom doors. It was littered with cards and flyers for Hollywood happenings. He sifted through idly until his eye was caught by a stack of cards for a burlesque show called 'Underground Cabaret.' He took one with him.

A little later, he walked up to the back door of a club on the east side of Hollywood. Glanced at the person selling tickets and did a double take. "Well, hello."

The hostile girl said, "Hello."

"You don't remember me, huh."

"Yeah, actually. Sorry about that. Bad night. One ticket?"

"Yeah."

"Enjoy the show."

He took his ticket and went inside. A short hall took him to a stairway leading down to a basement. The stairs opened to a large room, packed with bar-height two-tops, except directly in front of a sizable stage, where there were lounge-height four-tops. Each of those was marked Reserved. In the middle of the stage was a chrome dance pole. To the right of the stage was a long bar.

Vince found an empty table and hitched up on a stool. Within seconds a long-legged blonde in a bustier, tulle miniskirt, and fishnet tights was there to take his drink order. "What can I get you?"

"Hey, whiskey sour please, and a bottle of water."

"Whiskey sour, water, twelve dollars."

Vince gave her fifteen. "Keep the change. When does the show start?"

The waitress glanced at a bulky, rhinestone-encrusted wristwatch. "Um, thirty-five minutes. About."

"Great." She smiled and buzzed off to the bar, taking three more drink orders along the way. Long before Vince got bored with watching people, she was back with his drink order. "Perfect timing." She also placed a small plate of cheese and crackers on his table. "What's this?"

"Gift of the management." A saucy smile went with it.

Vince smiled back. "This is my new favorite hangout."

The waitress buzzed off again. The club was full and people were still coming in. Vince ate his snack and sipped his cocktail, enjoying the old-fashioned burlesque music being piped in. He turned at a tap on his shoulder; it was the pretty waitress. "Do you mind sharing a table?"

"With you?" That would improve the night even more.

She laughed. "I wish. This is a friend of one of the

performers, can he sit with you or are you expecting someone?"

"No, this seat is open. It's fine."

"Thanks!" She vanished again.

The friend said, "Hey, thanks a lot." He offered a hand. "I'm Will."

They shook. "Vince. Guess you just made it, huh?"

"They never start on time, but close enough. Marcy would've killed me if I missed her act."

"Have you seen this show before?"

"Not exactly. It's a company, kind of, but they don't do the same show every time." Vince made an inquiring face. "It's semi-pro, one of those labor of love things."

"But they're good?"

"Wait and see." Will smiled, looking confident. Vince was intrigued. A few minutes later, the lighting and music changed, and a flurry of activity was heard behind the curtain. "Sounds like they're about to start." Will was right; the house lights went down.

Vince watched with amusement, surprise, and enjoyment as the show progressed. Acts included classic burlesque, aerial silk, and aerial pole. The scantily-clad performers were all shapes, sizes, and colors.

Will said, in an undertone, "That's Marcy." Vince nodded, eyebrows shooting up as the tiny Asian woman on stage did a flagpole move. It was the most impressive of the acrobatics the dancers had shown off.

One act toward the end featured a pair of girls and a man, who mostly sat in a chair while the women danced around him. Will nodded toward the guy and said, again in an undertone, "He's one of their regular man props."

"Tough gig." They both stifled laughter. Vince felt someone pass behind him and saw the waitress go quickly by, whiffing her ticket book across Will's head. He ducked just in time. When the show was over, Vince applauded with the rest of the noisy crowd. "That was seriously cool. Sexy, but not skanky."

"Not what you expected?"

"I had no idea what to expect, picked up the card on my way out of a boring bar. Tell your friend I really liked her act. And also, major muscle tone."

"She teaches pole at one of the big gyms."

"Well, my hat's off. These ladies all look like they could bench-press my ass."

"Think you'll come again?"

"Definitely." Vince slid off his barstool and glanced toward the exit.

"If you don't have to go straight home, I could introduce you to some people," Will offered.

"Okay," Vince said, surprised but willing. "Great."

The next day, he dragged into the office. Elliott studied him for a second. "Was there a bachelor party I didn't know about?"

It hadn't been that long, but Vince was fully expecting the next bachelor party to be Elliott's. Instead of saying that, he said, "Went to a bar, got bored, on the way out picked up a card for a burlesque show."

"A what?"

"Burlesque. But it was more like Cirque du Soleil or something. Didn't start till 10:30, and then I hung around for a while after the show meeting people."

"People like girls?"

"Well, obviously girls. But a few guys too. Pretty much everyone in the cast plus their significant others plus friends and family plus random people like me. Turned into kind of an after party. Most fun I've had since you and Alicia shacked up." He hadn't meant to say that. He and Elliott were squarely in the 'don't let on how much we like each other' guy zone.

"What kind of show was it?"

"A little of everything. Some striptease, some pole dancers, a couple of aerialists, and a partner piece where a pair of girls danced with a guy. Pretty hot."

"Would I like it? How about Alicia?"

"Yeah, I think so. Their next show is in five weeks."

"Maybe we could go together."

"Cool." He woke up his computer and started reading through the email.

A week after his introduction to the Underground Cabaret, Vince met Will after work at the Lucky Strike. The other man was standing by the bar, waiting. "Hey dude! Great choice of venue. Thanks for coming downtown."

"Not a problem," Vince said as they shook hands.

"You bowl?"

"Never. When I'm down here, I'm usually next door at the Conga Room."

"Ah, a salsa man."

"Sí señor."

"I dated a girl who was majorly into salsa dancing. She dumped me when I kept not getting the difference between an inside and outside turn."

Vince laughed. "How much time did she give you?"

"Oh, she was patient. Three whole months. I'm not what you'd call gifted."

"You like dancing though?"

"I do, I just need structure. And a lot of patience!"

"Ever try ballroom?"

"Not yet."

"I've got these girl friends who keep telling me I need to go that way. Quote, you would be swarmed, unquote."

"But you're holding out for a salsa girl?"

"Not really." He looked away for a moment, debating whether to verbalize. "I guess I haven't made up my mind what to do with my life. My best guy friend shacked up with his girlfriend this spring, they'll probably be getting married, and it occurred to me I'm getting a little bored with hanging around in bars picking up chicks." *Maybe because I'm getting older and they're not*, he thought grimly.

"Well, there's always show business. David, the man prop in Marcy's last show? He's bowing out."

"Can't take the heat?"

"His boyfriend got a good job in Tahoe and they're moving."

Somehow Vince hadn't thought of that. He mentally smacked himself. "Huh."

"I know what you mean, though. At a certain point you do kind of look around and think, what's next."

Drinks and small plates were ordered and consumed as the guys continued getting to know each

23

other. "So I have two questions for you," Vince said, after a while.

"Shoot."

"The woman who was on the door at the last show."

"Oh yikes. You met Randa."

"I had the pleasure of dancing with her once at a club and then getting the verbal equivalent of a baseball bat upside my head when I offered to buy her a drink."

"Randa … has issues. She, um. There was a thing with a guy in a bar and it went really, really wrong."

"This, I could intuit."

"But she loves to dance and the only places to dance are bars, basically."

"She could try, I don't know, a dance *studio*. Whatever, moving on. The leggy waitress who looks like Marilyn Monroe. What was her name again?"

"Michelle."

"Is she part of the company?"

"Yeah. She's working on a piece for the next audition. Her specialty is aerial pole, same as Marcy."

"But completely different styles, I'll bet. Marcy's like." Vince thought for a second. "She reminds me of that Japanese backup dancer on Madonna's Girlie Show tour."

"Yeah! Though honestly, I can't believe I even know who you mean. I may have been watching too much girl-centric performance art lately."

Vince laughed. "Dude, is there really such a thing as too much of that? So, Michelle. I'll remember that for next time. Gonna bring a couple of friends."

Things were looking very slightly up in Kelli World. Work was going fine, and the performance class had won its event at the L.A. Salsa Challenge. She'd had a couple tolerable dates with straight guys and a fantastic night at a bar with a professional salsero she met at the Challenge. He was a friend of Sandra's, and if she were interested in pro-am competition she'd be all over him. But that shit got expensive fast. She booked a coaching session with him instead (mostly to impress her classmates with 'I took a private with Ricky Castillo'). And told herself very firmly to not be pissed at the guy for being gay, but *damn*.

On a week with no other social plans, she took Alicia up on the offer to join her and another friend at Monsoon for happy hour. If Kelli and the friend didn't click, she could always ease herself out. Go upstairs to the live-music room and dance a little.

They met up in the cramped bar, ordering a few appies to lay down a base for their drinks. Alicia lived in West L.A. like Kelli, but her friend Maria had to drive all the way down to Redondo Beach after this. She was making Alicia and Kelli laugh, telling stories about the negotiation between her and her husband. "He wanted to live down in the South Bay because he works in Long Beach. And okay, that makes sense. But I work in Beverly Hills, which let me tell you is a shitty commute."

Kelli didn't even want to think about it. There were days when the barely-a-mile between her place and Century City took half an hour. "You couldn't compromise on, like, Culver City?"

Maria made a face. "We couldn't find a place we liked. The nice neighborhoods are really high, and the affordable neighborhoods are really sketchy. Who knows, maybe someday I'll get a job down south and all my bitching will end." She drank some of her cocktail.

Alicia was looking sympathetic. "I feel really lucky that Elliott was happy to move in with me. He's got a low satisfaction bar for living space after working in real estate for so long." The other women made noises of amused comprehension. "It's like, if you can't see through the floor or walls or ceiling, and there's not an active drug den next door, snap it up."

Kelli snorted out a laugh. "I had a minute of thinking gee, maybe I should look into buying something. And then I looked for a minute and thought RUN AWAY." She didn't say it all that loud, but a few people around them turned to look. She made an 'eek' face at Alicia. "Was I loud?"

"Not really," Alicia lied, giggling into her drink. "You saw one of those Beverly Hills-adjacent tear-downs that was on the market for a million dollars, didn't you?"

"I did! It was terrible! A hundred years old and just needed to be scraped off planet Earth. The lot wasn't even big! Didn't have a single tree!"

"People who can pay a million dollars for an empty lot can buy full-size trees," Maria pointed out. "I feel you, though. Our place isn't very big, but at least we have a nice eucalyptus."

"Maybe you'll get lucky too," Alicia said with a sideways smile at Kelli. "Find yourself someone to move in with."

Kelli raised her glass. "From your lips to God's ear."

Alicia stared at her for a few seconds. "Hmm."

"What?" Kelli got excited. "Did you think of

somebody?"

"Elliott's got a friend at the office. Want me to send a note? If E tells him to come out here, and he's not doing anything else, he might. He's pretty easygoing."

Kelli tried to decode that. Did it mean 'doesn't have anything else to do' or did it mean 'desperate' or what? Well, whatever, never mind. "Sure, why not?"

Meanwhile, Vince was at home, flipping through channels on the TV, bored and generally dissatisfied with life. When his phone rang he barely glanced at it before picking it up. "Yo."

Elliott said, "Alicia has a message for you."

"She knows it's safe to talk to me herself, right?"

"Yeah, she's not here, she just sent me a text. Anyway she's out with friends at a happy hour and one of them is someone she thinks you would like. If you're interested, they're at Monsoon."

Santa Monica was a long way from West Hollywood. "Fuck me, all the way over there?"

"Get your lazy old ass out of the house," Elliott said, laughing. Vince grumbled his way off the phone, already heading for his closet to change his shirt and pull a sport coat off the hanger.

Not too much later, he walked out of the parking deck at Fourth and Wilshire and around the corner to the Third Street Promenade. There was plenty of foot traffic and the bar crowd was spilling out of several venues. He sidled into the packed bar at Monsoon.

"Vince!" Alicia waved at him from a tall table squeezed into a corner by the window. Two other pretty women were with her. Vince threaded his way through the crowd. He didn't see the look one of Alicia's friends was giving her.

Kelli had a lot of experience with 'you should meet my friend.' Sometimes it went fine, sometimes it was best forgotten. This was the first time she'd turned to the person setting the thing up and said "Are you serious?" in a way that did not mean 'you'll pay for this later.' Alicia snickered. "Is he really single?" Alicia nodded. It was too late to get more information, because he was there.

"Hey Alicia. You look gorgeous." She offered her cheek and he kissed it. "So should I pretend I just happened by?"

"We are all aware that this has been engineered," she said dryly. "Ladies, this is Vince, my boyfriend's best friend. Vince, this is my old friend Maria – I think you've met before – and my new friend Kelli."

Maria said, "Hi Vince, we met at the housewarming. Nice to see you again."

"Hi Maria." He leaned in to kiss her cheek, then turned to the new girl. *Wow*. "And Kelli, is it? With a Y or an I?"

"With an I, and it's my parents' fault. Nice to meet you. So Elliott called you?" She couldn't help sounding amused. "Does he always do what Alicia says?"

He couldn't help smiling at her. "Mostly." All three women laughed. "I was sitting at home, doing nothing, so when I got this life-saving phone call telling me there was someone I need to meet down here, I was like, sign me up."

"Gives me a whole new appreciation for the social network." She was still amused, but she liked his candor. And his face. And what she'd seen of his body as he slithered through the crowd.

Vince was appreciating the network, too. He noticed that Kelli looked him in the eyes with her chin tipped slightly up. The posture showed off her slender neck. "Are you a dancer, by any chance?"

"As a matter of fact." Kelli thought he must have a reason for asking, and hoped it was the reason that came to mind.

Alicia answered the question by noting, "I have it on good authority that Vince is an excellent dancer."

"And if I'm not mistaken, the band is due to start upstairs in about fifteen minutes," Maria said helpfully.

Vince was still looking at Kelli. She had braided black hair, light brown skin, and big Bambi eyes over high cheekbones and that luscious, smiling mouth. He was a little dazzled. "Then we might have time to squeeze in there. If you'd like to."

Would I huh. Kelli hadn't been introduced to someone like this for quite a while. Or ever. "I'd love to. Ladies, it's been a pleasure and I'll hope to catch up with you soon." The women all shook hands in a businesslike way and then dissolved into giggles.

Kelli slid off her barstool and Vince saw that she was wearing dance-friendly high-heeled shoes. She was the perfect height for him. He looked at Alicia and Maria again. "Great to see you, ladies. Drive safe home." He pressed a hand to his heart and shaped the words 'thank you.'

"Will do," said Alicia, giggling.

"Bye, Vince. Have fun."

Vince nodded and turned away, making a path for Kelli to precede him to the stairs leading up to the mezzanine. "Are you looking at my ass?" she said over

29

her shoulder.

"Of course." *Slap or laugh?* he wagered with himself, and won. He kept winning all night. They laughed at each other's jokes, figured out their lead and follow in about five seconds, liked the same songs. Vince was glad the music room was so small. Usually he preferred having some extra space to maneuver, but he liked being close to Kelli. Liked it so much that by the time the band shut down and the DJ came on, they weren't really doing salsa at all. It was more like an animated hug: body to body, keeping time to the music. Not looking at each other, because they were too close.

She sighed at the changeover. "That probably means it's time to go home."

Vince slowed, then stopped moving. He didn't want to go home. He wanted to stay out all night, doing exactly this. Instead he said, "Probably so. Can I walk you to your car?"

Kelli eased back, just enough to make eye contact. "I'd like that."

CHAPTER 3

All the way home, Kelli was trying not to freak out. It was half delight and half panic. When she got home she sent a text to Alicia: *I hope you don't get this till tomorrow because your phone should be OFF by now young lady but HOLY HELL what is wrong with him because I didn't spot anything and if nothing's wrong WHY IS HE SINGLE because DAMN*

The reply was waiting when she turned her phone on in the morning: *LOL OMG I know!! He and Elliott used to pub crawl, they've worked together for a while, AFAIK he is only single because he doesn't know what to do next*

Next since what

Next since Elliott isn't pub crawling any more. I asked E if he thought V was ready to get serious with someone and he said he honestly didn't know, but that V hasn't been dating around the way he used to. So maybe?

Is Vince short for Vincent? I forgot to ask

Short for Vicente. His mother's from Mexicali

Oh lord that explains the hair skin eyes mercy me those eyes yummy yum yum

LOL don't you have a job to get to?

Yeah but whatever. Thanks for the intro chica!

YW TTYL. Kelli could have kept chatting with Alicia all day, but she put the phone down and started getting ready for work. Her concentration was going to be crap today. It might have been screwed anyway by the great night of dancing, but the gentlemanly escort back to her car, and the complete lack of pressure, and

31

the invitation to dinner on Friday: she was toast.

Her mind was a little more clear this morning than the night before. She could more rationally appreciate the way that man demonstrated attraction without ever once being skeevy or gross. None of the usual not-so-sly innuendo or blatant propositions. Only the gaze and touch and body language that said 'you're sexy' and 'you're fun' and 'I like you.' He was definitely interested, and he could probably tell she would have gone home with him. But instead of asking for that, he asked her out to dinner. "Keep a hold of yourself girl," she said out loud. "And keep it *to* yourself." If she started telling people, she'd look like a fool if it didn't work out. And even though her connection with Vince felt very different from the usual, it still might not work out. She'd know better on Saturday. Either way, she'd be on the phone to Diana after their dinner date. *God I hope I have something good to tell her.*

Vince had been at work for two hours when Elliott loped in. "Hey. Early showing?"

"Yeah. Finally, some action in the market."

"No shit. I feel like all I've done for the last eighteen months is refer for re-financing."

"So how'd it go last night?"

"That is one *hot* chick. Tell Alicia I appreciate the setup." He tried to sound casual.

"Did you score?"

"Jesus, Elliot. What are we, sixteen?"

"I take it that's a No."

Vince laughed. "Fuck you. I'll have you know that I walked her sedately to her car and held the line at a gentlemanly peck on the cheek."

"Who are you and what have you done with my friend Vince?"

"Your friend Vince had a revelation last night."

"Going to see her again?"

"Dinner Friday."

"Dinner?" Elliott was still skeptical, but also very interested; Vince hadn't been on a serious date for nearly a year.

"Yeah. She's a great dancer but actually I want a chance to talk to her."

"*Talk*?"

"Shut up." Vince turned back to his work, ignoring his laughing friend, already counting the hours.

A few days later, Vince was leaning against the bar at Morton's when Kelli walked in. The bartender gave himself whiplash getting an eyeful of her curves, well-packaged in a scarlet wrap dress. Kelli gave a pleasant nod to the host and looked past her into the bar. Vince took an involuntary step toward her. "I'm meeting this gentleman," Kelli said, looking straight at him. He was wearing a suit, the color somewhere between charcoal and navy, with a blue paisley shirt and no tie.

"Welcome," said the host.

Kelli smiled at her absently, then walked up to Vince. "I've been looking forward to this."

"Me too." They looked at each other at close range for a moment. Her gaze dropped to his mouth, then lifted to his eyes. She wasn't quite smiling. Vince wasn't quite breathing. He had to clear his throat before he spoke. "I believe our table is ready. But would you like a drink first?"

"No, let's go on in." He nodded to the bartender

33

and put a hand lightly on Kelli's back as the host ushered them into the dining room. They settled into a big, curved booth. "Oh my. We get all this?" It was nice to have some space between them; on the other hand, it seemed like a little too much space. She scooted toward the inside.

Vince slid in, not crowding her. "The benefit of making a reservation for an early seating."

"I'll have to remember that. I've been going to places that don't take reservations for so long, I forget how it's supposed to work."

The host handed them menus and said something pleasant about their server before walking off. Vince took a moment to comprehend how close Kelli was, consider how little he cared what he ate tonight, and make a decision. "Let's look at these now, okay? I think I want to minimize service interruptions."

She'd been watching every move he made, noticing how he moved in close (but not too close). Noticing how this man, with his excellent manners, had acknowledged the host in a very distracted way. *He is caught.* It was a thrill. After a second she remembered he'd said something. "I think I know exactly what you mean."

They concentrated. They gave their orders. And then they gazed at each other again. "You look spectacular tonight," he said.

"Thanks. So do you." She smiled.

So did Vince, before realizing he was leaning toward her and straightening up. There was some ground he wanted to cover. So many things they hadn't asked each other yet. "Okay, top five answers, let's get them out of the way. One, not religious. Two, never been married, no kids. Three, no siblings, parents

34

divorced, Ma lives in town and taught me how to salsa. Four, mortgage broker. Five, thirty-two and intensely attracted to you."

Kelli fanned herself a little. "Woo! Let me catch my breath a second here." She was given a break as the wine arrived. They waited for the bottle to be opened and approved, for the glasses to be filled, for the server to leave. "Okay." She took a deep breath. "One, ex-Catholic. Two, never married, no kids. Three, two sisters, one brother, parents still married and live in Baltimore. Four, human resources admin. Five, thirty-one and is it hot in here?"

"Yes. Yes, it is." Vince was sitting back against the upholstery, one arm stretched across the top of the banquette. Kelli was sitting forward, holding her wineglass between both hands. "Have you ever seen 'Annie Hall'?"

"Not for a long time."

"There's this scene where Woody and Diane are walking down the street on, like, their first date, on their way to dinner, and he says something about how they should kiss now and get it over with so they can digest their food."

"I did not remember that. But it sounds like a decent strategy." She so hoped this was going where she wanted it to. Her gaze dropped to his mouth again.

"May I?"

Oh thank you Jesus. "*Please.*"

Vince leaned forward, and Kelli turned toward him. He lifted a hand and placed it lightly on her face, his thumb brushing her mouth. Her lips parted, and he didn't hesitate. Neither did she. They kissed. And kissed. And kissed.

Much later, they left the restaurant carrying to-go packages and suppressing laughter. "That is possibly *the* best restaurant in Los Angeles," Vince observed.

"Oh my lord. I came up for air and there was that nice waiter with our salad and he's so matter of fact! Like Nuyorican chicas are climbing all over people in his booths all day long, no big deal, enjoy your dinner!"

"The quintessence of good service." He started to snicker and in another second they both lost it. After they settled down, he said, "I swear to you, I have not behaved that badly since I was, like, eighteen."

"I'm going to take that as a compliment. And personally, I think I deserve some kind of award for not jumping on you right in the bar."

Vince laughed. "I wish you had. You want to walk around the block before we get our cars?"

"That's a good idea."

They walked slowly, Vince watching out for uneven sidewalk. They didn't talk much. Maybe both of them felt they needed to give themselves time to consider all the things they'd talked about over dinner. As they came back around to the valet, he gently stopped her. She turned toward him. He wrapped his free arm around her and held her close for a long moment. Then he dipped his face into the curve of her neck and spoke. "I'm not going to risk kissing you again right now."

Kelli said, a little breathless, "Probably wise."

"I'll call you tomorrow afternoon."

She believed him. "Okay." He slowly stepped back and they looked at each other for another long moment. "Let's get our cars. Before all these good intentions go to hell."

He huffed out a laugh. "Yeah."

There was a text from Alicia waiting when Kelli checked her phone: *Well??*

She wrote back immediately because she couldn't stand not to: *OMG OMG OMG*

LOL so I guess it was a good date?

Girl please I almost banged him right there on the table

ROFLMAO did he kiss you?

DID HE EVER

LOL OMG Kelli you crack me up what's next?

He said he'll call me tomorrow. If he does, then I will know he actually is perfect and I can commence planning our wedding. JK but OMG. Btw that reminds me

No not yet, we haven't even lived together for six months, give him a minute!

LOL okay. I have to do something right now

Not asking, don't want to know, see you soon!

The next morning, Kelli got on the phone with her sister. She hadn't called after the salsa night, even though she'd been longing to squee to someone besides Alicia, only because there was still so much that could go wrong. But now, "Oh lord, Diana, this guy!"

"Tell me about him."

"He looks like Antonio Banderas, he's a great dancer, he's a mortgage broker and he kissed me in the restaurant."

Diana laughed. "Did you have dinner too?"

"Yes we did and it was mighty good. But holy hell, girl. If the waiter hadn't come up with our salads I don't know *what* might have happened! I've never been so mortified!"

"Lost track of time a little?"

"Lost track of *everything* a little! Damn it, my first time going to Morton's and I can never go back!"

"Oh come on. You think a swanky restaurant in Beverly Hills hasn't seen worse than a little kissing?"

"Girl, this was not *a little kissing*. This was, like, *get a room*."

They both laughed. Then Diana said, "So did you?"

"No. He was a perfect gentleman. Damn it." Diana was laughing again. "Lord have mercy. Tell me what's going on with you." Trying to be polite and change the subject.

"Oh, old married lady stuff. Nothing new. When are you going to see him again?"

"I don't know yet. He said he'd call this afternoon."

"Think he will?"

"I think he'd've called this morning if he didn't know it would make him look desperate." Kelli heard her sister giggling. She tried again to change the subject, but she couldn't. "Don't tell Mom yet."

"What?! Why?"

"Because I can't talk about this with her. She'll be all how many children does he want and I'll be all mind your own business and we'll have a fight and then I'll feel guilty and I'll act weird the next time I see him."

Diana was laser-focused. "Have you already talked about that stuff? Did I hear you right, this was the second time you've seen him?"

"You heard me right. I swear to God, Diana. The

night we met felt like our fifth or sixth date, it was so easy. This time it was like he'd spent the whole time in between thinking about what I needed to hear to know he was going into this seriously." And the fact that he would put that much thought into it so early, or at all, was still blowing her mind.

"Wow."

"I know!!" Kelli blew out a breath. "It was like the difference between a candidate who's just kind of seeing what's out there, and a candidate who really wants the job. Not just any job, the specific job."

Diana didn't blame her sister for not wanting to have this conversation with their mother yet. "Can I tell Steve?"

"Oh, sure. What's new with him?"

Diana sighed. "The medical center softball team is trying to recruit him."

"That's a terrible idea!"

"I know!" Diana launched into the story. Kelli settled back in the corner of her couch to listen.

Meanwhile, Vince was on the phone with Will. "So what's up?"

"Michelle asked me if I would call you. She's having trouble with her new piece. She was hoping to work with David on this one and since he skated she's freaking out a little. I might have mentioned you were a dancer and she kind of squealed and made that puppy noise, so I said I would call you," Will said.

Vince blinked, trying to decipher that. "Uh, so she needs a, what did you call it?"

"A man prop."

"Well, I don't object to talking to her about it, but

I kind of doubt I have the right skill set," Vince said.

"She probably just needs some help sparking some ideas."

"Give me the digits." Will gave Vince the phone number and they ended the call. Vince thought for a few minutes. He became aware of the music he had playing and smiled to himself. When the song ended, he dialed the phone.

Vicky answered. "Hey chico! What's up?"

"I have a really far-out proposition for you."

"Vince, we've been over this." Her tone was dry.

He laughed. "You've heard that one so many times it doesn't qualify as far-out. There's this burlesque outfit I went to see." He told her all about it, and then about the Michelle situation. Vicky didn't take much convincing, though she did give him some crap for not mentioning the burlesque thing before. "Whatever, pick me up when you get to WeHo."

"Sure, fine. See you later."

Around noon, Vince, Vicky, and Sharon rolled up outside a West Hollywood apartment building. They all piled out of Vicky's car and walked up the stairs to the door. Michelle flung it open. "My heroes!!" She stood back to let them into an almost bare studio apartment.

A daybed was pushed up against one wall, a chair and a small table were in the opposite corner underneath a couple of shelves with a small stereo and a few books, and in the middle of the old hardwood floor was a tension-mounted dance pole. "Wow. Is that safe?" Sharon sounded doubtful.

"So far. Thank you so much for coming. Can I get you all anything to drink?"

"No, we're good," said Vince. "Listen, Will kind

of gave me the background but I wanted to ask how far along you were with your piece."

"I had some music picked out but I had David in mind, and without him it just sucks, and frankly I haven't been able to settle on anything. I'm desperate."

"I was listening to something this morning and, you gotta understand I know nothing about how to do what you do, but I thought maybe this had potential so I brought it over. If you like it, Vicky and Sharon said they would dance one style to it for you, and then Vicky and I will dance a different style, and maybe that'll get the juices flowing."

"Sounds awesome. Thank you, thank you. CD or iPod?"

"CD. Here, it's track four."

Michelle looked at the track title. "Well, it certainly sounds promising." She loaded the CD and cued the track. Big Bad Voodoo Daddy's '(Don't you) Feel My Leg' started to play.

They all listened to the spoken introduction and Vicky snickered, kicking off her loafers. "I remember this one! Come on, Sharon, get those shoes off." She and Sharon started dancing in their sock feet, doing a bluesy foxtrot to the slow swing. Vince and Michelle backed up to the wall to give the other women space.

"That is so cool," Michelle said, almost wistfully.

After a minute or so Vince cut in, leading Vicky in a West Coast Swing. Sharon said to Michelle, "What do you think?"

"It's awesome. It's hilarious. I love it. And you two are so great. How long have you been dancing?"

"Just a year or so, but we take a lot of lessons."

"That's the way."

Vince gave Vicky a spin and a drop as the music ended. "Whee! Man, you're strong for a short guy."

Vince laughed. "Bite me, glamazon."

"We need to do that drop. If we're gonna do this competition crap we've got to have a big finish," Sharon pointed out. Vince caught her hand and spun her into the ending position; she squeaked with alarm and Vicky laughed. Vince set Sharon back on her feet and she scurried over to Vicky.

"So, Michelle." Vince gave her an inquiring look.

"It's perfect. You're a genius. Would you, um." Michelle shook herself, giving a very strong impression of 'nothing ventured.' "Would you consider doing it with me?"

He blinked, a little surprised that she was actually asking. Thought about it, made a 'maybe' face. "If you had asked a week ago there would be absolutely no question in my mind. But there's someone else in the picture and so I can't say yes right away. I'll call you tonight to let you know, though. Keep the CD for now and get started."

"Yes sir. Thank you all so *very* much!"

"Our pleasure," said Vicky, staring at Vince. "And now we're all warmed up for our practice."

"Which we had better get going for. When's this show supposed to be, again?" Sharon directed that at Michelle.

"Oh jeez, it's in three weeks."

Sharon looked at Vicky. "Think we can go?"

"I don't see why not."

"I'll call you later," Vince said to Michelle. "Bye for now."

The friends collected hugs from Michelle and then

took off. They heard the track start to play again as they walked to the car. Vicky said casually, "So I am absolutely dying of curiosity about this person you need to check with."

"Yeah, I knew you would be. I hope you'll be meeting her soon."

"And you've known her a week?" Sharon said.

Vince could tell they were skeptical. Or something. "Weird, right? I just feel like there's something unusual going on, and I don't want to be casual about it. Come on, snoopies. I'll walk home from the studio."

Vicky put the car in gear. It wasn't far to the place they were taking lessons. "What else are you doing today?"

He ran a hand through his hair. "Might go get a haircut. It's getting rowdy."

"No, leave it," Sharon said emphatically.

"Say what?" Vince usually didn't pay attention when these two busted his chops, but he had a sense that things were changing. Sharon hadn't sounded like her intention was to give him a hard time. And he knew that however snarky they all got with each other, she and Vicky only wanted the best for him. "You think it would be better longer?"

"Let it grow. Trust me."

When he got back to his apartment, Vince couldn't settle down. He fidgeted, looked around and did some basic tidying-up, checked the time and thought *not yet*. He was desperate for something to do to keep from calling too early and looking desperate.

It occurred to him that his apartment looked like a bachelor pad. All of a sudden this was not good enough.

43

He picked up his phone and dialed. His mother picked up on the second ring. "Hey, Ma. Are you busy tomorrow afternoon? Great, wanna go shopping with me? No, not for you, for me. I'm sick of my place." He laughed, listening. "Maybe. I'll tell you tomorrow. Te amo." He hung up, then looked around again, thinking. By late afternoon, a variety of junk had been removed from the apartment, some furniture had been shifted, and he had formulated a plan. He poured some coffee over ice and sat down. Then he picked up his phone, took a deep breath, and dialed.

She answered, like his mother, on the second ring. "Vince."

"Hey, Kelli."

Oh lord, Kelli thought on the other end of the line. *How can 'hey Kelli' sound so much like 'get in my bed Kelli.'* Hoping that was what he really meant, she said, "I'm glad you called."

CHAPTER 4

August 2011

Midway through Vince's show prep, he and Kelli went to Café 50s for Sunday brunch. They sat across from each other in a booth. After the busboy came by to get their drink order – a latte for Kelli, black coffee for Vince – he said, "I used to always sit next to my dates in a booth."

"But?"

"I like being able to look at you. Also, it's ten percent easier for me to keep my hands off you this way."

Kelli was tempted to put her feet up on the seat next to him. If her shoes didn't have buckles, she might have, but fiddling with your feet under the table wasn't a good look. "So tell me what you've been up to for the past week."

"Work, work, rehearse, work, fantasize about you, work, rehearse."

"I like that middle part."

"I do too."

A waitress came over to get their order. "Blintzes, please. Side of bacon," said Kelli.

Vince said, "Steak and eggs, medium and sunny side up, tomatoes."

Order given, they sat back and smiled at each other. "You order like someone who's been here before," Kelli observed.

"A bunch of times. Not you?"

She gave him a look under her lashes. "I don't usually go out for breakfast."

"It's one of my favorite things. 'Cause otherwise my options are Frosted Flakes or a bagel."

Kelli laughed. "You don't cook?"

"Nope."

"Me neither, really, but I can scramble an egg."

"Overachiever." He smiled at her.

"And how are the rehearsals going, speaking of overachievers?"

"Hell, I don't know. I've never done any kind of performance thing before. There's only a little bit of my kind of dancing in it, so I'm just trusting Michelle knows what will work."

The coffees arrived. Kelli took a moment to taste her latte, stir in some half-and-half, and taste again. "I appreciate you asking me about that. You didn't have to."

"Well. I told my friends, there's something kind of unusual, for me, going on here and I don't want to be too casual about it. I mean, I want you to know I think," he paused. "I don't even know how to put this."

"I know what you mean. Something's different."

God, what a relief. He'd been thinking it couldn't possibly be just him, but still. "Yes."

"And by the way I am *totally* jealous of Michelle."

He barely avoided inhaling some coffee. "What? Wait!"

Kelli was laughing. "Only because I've been doing this performance class for a couple of years and never got to do a partner number."

Oh. He relaxed, sat back, breathed. "What's wrong with those guys?"

"There are usually only a couple of guys in the

group and the long-timers always get 'em."

"The nerve."

"I know, how dare they." She waved it off.

Vince laughed. "Is that the main thing you do outside work?"

"Well, I've been dating," she pointed out. "So I've been to a ton of movies and clubs and museums. Greek Theater, the Bowl. There's a lot to do in L.A." He was nodding agreement. "But yeah. I love it. There's nothing like dancing to make me feel alive. Well, almost nothing." She couldn't help it if that sounded a little suggestive.

Vince definitely thought it did. "Knock it off, I'm trying to be restrained here. Find us a class or something for after the show."

"Us, huh?" Kelli said softly. Did he mean he wanted to be exclusive? Should she ask? Should she tell him she hadn't even thought about seeing anybody else since the night they met?

"Don't you think?" After a second, Vince gave in to the look on her face. "I don't want to date anyone else."

She blinked, bit her lip, shook her head slightly as if to say 'neither do I.' She thought he read her mind; it looked as though he was about to lunge across the table. "Damn it, why are you so far away?" She was about to get up and move, slide in beside him, touch him. The waitress brought their breakfast just in time. After slathering her blintzes in sour cream and blueberry sauce, Kelli glanced up at Vince. "Sandra would kill to get you in this class. There's always a few guys but none of them look like you." That made him laugh again. He asked her about how she found the class, did

47

they compete, where and when. Kept her talking about herself and her dancing all the way through breakfast. Didn't mention sports once. Kelli was pretty sure she'd found the perfect man.

"Jesus. You need air-conditioning." Vince signaled a break and headed for a towel to mop his face and neck. He was covered with sweat; this number was hard work.

Michelle bent over to touch her toes, then reversed and twisted her back. "Yeah, I know. This place is just so convenient to my job. And since it's over the garage there's no downstairs neighbor to bitch about noise."

He retrieved a couple bottles of water, handed her one, drank half of his. "How do you even stay on that damn pole?"

"I've got this sticky gunk on me, didn't you notice?"

"I'm still having to think too hard about what I'm doing here. Am I doing it right?" He dropped the towel on top of his gym bag. It was a good thing he'd brought along a fresh tee shirt to change into when they were done.

Michelle was giving him a look. "Are you serious? You're doing incredible. I can't believe how good I used to think David was."

He couldn't help but be flattered. Might have blushed a bit. Tried to wave it off. "Well, you're the expert, so okay. Dress rehearsal tomorrow, right?"

"Yeah. One o'clock at the club. Then two shows, Sunday and Monday night."

"All this work for two shows!"

"I know, right? It's one of the reasons the cast

changes every time. But you never know. A member of the company got picked up by Cirque last year, and another girl got hired for a Vegas show."

He wondered if that's what she wanted. She was much too good a dancer to be working for a car-rental place. "I guess I'm glad the number got put in."

"Me, too. I needed to do something different. And you're gonna kill it." She regarded him for a minute. He was leaning against her kitchen counter, both hands on the edge. Fit and handsome and sexy as hell in that sports tank and jeans. "Vince, can I ask you something?"

"Sure."

"The first time we met I thought you seemed kind of into me. And that was fine. You're different now. And that's fine too," she assured him hastily, realizing that this was a very awkward conversation to be having during a rehearsal.

He didn't seem to think so. "You're a beautiful woman. But I'm in love with somebody else." He glanced over at her almost apologetically, hoping she wasn't offended.

She wasn't. Disappointed maybe, but not offended. "How long have you known her?"

"Not nearly long enough." She laughed, and he smiled. "Let's run this damn thing again."

On Sunday night, Vicky, Sharon, Kelli, Elliott, and Alicia were all seated at lounge tables in front of the stage at the club. It was a few minutes to showtime. Vince was pacing restlessly around the room, circling back from time to time. Michelle looked around the wing curtain and caught his eye, tipping her head to indicate he should get backstage. "Ah, fuck me." He looked for a moment as if he were going to bolt.

"Get back there," Elliott said sternly, pointing at the stage door.

Vicky said, "You'll do great, chico." Vince shook his head, took a deep breath, and marched away.

"God *damn* he looks good tonight," Sharon stated.

Alicia laughed. "Letting his hair grow out was a good choice, huh?"

Vicky and Sharon answered together. "Yes."

"How long have you known him?" Kelli asked.

"About a year and a half. Huh, seems longer," said Vicky.

Sharon cut her eyes over at Kelli. "So, how's the dating going?"

"Girl, I am about to *explode*." All the women laughed.

Vicky said, "I can assure you, when you finally do get to bounce on that, it will be worth the wait."

"Ladies, please!" Elliott was blushing.

Alicia said, "I warned you. This is what you get when a gang of women goes out."

"I honestly had no idea."

Kelli said, looking from Vicky to Sharon and back, "I'm confused, I thought … ?"

"You thought correctly, but before Vicky came to her senses she had a little fling with the Vincinator."

"And I'm sincere when I tell you that he's the best guy I know – no offense, Elliott – and also the best guy I've *known*."

All the women laughed again. "I believe I need another drink," Elliott announced, and fled to the bar.

As a waitress dropped off the ladies' second round, the music and the lights changed. Elliott judged it safe to join them again, and the friends settled down to watch the show.

It was a mix of performance styles, with the partner number slotted in toward the end. Kelli gave a little sigh of impatience and Alicia patted her shoulder sympathetically. Kelli said, in an undertone, "I appreciate this other stuff but I am just dying to see Vince and Michelle!"

"Only a couple more."

"Hmph!" All the women snickered.

Finally, the trapeze artist finished and two stagehands stowed the rig, then brought in a portable bar and two stools which they set upstage left. The music started and Vince slouched on to the introduction. He was wearing an open-necked white dress shirt with suspenders over pinstriped slacks and dance boots.

The friends hooted, whistled and clapped. Then Michelle slunk onstage, wearing an unbelted leopard-print trench coat over a black pole bikini and lace-up knee-high black vinyl boots. Her body was incredible. "Holy shit," Elliott said blankly.

Alicia shot him a look. "Watch it, buster."

The number went on with action perfectly matched to the lyrics. The pole, the bar, the stools, the suspenders, the coat, and Vince were all props for Michelle. They worked some swing choreography into the jazzier pole-style action. At one point Vince boosted himself up on the bar, and Michelle pushed him onto his back to the lyric 'if you keep drinkin' you're gonna get fresh,' using hidden stairs to step onto the bar and strut over his body to 'and you'll wind up

51

begging for my fine fine flesh.' Elliott couldn't resist joining a chorus of wolf whistles, and Alicia laughed.

Then Vince rolled off the bar and lifted Michelle down, his hands suggestively under the coat. They swung around the pole for a few seconds, Vince flying over Michelle as she crouched on the stage. When he landed, he pulled her to her feet and peeled the coat off her shoulders. She leaned in so close they were nearly kissing, then retreated. He threw the coat over the bar and grabbed her again.

"This thing is fucking *hot*," Vicky muttered, fanning herself.

"You said it, sister." Kelli never took her eyes off the stage.

The number finished as Michelle tossed one of her long legs up on Vince's shoulder and he dragged her across the stage, then flipped her into a drop, to a roar of applause from the house. Vince and Michelle took a couple of bows, then the stage was re-set for the final number. There was more enthusiastic applause at the end of the show, with an extra burst as Vince and Michelle joined the line.

Sharon said, "I feel like I did not properly appreciate that last thing. What was it again?"

"Was there another number?" Kelli remembered seeing something but it really hadn't registered.

Vicky said, "A kickline number. Very cute. But my vision was still a little blurry."

"All I'm gonna say is, no wonder you liked dancing with him so much," said Sharon.

Alicia looked at Elliott. "Honey, you know I love you as you are, but could we talk again about taking dance lessons?"

"If you'll wear an outfit like that."

The other women all laughed while Alicia said, "We can negotiate." Everyone stood up, stretching and shifting, draining their glasses as they waited for the company members to come out. Finally, Vince and Michelle joined them. Michelle looked giddy and happy. Vince looked wired.

Elliott shook hands with Vince. "Good job, man."

"You are such a *guy*," said Alicia. "Wonderful, both of you!" All the women piled on Vince and Michelle in a group hug.

Michelle said to Kelli, "Thank you so much for letting me dance with Vince. He's been terrific."

"I have to agree. I'm coming back tomorrow to see it again!"

Sharon said, "It's a damn shame that's only going to be performed twice."

Vicky went on alert. "Doesn't the company take video?"

"Not usually, not official video. We looked into it, but it was too expensive," Michelle explained. "People sometimes have friends record certain numbers."

"So I could record it tomorrow?" Kelli asked.

"Sure."

"Hmm. I'm having a thought," Vicky said, looking crafty.

Sharon said, "Uh-oh."

"No, I think you'd approve. Let's talk on the way home."

"Vince, are you gonna be here a while? Should I have Elliott and Alicia drop me off?" Kelli put her hand on his shoulder and he turned to her.

"Huh? Oh, sorry. My brain is fried. No, let me take

you home, I'm done for tonight. I've got to go to the gym or something though." He looked at Michelle. "How the hell do you get to sleep after this?"

"Excedrin PM and a cup of herbal tea."

"Seriously?"

"Or sex," she said helpfully. "When it's available."

Vince looked at Kelli. She blinked, then let her gaze drop to his mouth ... to his bare throat ... and lower. She looked up again. He was slightly flushed. She opened her mouth to speak.

Vicky got in first, saying briskly, "And this was a wonderful evening everyone, see you soon, good night!" She grabbed Sharon's hand and they scampered out, laughing. Alicia congratulated Michelle again and towed Elliott away.

"I'll see you back here at eight tomorrow, okay Vince?" Michelle looked amused.

"Yeah. Eight. Okay."

Michelle flapped a hand at him and went backstage. Vince was still looking at Kelli. "Shall we?"

"Please."

Not very much later, Kelli opened her apartment door and waited for Vince to follow her in. As soon as the door closed, she was in his arms. "You're shaking," he said softly.

"I'm so hungry for you, I'm about to *die*."

"I don't want to rush this." His hands were moving, his mouth was on her throat, and Kelli thought she might faint for real. "But I don't know how slow I can go."

"Go slow the second time," she said huskily. She put a hand on his face and brought his mouth to hers.

54

He made a low hungry sound. Kelli started backing toward her bedroom. Somehow he steered around the furniture and they made it through that door intact, still kissing, both panting. They were tearing off their clothes as soon as Kelli's legs made contact with the bed. "Oh my lord, Vince, I should have known."

"Should have known what," he said, one knee on the bed, tossing a condom on the side table. She collapsed onto the bed, reclining, reaching for him.

"Should have known you'd be perfect." She drew up a leg and he was on her.

"You still have your shoes on." Those high-heeled sandals in peacock blue. He'd been thinking of them, of her legs, of her body, of her beautiful face all night except when he was actually onstage.

"Well they have buckles." He laughed against her breast, kissing his way down her body. "Oh my *God*."

"I should have known," he said indistinctly, right up against her.

"Should've known wha, ngh, oh my *Jesus*."

"You'd be perfect." He moved up then, bracing himself over her, looking directly into her eyes as he sank into her. Watching her eyes close, watching her lips part. "Kelli." She hooked her foot over his thigh and pulled him deeper. He kissed her again.

Early the next morning, Vince opened his eyes. Light was falling across the unfamiliar room at an unfamiliar angle. His body was pleasantly sore. And beside him Kelli was … not asleep. "Good morning."

She smiled. *Yes it is.* "Good morning."

"I'll be right back."

He slid out of bed and walked, naked, out of the

55

room. Kelli watched with appreciation. Then she also got out of bed, stretched, and went out to the kitchen to make coffee. It was a very good morning, but it was a workday. The temptation to call in sick was strong.

As she punched the start button, Vince came up behind her and wrapped his arms around her, pulling her back against him. He dipped his head to press his lips against her neck. She inhaled slowly, angling her head to give him better access, purring. "My turn. Hold that thought."

She slipped away, went down the hall and into the bathroom. Vince returned to the bedroom as the scent of coffee started to fill the apartment. He was looking over a cluttered bookshelf when Kelli came back in. It was her turn to hold him, her turn to press her lips to his spine. Her hands roamed around his chest, sliding down his body. He inhaled sharply, then tipped his head back, eyes closing. She went up on her toes to kiss his neck, burrowing her face into his not-so-short hair. "Does that coffeemaker have an automatic off?" he said.

"Yes."

"Just checking." He turned around and they started again.

CHAPTER 5

September 2011

Not long after his Underground Cabaret debut, Vince and Kelli were sitting on the couch in his redecorated apartment. It was early evening on a weeknight. Takeout containers were stacked on the coffee table beside a DVD case with no title. The cover image was of several sets of legs, in fishnet tights, tangled together. "It was so cool of Vicky to set that up," Vince said, nudging the DVD case.

"I can't believe how fast she got it done."

"I guess one of the people they know from ballroom has a side business doing video and just by luck he wasn't booked with anything that night."

"So do you want to watch the whole thing, or just 'our' part?"

"Let's watch our part first, then the whole thing. Man, I'm nervous all over again!"

"What for? You were awesome. Michelle was incredible. It was the best number in the show." She could say this with some confidence, having seen the entire thing twice. The second time through, she even managed to pay attention to the closing number.

"Well, you gotta understand I only ever saw a phone video from a practice in her apartment, and it was not exactly ready for primetime."

"Well, cue it up, but I warn you right now you are not allowed to say anything bad about yourself. Because honestly, even the gay women in that room were ready to jump on you."

Vince waved that off. "If you say so." He got up

and loaded the DVD, then sat back down with the remote. Pulled Kelli tight against his side as he accessed the menu. "This is really well put together," he said, stalling.

"Hush up and press play already!" They watched the performance. When it was over Kelli took the remote out of Vince's hand, pressed Stop, and lunged for him.

Some time later, Kelli stretched out on top of Vince on the couch. His hand rested on her bare bottom. Her head was propped on her hands, her elbows planted on each side of his head. "This was an excellent choice of a couch," she remarked.

"The mamacita helped me pick it out."

"Oh really?"

"Yeah. The Sunday after our date at Morton's."

"I thought things seemed kind of new in here."

"I've lived here a long time, but the day after that date I looked around and thought, this is not someplace I want to bring that delicious woman."

"Ooh, that's nice." *Speaking of delicious*, she thought, lips brushing his face.

"So I called up Ma and told her I needed help turning this into a home for an adult."

"Well, good job with that." She was half listening, half preoccupied with writing her name on his chest with her fingernail. *Wish I could brand him. Property of Kelli L. Hands off, bitches.*

"Want to meet her?"

She looked up, startled but pleased. "Of course."

"Cool. 'Cause she's been harassing me ever since we went shopping. I'll set that up."

Already?! Going to meet his mother! Diana was not going to believe how calm and cool she was playing it. "I'll look forward to it. So how did you like the performance?"

"I think I need to watch it a couple more times to desensitize myself, but I didn't hate it." It was strange to see himself like that, onstage performing. He'd seen videos plenty of times when somebody'd caught him accidentally, out at a club or at a swing or salsa event. It wasn't the same.

"Good, 'cause I'm gonna be watching it a lot." Kelli wondered if he realized how good that number was. She was dying to do something like it. She tried to sound casual when she said, "So how would you feel about doing something like that with me? Only more, you know, caliente?"

Vince imagined doing that same routine with Kelli (maybe minus the actual pole dancing) and realized he was getting turned on again. "Well, anything with you is going to be more caliente. You mean something salsa?" She moved, one knee sliding off to the side, and lowered her head. He brushed his lips against her cheek, fitting himself against her.

Oh lord, move like that again, holy hell. "Yeah, maybe. Maybe something for one of the contests at the Mayan, or the Granada?" She was breathless again, hungry again, wet again.

"Could be fun." He ran his hands up her ribs and she kissed him.

Counting back the weeks, Kelli almost couldn't believe they'd known each other for such a short time. She'd dated Hunter for nearly a year before they had the 'are we exclusive' conversation, another year before he proposed. When it happened, it felt like the next step in their relationship. But if she was honest with herself – which she needed to be right now – she hadn't been waiting for it. Hadn't been wishing for it. Hadn't thought what she texted to Alicia: *Amiga if this isn't love I don't know what is*

It took a couple of hours to get a reply, probably because she'd texted right after work: *How many bad decisions so far?*

LOL no bad decisions but some close calls. I went back on the pill ASAP, TG I still had some that weren't expired!! But let's just say it's going to be pure luck, you know they say two months for best results and he gets me so hot I'm like wow and well we are not always as careful as we should be. Eeek

What happens if, you know?

Would you believe we did talk about that? At a time when we were clothed and in public?

Wow Kelli good for you, I wasn't sure you ever were clothed when you were with this guy

LOL OMG I don't blame you!! All I ever do is talk about sex! But LOOK AT HIM

LOL I know. I love E but one cannot fail to appreciate

Anyway if we get caught we have a plan, because you know I want kids and no way no how is there better genetic material. Btw he is taking me to meet his mother

Already?!

I KNOW

A few days later, Kelli was in her apartment, looking around and thinking. She roamed around studying the layout, then went outside, shut the door, waited a few minutes, and went back in. "It *does* look like crap."

She plopped down on her couch, which she noticed was not all that comfortable. Everything in the room, which seemed fine a few weeks ago, now annoyed her. "Hmph!" She took her phone off the end table and dialed.

Her sister answered. "Hey baby. What's going on?"

"Do you have a few minutes to talk?"

"Sure. The kid is at band practice and Steve is messing around in the backyard."

"Can I bore you with more about Vince?"

"Where do you get the idea I would be bored? I'm *fascinated*."

Kelli laughed. "I guess I haven't been too talky about guys before."

"You could have been a nun for all I knew."

"Well, how many times does anyone want to say I had a few dates with this guy and then one or the other of us didn't return a call and that was that."

Diana laughed. "Tell me all."

"I told you already about the show. That was pretty amazing."

"And then there was some major action immediately after that, according to your text."

"Um yes, you could say that! It was all I could do to go to work the next day. I had to leave him in my apartment and I was *still* late."

"And since then?"

"Well, there was the show again that night. Even better, by the way. Since then we've talked every day and I've seen him a bunch of times and each time he looks better to me. There is *nothing* wrong."

"Are you sure he's a guy?"

"Believe me, I am *sure!*" They both giggled.

"How do you even stand somebody so perfect?"

"He's just, I don't know, *nice*. He's thoughtful. He can talk about anything. He's gentle, except when he's not, and when he's not, it's because I don't want him to be."

"Well, don't be shocked, but I know what you mean. It's probably politically incorrect, but there's something to be said for being manhandled occasionally."

Kelli snorted out a laugh. "I mean, I've been manhandled before, but there was always something I didn't like about it."

"You like the way he does it, huh."

"Ooh child." They both laughed again. "It's like he can't get enough of me, not like he's being macho."

"I get it."

"And he's always so calm. There's never any drama. I can just be me and not have to worry about my silly shit setting off any bombs."

"Are you silly?"

Kelli gave her phone a look. "You of all people should know."

"I can't wait to meet him."

"I was over at his place the other night and he's recently redecorated. He told me that he started fixing it up the weekend after our first date."

"And it looks good?"

"It looks like a design house, except there's

nothing designery and everything is comfortable and it all works. He went shopping *with his mother*."

Diana sucked in her breath. In their world, that was significant. "Oh, my lord."

"I'm meeting her next Sunday."

"Already?!"

"I know!!"

Meanwhile, Vince was strolling in the park along Ocean Drive in Santa Monica. Vicky walked beside him and waited for him to speak. Eventually he said, "Thanks for meeting me."

"No problem. Sharon's doing some homework, it's probably good that I'm out of her way."

"She's doing that paralegal course, right?"

"Yeah, it's evenings and online." She smiled. "But you didn't call me so we could talk about Sharon."

Absolutely true. "Remember when you two were dating?"

"Yep."

"You kind of gave me the idea."

"The delayed-gratification idea?"

"Yeah. You know, I've always been the 'let's get down to business' kind of guy."

"Chico, every guy is that kind of guy."

Vince laughed. "I know, and I totally could have gone there. I know I could have. There was a 'yes' in her eyes every time I saw her."

"So why didn't you? Really."

"Because ... I'm still trying to figure this out. Because I wanted to know her better, I think. I didn't want to skip over anything. I wanted to experience her in a lot of different ways and not just in bed."

Vicky mentally collected on a bet she had with Sharon. "That Kelli is one lucky woman. You know, I told Sharon you were going to make someone very, very happy someday."

"So is that kind of the same?"

"As what we did? Yeah, I think so. I mean, I was still getting used to the whole idea. I didn't have any strong feelings either way about gay or straight, it just honestly never occurred to me that I might fall in love with another woman someday. So even though we were already best friends, and already roommates, and we got along really well at work, I think yeah. I wanted to do a few things differently so that we could both *see* each other differently."

"That's it, exactly."

They walked on for a few minutes. "So. Is she The One?"

"I never even believed in that. But." He shook his head.

"But you can tell, right? It really is different."

"It is *so* different! She makes me feel good. Just having her in the same air as me." *And I miss her*, he thought but didn't say. It was way over the top. How could he miss somebody he'd only known for a few weeks? He glanced over at Vicky, who made an encouraging sound. There was more to say, so he said it. "She feels *right*. She smells right, she tastes right, I love the way she looks and the way she moves and the way she fits me."

Vicky took his hand and squeezed it, then released it. "Ever said that – or thought that – about anyone else?"

"Nope. Not even you."

"Stick a fork in you. You're done."

The next Sunday, Vince and Kelli pulled up outside his mother's neat little bungalow in Westchester. "This is one of those neighborhoods that kind of hides in plain sight, isn't it?" Kelli looked back along the street.

"Los Angeles is full of them. I actually met Elliott when he sold me this house."

"And now you're working together! That's so cool."

"Yeah. Ready to go in?"

"Kiss me first."

Vince laughed. "No way, she's watching us right now." She made a terrified sound and reached for the door handle. "Hold on, I have to do this right." Vince exited the car and came around to help her out. Vince's mom threw open the door as they walked up the path to the house. She was tiny, curvy, and cute. "Hey, mamacita. This is Kelli Lopez. Kelli, meet Esmeralda Madrigal."

"What a beautiful name! I'm so happy to meet you!" Kelli put out a hand and Esmeralda took it in both of hers.

"Come in, come in! I've been looking forward to this for so long!"

"It's only been a couple of months," Vince objected.

"Muchacho, it's been thirty-two years!"

Kelli and Esmeralda laughed as Vince rolled his eyes. They all went in, and the women immediately fell into easy chatter as Esmeralda gave Kelli a tour. Vince followed along, listening with amusement. "Who is this a picture of?"

"That is Vicente with his dad."

"How old was he?"

"In that picture? Twelve. We were still married then."

"Vince, your dad is a handsome guy too."

Esmeralda nodded. "He is part Navajo. A good man, hard-working man."

"But you got divorced? If you don't mind my asking."

"No, no. It was me. Once Vicente went off to college and Adam was still on the road all the time, I was lonely and I wanted to move to the city. Adam didn't want to so I came by myself."

"And she's been breaking hearts ever since," Vince said dryly.

"Hush, m'hijo!"

Kelli laughed. "Do you still see your dad?" She hoped so.

"Once in a blue moon. We met by accident once in Las Vegas. I was there for my birthday, he called to say hi, I told him where I was and he said no way, me too. Got to spend the evening hanging out. That was pretty cool." Vince could tell that reassured Kelli somehow.

They went outside, where Esmeralda had laid a casual dinner setting on the west-facing covered patio. The sun was barely below the overhang. Esmeralda said, a little anxiously, "It's so early, too early for dinner, but I went ahead and set things up in case you can stay."

Kelli looked at Vince, eyebrows raised in a question to which the desired answer was clearly 'yes.' He smiled. "We can stay, Ma. Thanks."

"Oh, I'm so happy! There is so much to talk about!"

As the sun slowly descended, the conversation

ranged widely, always coming back to Esmeralda's transparent delight. Kelli took advantage of a moment when their hostess was in the kitchen to speak quietly to Vince. "I can't help wondering how often you've brought a girl to meet your mom?"

"That would be never."

"What? *Really*?" She somehow managed to say that softly.

"She was probably starting to wonder if I was gay."

"You're the opposite of gay. But really, *never*?!"

"She met my date for high-school prom, and my girlfriend at my college graduation. But otherwise, yeah."

"Wow."

Esmeralda came back into the sitting room. "Dinner is almost ready."

"I know Vince is looking forward to this, he doesn't get many home-cooked meals."

"Yeah, my cooking skills don't go much farther than nuking something."

"Mine either," Kelli said.

"At least you can scramble an egg."

"It's different when you work full time. I remember!" Esmeralda shook her head.

"How do you stay busy these days?"

"I work part-time at the Home Depot!"

"She's being modest. The mamacita is a designer. She does all the work on the house. Unless she has to lift something bigger than she is." Vince gave Kelli a sideways look. This was clearly a standing joke he had with his mother.

Esmeralda was laughing. "Which sadly happens a lot! But I have many friends, to help me. Now, let us go and have our dinner with the sunset."

Conversation slowed down as they enjoyed traditional carnitas with non-traditional sides. "I love this black rice," said Kelli. "I've never had anything like that before."

"A friend gave me some and told me I had to use it instead of white rice! He said, Esme, that white rice is just like eating white bread, it's no good for you!"

"I like it, too. And the squash thing is great," said Vince, taking another bite.

"It's maybe a little like Thanksgiving dinner? Too much?"

"No, it's delicious," Kelli said. "That little hit of ancho on there is perfect."

"Thank you, m'hija. Whew! So. I am still so excited, I forget all the things I want to know about you! Where do your parents live?"

"They live in Baltimore. Used to be New York, then Dad got a job with Amtrak and after a few years had the chance to transfer south."

"And brothers, sisters?"

"Two sisters and a brother. They're all married. I have a nephew and two little nieces and my mother is being Very Patient With Me because I'm the baby of the family."

"Oh, she wants you to give her some more grandchildren?"

Vince gave his mother a look. "Is there a Latina mama on the planet who doesn't?"

"You mean to say your own mamacita has been Very Patient With You?" Kelli knew she was being mischievous.

Vince made an incredulous sound. "She hasn't

been the *least* bit patient with me."

Kelli and Esmeralda laughed. "It's true, I am always pestering poor Vicente. Which is why I am so excited when he brings this beautiful young lady to meet me."

"Well, it seemed like the thing to do." He looked at Kelli in a way that seemed very serious, almost grave. Kelli caught her breath and reached for his hand. He lifted their joined hands to his lips, watching her steadily. Kelli could see only him for a long, long moment. "Mi corazón," he said softly. His eyes warmed with the hint of a smile.

Kelli blinked back sudden tears. "Um. Woo! My goodness."

Esmeralda stood up and came around the table. "I'll get the coffee."

"Esmeralda?"

"Sí, m'hija?"

Kelli looked up at her hostess, reached out with her free hand and captured Esmeralda's. "You know we haven't known each other very long. But just for the record, I'm prepared to say yes to pretty much anything Vicente asks me."

Vince smiled. "That's good to know."

Kelli was a mess. All the way home from Westchester she'd been quiet, thinking about the difference between that day and the day she'd met Hunter's parents. His white, country-club parents, who spoke to her with chilly politeness and to him with thinly-veiled criticism. From this distance, she wondered if their whole relationship was his way of rebelling. He married a white girl eventually. Kelli would never have been happy in that family. She was already crazy about Esmeralda. Could easily imagine how they would all be together, at a big family gathering someday. Could easily lie here on her bed, wishing Vince was with her, imagining a big family wedding. Clutching her phone. *Alicia I met his mother today she is adorable and he loves her and OMG*

Alicia was surely already in bed but she answered anyway. *You think he's serious don't you*

He called me his heart

OMG

I'm the first woman he's ever taken home

OMFG

I know. I'm freaking out a little. Has he talked to Elliott?

Let me check. "Honey?"

"Mmm?" Elliott was half-asleep.

"Has Vince said anything to you about Kelli?"

Elliott was wide awake now. Vince had, in fact, said something. It was more along the lines of 'get your ass in gear with Alicia' than any statement of his own intentions. Elliott had, however, taken his meaning and made certain plans. Which he had not yet communicated to Alicia. She was looking at him with that tolerant impatience he loved. "Things have been said," he admitted finally. "He talks about Kelli a lot. And not just when we're making plans to go out." There had been a few double dates. Alicia looked as though she would like more detail. "Can't tell you any more. Bro code."

"Oh for God's sake," she said, laughing, and texted back to Kelli: *E says things have been said and apparently they are top secret which IMO means one or the other of them is planning to propose*

Well we already know E is going to do that any day now

I hope!

V can't go first. E would kill him

LOL I know. Sweetie I don't think you have anything to worry about here. How soon would you want him to ask?

IMMEDIATELY

LOL oh okay well be patient if you can

Thanks chica TTYL

CHAPTER 6

October 2011

Vince had known, in a vague way, that there was a dance studio in his neighborhood. It wasn't until Vicky and Sharon started taking lessons there that he realized how close it was. After he pointed it out to Kelli, she suggested joining one of the group classes. Neither of them could have said whose idea it was to do extra practice there, but it had rapidly become a part of their routine.

They were practicing one night when a wedding couple was getting a lesson. It made Kelli uncomfortable in an excited kind of way, thinking about 'maybe someday.' That was based partly on the way Vince looked at the couple. It wasn't an Oh God Hope She Doesn't Want That kind of look. More like Hmm What Kind of Wedding Dance Should We Do. She didn't want to get ahead of herself; it seemed like living together should come first, and they hadn't even said I Love You yet.

Vince's mother had not let up since their visit. He'd fielded several phone calls in which 'when are you going to ask her' was the primary topic of conversation. Watching that other couple gave him ideas. Starting with choosing something other than a big diamond solitaire that was going to catch on every damn thing all the damn time. If it were on her right hand, that poor guy would be cut to ribbons.

Kelli didn't say or do anything to hint at 'that could be us.' He really didn't want to get ahead of Elliott and Alicia. Wondered if Alicia and Kelli were talking about these things. *Of course they are.* The thought almost made him laugh. It was time to talk about what came next. When they walked out to the parking lot he leaned against her car. "Can I say I'm starting to think we should move in together?"

She tried to play it cool instead of bouncing up and down shrieking. "It's kind of a drag doing this juggling act, isn't it?"

"You want to talk about it? We could go get dinner." The neighborhood was full of restaurants.

"Okay." She smiled up at him. He bent to give her a kiss. She locked the car again and they walked down the street. Over dinner at the Mexican place, it seemed there was only one real question. "Okay, so your place or mine? You have much better furniture," Kelli pointed out.

"Your apartment is bigger."

"But you have off-street parking. And central air." That had been really nice on a few hot September nights.

"Hmm, yeah. Parking and air-conditioning versus a few square feet." Plus his place was in this great walkable neighborhood.

Kelli would have moved in together weeks ago, and definitely preferred his place. She liked this neighborhood, and it was still convenient for her job. "I mean, we both work full time, and we practice at the studio, and we don't exactly host big parties at home."

"No, I've always preferred to have parties at bars."

"Somebody else gets to do the clean-up." She thought of the clincher. "And you're walking distance from the studio."

Vince nodded. That did seem significant. "Okay, let's make it official. Kelli, mi corazón, would you please come live with me?"

"Sí Vicente mi amor, nothing would make me happier."

"I really love you, you know." He hadn't said it before, and wondered why.

Oh my God oh my God oh my God. "I love you too." They smiled at each other across the table. "Now take me home to bed," Kelli demanded.

"Your place or mine?"

"*Damn* it!"

A week later Vince was lying on the couch, talking to Elliott on the phone, calm in the midst of chaos. His apartment was strewn with moving boxes. "Yep, we pulled the trigger. Kelli's moving in at the end of the month. Officially."

"Meaning she's pretty much there already?" Elliott had put the call on speaker so Alicia could listen in.

"Yeah, she said I have better furniture – "

"*Now* you do."

"Shut up. So she's curb-marting most of hers. Our only real issue's been – "

"Closet space." Alicia had her hand over her mouth to stifle the giggles. Elliott was close to giggling too.

"I forget you recently did this yourself," Vince said. The thought made him smile; he'd been so bummed out then, watching Elliott's life take a turn while he stayed on the old path. Well, they were headed the same direction now.

Elliott was saying, "So, moving-in party?"

"Yep. Halloween. But it only starts here, then I have a car coming to pick us all up and take us out to the Underground Cabaret show at Level."

Elliott glanced at Alicia. "Good, somebody's been bugging me to take her to another show." She swatted his arm.

"Dude, taking her out is supposed to be *your idea.* Have you learned nothing?"

"Apparently, that's exactly what I've learned."

Kelli came in from the back. She was wearing nothing but one of Vince's dress shirts, unbuttoned, and a pair of high-heeled shoes. She struck a pose. Vince propped himself on an elbow. "Yowzah. Listen, something's just come up, I'll see you at the office."

Elliott laughed. "Right." He disconnected before Vince could hear Alicia laughing.

Vince put down the phone. He hadn't heard a thing. "Come here, beautiful."

"That was the general idea," she said, on her way.

Putting together a number for the Underground Cabaret was one of those 'oh wouldn't it be fun' ideas. Half-serious, at most, because Kelli was genuinely up for the idea but she didn't quite believe Vince genuinely felt the same way. She changed her mind in a hurry after their first brainstorming session. It seemed like there was no gap between getting the email from Michelle – the one about Halloween – and the two of them being on a call with her, rapidly followed by digging into their music collections.

"He called my bluff in a big way," she told Diana on the phone. "I mean, not that I was bluffing."

"Uh-huh."

"Quit laughing at me! Come on, what were the odds? It's one thing for the guy to go up on stage with someone like Michelle. She's the real deal. I have no idea why she's not in a pro company somewhere." That wasn't quite true. For one thing, Michelle was a couple years older than Vince, an age when many professional dancers began to consider retirement.

Diana made a dismissive sound. "How did the conversation go?"

"Well, we tossed the idea around a while back. Like, wouldn't it be fun, right. And then she sent the audition flyer and he was like oh, hey, look at this. Do you want to. What was I going to do, say no?" Diana laughed again. Kelli didn't blame her. "He threw them a few bucks to add some hardware. Lighting shit and some drapery, these things called legs? Panels that go along the sides of the stage. Oh and a fog machine. Michelle was like uh what and he was all dude, you've got a real stage, make the most of it. He was on the phone with Vicky, the one who organized the video that time, getting the 411 on stage mechanics. God knows how she knows that shit."

Diana noted that Vince was friendly with his ex and moved on. "Jay's school just upgraded their auditorium. They got a fog machine too, and he was so excited. He's going to be in the school play, it's this thing about a summer camp for baby monsters. He's out of his mind. But anyway, so what are you doing?"

"Creepy thing. Not like zombies or vampires, but still kind of a horror story. It's all in the song, we're just acting it out."

"Having fun?"

"Oh my God so much fun. It's mostly West Coast Swing, which he's awfully good at – I guess he used to go out dancing a lot with Vicky – but we're working in some ballroom and salsa stuff, plus a little bit of tango

76

styling I picked up from Sandra's class. Well, I say *we*. I mean we go in to our coach and say we were thinking about this and he goes oh great idea, do it this way, which is completely different, and it's a hundred percent better." Diana was laughing. Kelli rolled her eyes. "Dmitri's awesome. He's always so serious but he's never mean. Such a good teacher. It's like he knows how to make the most of what we can do but he's always upping our game a little."

"I'm so glad you're getting to have this experience, honey. I know how much you love dancing. Is that pretty much all you do?"

"Mmm, no," Kelli said. "We hang out with friends, we watch movies, we fool around. Like, a *lot*." Diana laughed again. Kelli was grinning. "I'm living my best life."

"Sounds like it. Are we going to see you for the holidays?"

"Thanksgiving. I'm so excited already. I asked him do you usually have T-day with your mom and he said yeah, but do you want to go see your folks, I'd like to meet everybody."

"Aww."

"I know!!"

"Can I tell Mom?" Kelli made a horrified little sound; Diana laughed some more. "Come on, Kelli. You better let this cat out the bag. People need to *know*."

That was so true. She'd been hoarding it because they were so busy, and it was so precious, but she was going to be in all kinds of trouble when their mom found out she was about to move in with the guy. Didn't even need to say that out loud. "You're so right. I had the East Coast in one box and West Coast in another. I'll call her as soon as we're off the phone. And

I'll be sure to tell her you've been hearing all about it." Before Diana could yell at her about that, Kelli disconnected. Blew out a breath, thought for a few seconds, went to pee and then to get a drink of water. Finally she settled herself down and made the call. "Hey Mama. Oh, I'm good. You good? Great. Listen, I have some news for you."

She had a lunch date with Alicia the next day and they spent almost the entire hour laughing about that whole situation. "Girl, I haven't had an ass-whuppin' like that since I came in at two in the morning one time in high school. Woo!" Kelli laughed some more, dabbed at her eyes, drank some of her iced tea.

Alicia couldn't get over how long Kelli managed to keep it quiet. "That only worked because you're three thousand miles apart."

"Don't I know it! But, oh my lord. I knew my mother was going straight into is he the one, does he want kids, if not why not, have you met his family. All these questions. And okay, I know the answers. But just because we figured that shit out fast doesn't mean I wanted to share it right away. I just wanted to *enjoy* it for a while. I was single for, damn, longer than I wanted to be." She fiddled with her fork, decided she was done eating, glanced up to make eye contact. "The truth is, they have to stop hoping I'll move home now. I'm about to move in with him. They know what that means. Even if we never get married –"

"Oh, right."

Kelli snorted out a laugh. "But for real. His life is here, and my life is here, and that means those three thousand miles are between us for good. From here on out, visits are all there is. So, I mean, I get it. She's upset about that. She was always going to be upset

78

about that. They all hoped I would give up on La La Land and come on home. It's really got nothing to do with Vince or whether he's the right man for me."

"Which he is." Alicia was giving thanks that her family and Elliott's were all right here in L.A. County. "I mean, you're pretty sure of that."

"I am *sure*." She sighed, leaned back in her chair, gazed fondly at her friend. "And I owe it all to you." Alicia tried to wave that off. Kelli insisted, "I do! And I will never stop appreciating it! So are you gonna come and see us dance?"

"Would we miss it? E started giving Vince crap about it immediately. He comes home and he's snickering about some snarky thing he said." She rolled her eyes. "Men and the ways they express affection." Kelli cracked up again.

Ever since Kelli mentioned possibly doing a show routine together, Vince had been scouring the internet for ideas. Watching somebody else execute a move was not the same as practicing it himself, but he managed to get to Shall We Dance on his own a few times to work with Dmitri. "She didn't think I was serious," he said during one mid-week session. "I think she thought I was just going along with it to get in her pants." He was starting to know what a laugh from Dmitri usually looked like. If he ever made the man laugh out loud, it would be a victory. "So am I crazy throwing all this stuff in the mix?"

Dmitri gave him one of those warm looks that Vince was starting to love. "Ambitious. Not crazy."

"All right. Well, come on. She spins better than me. Let's fix it." This was like the old days. Hanging out with his dad, learning how to do things around the house or with the car. Vince had not been conscious of missing his father, but this experience, working with Dmitri this way, was telling him he did. He made a point of texting a little more often. Bringing Adam up to date on the whole Vince-and-Kelli thing. He might not have been able to say certain things face to face, but in a text he could come right out and say *I really appreciate all the time you took teaching me how to do stuff. Most of my life skills are down to you*

The reply he got was one of those he figured he'd never delete: *I always appreciated the way you wanted to spend time with me. Glad we got so many chances. Looking forward to meeting Kelli sometime soon*

A couple days later, Vince and Kelli were at the dance studio to do a run-through of their number. Dmitri was standing in a corner next to Michelle, who was recording the routine with a small video camera. After they finished, she applauded. "It's really good!"

"In all seriousness, is it appropriate for the show?" Vince mopped his forehead with a bandanna.

"We don't want to get in just because Vince put some money into the company. Well, we *do*, but we don't," Kelli clarified.

Michelle made a complicated gesture, communicating understanding. "Well, I'm now one of the partners in the company and I think it's a great number. Even more to the point, it's something different, and that's what our fans like."

"Every entertainer knows this. Cannot do same show over and over again." Dmitri extended a hand and Michelle put the camera into it.

"Exactly! I'm sorry, I didn't catch your name. I'm

Michelle Walker."

"Dmitri Vasko." They shook hands, then he returned his gaze to the little LCD screen.

Michelle returned her attention to Kelli. "Anyway, I'll show it to the other girls tonight but I'm pretty sure they'll be happy to have this. We're a little thin right now since Marcy got that gig in Miami, and I've been so tied up at work I haven't had time to put together a number."

"Promotions are always like that," Kelli said. "Yay money, boo time. Or your brain is just too fried."

"For real." Michelle rolled her eyes. "I might invest in a new dance pole at home."

"You are a pole dancer?" Dmitri said, handing the camera back to Michelle.

"Yes, I am."

"I would like to talk with you about this."

"Any time."

"Now? I am finished for the day."

Michelle looked at Vince and Kelli in surprise. "Do you mind?"

"Not at all," Kelli assured her. "Thanks for all your help and advice. And give us a call so we're not in suspense all night!"

Vince and Kelli held hands walking back to his – *their* – apartment. He was carrying both their shoe bags in his other hand. "I still can't believe that studio's been right around the corner. Never heard of it until Vicky and Sharon started taking lessons there." And now they were in there all the time.

"Well, you weren't really the studio guy, were you?"

"No, I did most of my dancing in clubs."

"How did you get so good, though?"

He liked that she thought he was good. "Went to those swing and salsa weekends a few times, you know, take workshops or private lessons all day and then dance all night like a maniac."

Kelli laughed. "Me too. Those were fun for a single girl. I always ended up meeting someone."

"I'll bet you did."

"Too bad I never met you!"

"Just as well. I might not have appreciated you." He pulled her close and kissed her. She stayed close, her arm around his waist. He breathed her in. "On the other hand, you might have saved me some mostly boring years."

"No, you're right. This is better. I needed to go through some shit and figure myself out. I spent a lot of years looking for someone else to make me happy."

"You seemed pretty happy when I met you."

"Well, I decided to have fun with life, and I figured out how to do that, and aside from one little thing I was happy. Then I met you, and now I'm completely happy. And in love." She kissed him again, then let him go so they could walk on.

"Well, I think I was happy too. I was enjoying life. But I'm sure enjoying it a hell of a lot more now."

Later that evening, Kelli was emptying out moving boxes, going back and forth between the rooms as she found homes for various items. Vince was reading on the couch but looked up often to watch her work. She glanced over. "Is this bothering you?"

"You're kidding, right?" he said, smiling. Then his phone rang. He glanced at it and picked up. "Hey, Michelle. What's the word?"

"The word is, where the hell did you pick up all the jazz stuff, and welcome to the show."

"Awesome. Tell the girls we stole all those moves from the August show." Plus the internet, plus the dance encyclopedia otherwise known as Dmitri.

Kelli said, pitching her voice to be heard, "We've been studying!"

"Boy, I guess," said Michelle. "Dress rehearsal next Saturday."

"See you there." He hung up the phone and looked at Kelli, smiling. "Guess we'd better figure out our costumes."

After the dress rehearsal, the cast relaxed in the club, chowing down on pizza delivered from the joint next door. Michelle pulled a chair over to join Vince and Kelli. "So I have to ask where the inspiration for this number came from."

Kelli said, "Well actually, we'd talked about putting together a routine for a salsa contest. We were listening to a ton of music – "

Vince continued. "And we weren't really feeling any of the hard-core salsa stuff – "

"So we went a little deeper into the collection trying to look for a storytelling kind of song, something like the Voodoo Daddy one – "

"And I dug up the Squirrel Nut Zippers – "

"And first we thought, you know, 'Hell!' because it's a mambo – "

"But we got further down the CD and this one really rang a bell for me, a story I heard recently," Vince finished.

Michelle nodded, swallowing a bite of cheese and

mushroom. "It's perfect for the theme night, that's for sure. Your music sense is great."

Kelli nodded. "He likes the songs that are kind of … cinematically evocative."

"Movie fan." Michelle smiled.

"Yeah, it was fun putting this number together. Good thing we hooked up with Dmitri, though, because all these lifts are a bitch and a half. I really needed the coaching."

"You've done that stuff before, Kelli?"

"Some. I've been working at a studio out in Santa Monica for a while in this performance class." She gave Michelle the details. None of the Underground Cabaret people seemed to lean Latin but you never knew. "I volunteered to understudy the partner routines. Never ended up performing but I did get to sit in on a lot of rehearsal and coaching."

Michelle said, "That was smart. Obviously you picked up a lot of good information."

Vince changed the subject. "So, you talked to Dmitri about some stuff?"

Michelle told them about the half-serious discussion of adding pole dance or a burlesque jazz class to the roster at Shall We Dance. "But it's all a maybe. Depends on how much time I have. I'm determined to get a number into our December show. No way it'll be as good as the last one." Michelle did a 'that was all you' thing toward Vince. He shook his head, laughing.

"You could ask Dmitri to do one with you," Kelli suggested. "I'll bet he would. We've only seen him perform once, at a studio party, but he's kind of amazing. Dancing with him is an *experience*."

"Hey." Vince tried to look insulted; Kelli just laughed.

He rolled his eyes and turned to Michelle. "That's a good idea, actually. I'd pay to see that." She had her eyebrows up. "No, really. You should ask him."

"She really should," Kelli said later. They were back at Shall We Dance for a social, even though the smart money was probably on staying home to stretch and rest. Both wearing yoga pants and sleeveless dance tees, Kelli in flat swing shoes, eye makeup smudged because – she said – why bother fixing it when she was only going to get sweaty again.

Vince thought she looked beautiful. He always thought so. Even when she was gazing across the room at another man. Impossible to get bent about that when the man in question was their coach, dancing with another student. "I've been coming in for some extra coaching," he said.

That brought Kelli's attention back in a snap. "You have? When?"

"Here and there in the afternoon. I'd see something online and think it would be cool to do with you, take him the video, he'd teach me how to do it." After a few seconds of maneuvering – ballroom dancers traveled more than swing or salsa dancers – he made eye contact again. She was giving him a complicated look. "What's that face mean?"

She huffed out a laugh. "It means you're awesome, and you're sneaky, and you really didn't have to do that. I've always loved dancing with you."

"But I want to be the best possible partner for you."

Oh lord, there was so much subtext in that. He had to know it. Kelli stared at him for a few seconds, still dancing. Following without thinking about it because it was so easy with him. "You already are," she said finally, sliding her left hand up behind his neck. It wasn't the correct dance hold for rumba, but she didn't care. Judging from the way he slid his arm all the way around her and kissed her cheek, he didn't either.

On show night, the lounge section at the nightclub was packed with Vince and Kelli's friends. Michelle was waiting tables again. Vicky's video guy was there, since this was a one-night show. He was already set up, taking footage of the activity in the bar.

Sharon looked around and said, "I can't believe the crowd in here."

"I can't believe how domesticated Vince is." Vicky's tone was half affection, half mockery.

Alicia looked amused. "The apartment looks great, doesn't it?"

Will nodded. "Wish mine looked like that."

"I'd like to say that I gave him the idea," Elliott began.

Alicia gently cut in. "But that would be a lie."

Elliott sighed, "Yeah," and they all laughed. "But! I do have the occasional idea, and one idea was to take advantage of this occasion to say, Alicia, I have signed us up for a series of private lessons with Vince and Kelli's coach."

Alicia was thrilled. "Oh! Honey, that's so awesome!"

"And then, um, after I learn to dance." A ring box had appeared in his hand. He opened it and a hush fell over the group. He cleared his throat. "Will you, um, marry me?"

Alicia stared at Elliott for a second, then said, "Oh my *God*, yes!!" She threw her arms around him and he kissed her.

Sharon rescued Alicia's cocktail from impending doom, giving Vicky a sideways glance. "Now *that's* a good idea."

"Someday, sweetie. Someday we can. That Prop 8 bullshit is going down." They kissed. Elliott and Alicia were still kissing. Will, slightly forlorn, headed for the bar.

By the time the lights and music changed to signal the start of the show, the friends had composed themselves. All watched with growing anticipation. Every number – some dark, some funny – had been designed to fit the Halloween theme. Sharon leaned over to Vicky between numbers. "Any idea what this is going to be like?"

"I don't have a clue, and I'm really pissed about that."

Sharon snickered. "You're all proprietary about Vince."

They watched the antepenultimate number, featuring a pair of trapeze artists dressed as ghosts. Finally, the stage was re-set and it was time for the partner number. The chatter in the house dropped as a spotlight hit Vince and Kelli onstage, and the vintage sounds of Squirrel Nut Zippers' 'Blue Angel' started to roll out. 'Your mama never told you how you were s'posed to treat a girl … .' There was silence from the audience as Vince and Kelli danced, using the music to tell a story of domestic violence and revenge.

The choreography was jazzy and slinky, emphasizing rotating, curling, looping movements that suggested constraint, bondage, and strangulation. Vince rolled and flipped Kelli into lifts and drops that seemed to invite catastrophe. Then the tables turned. At the end, Vince was crumpled on the stage with Kelli standing beside him. To the final lyric 'devils are dreaming,' a lighting change turned her blue-white dress to flaming red.

For a moment there was nothing, and then a roar of applause filled the club. The friends were on their feet. Michelle was standing with them. "Jesus *Christ*!" Sharon looked astounded.

Vicky was shaking her head in disbelief. "I am so fucking glad I got Jim here to do the video."

"And you'd better take back that thing you said about 'domesticated.'"

"God, I know." Vicky glanced over at Sharon with her eyebrows up. "What the fuck."

"I feel really sorry for the closers," Will commented.

Michelle nodded, still applauding. "No kidding! If they ever get to go on!"

The applause continued. Kelli pulled Vince to his feet and they took a bow, then left the stage. Still the applause went on. They came back out, laughing and excited, to take another bow, then ran off as the stagehands come on to create a graveyard set.

The final number was a Fosse-style group cabaret routine set to a remix of 'Monster Mash.' It looked like 'The Frug' crossed with Wade Robson's 'Ramalama,' and was a hit with the crowd. But at the final curtain call, the biggest applause was again for Vince and Kelli.

"Did you ever think?" Alicia said to Elliott.

"Who would? I mean, he's got a lot to him, but that was pretty intense."

"He's a natural, but it was really well conceived," Michelle agreed. "And well executed. I'm glad everybody liked it."

Will said, "I think I know where some of it came from."

"I think I do, too." Vicky looked at Sharon.

Sharon nodded. "The after-Valentine's-Day story."

"What was that about?" asks Michelle.

"Randa." Will was looking around.

"Oh. Oh!" Michelle looked around too. "She's here tonight."

"I know."

"Do you see her anywhere?" The club was starting to empty out. Michelle spotted Randa standing at the bar. She was clutching a bottle of Pellegrino and looking a little bit lost. "Do you think she's okay?"

"I'll go see," said Will. "Tell Vince and Kelli how great they were, for me, will you?"

"Absolutely. Thanks, Will." She watched him go, but a moment later Vince and Kelli joined the group and a celebration began.

"Some party, dude," said Elliott, shaking Vince's hand.

"Yeah? Top *that*."

"Actually, he kind of did," Alicia said, displaying the engagement ring.

Vince stared at Elliott, who broke up laughing. Kelli exchanged a glance with Alicia, bit her lip, and patted Vince's back. "Yes, baby. You can discuss his timing later."

"Oh, we will." Vince rolled his neck, settled his shoulders, and looked around for something to drink.

"A toast?" Michelle headed over to the bar and

picked up a bottle of champagne and a stack of plastic glasses. Will and Randa had gone. The bartender was starting to wind things up. Michelle opened the bottle and poured for everyone. "Here's to Vince and Kelli, and Elliott and Alicia."

Kelli grinned. "And to the Underground Cabaret!" They tapped glasses and drank. She felt the heat of Vince's body alongside hers, made a happy/thrilled face at Alicia, and let herself be excited. Everything was going so damn *perfectly*. And that applause was such a *rush*. If they never got on stage again, she was glad they did this. It would be something to tell the kids someday.

Two weeks later, Vince and Kelli were hosting dinner at home. This was a new thing, so everyone involved was a little excited. Kelli and Alicia had retreated to the bedroom to talk in private. Vince gave the chili a stir, then picked up his glass and leaned against the counter.

Elliott looked over his shoulder to make sure neither of the women was in earshot. "So when are you going to do it? I mean, now that I cleared the way."

Vince laughed into his glass. "Haven't decided. We're going over to Baltimore for Thanksgiving and I don't want to do it before that."

"Mmm, yeah. First time meeting the family. Not Christmas?"

"Then it's like I'm doing that instead of getting her an actual gift." Vince grimaced.

"Do you have it already?" Elliott lowered his voice even more.

Vince knew he meant the ring. "Got it picked out

and paid for, it's still with the jeweler." A slight increase in volume from the women; they were giggling. It made him smile. "What do you want to bet they're talking about the same thing."

Elliott nodded, grinning. "Alicia says she's been crazy about you from day one."

"Mutual."

"Yeah, I know." Elliott sipped his wine. "Okay, so Christmas. I covered my ass pretty well with the dance lessons, but her parents will judge me if there's not something in the stocking, so I went with tickets."

"To what?"

"Like, everything." They both snickered. "Since we met down at the Music Center, I did a selection. A play, an opera, a ballet, and a concert."

Vince raised his glass approvingly. "Well done. Maybe," he hesitated, thinking it over. He was pretty sure Kelli would want to dance more, not less, in 2012. How to make that easier, or more fun? Lessons were a given, not a gift. "Worldtone gift certificate? Massages?"

"God, yes. Wait, what's Worldtone?"

"Place that makes dance shoes. Where I got mine for the things." Another increase in volume. This time it meant the women were leaving the bedroom. Vince set down his glass and stirred the chili again. Elliott started talking about something he'd seen on HGTV. By the time they sat down to eat they were all debating the pros and cons of fixer-uppers.

Kelli looked across the table at Vince, thought *this chili is damn good*, and realized they were officially grown-ups now. Sharing a meal they cooked themselves, talking with their engaged-to-be-married friends about what exactly went into a dream kitchen. Vince was telling Alicia about the Westchester house and the state it was in before he turned it over to his mother, and Kelli couldn't imagine being more in love.

CHAPTER 7

Thanksgiving 2011

The holiday traffic was hell. Vince and Kelli were in a town car, heading to the airport, along with apparently every other inhabitant of L.A. Kelli stretched her legs. "You know, you're getting me thoroughly spoiled. The last time I flew out, I took Super Shuttle."

"One of the advantages of being shacked up, doll. Half the rent." He was smiling, because they hadn't been living together long enough to really notice that benefit. There were so many other benefits they hardly cared about the rent.

Kelli had a thought. "You've always played the angles, haven't you? I mean, I'm in pretty good shape but I sure couldn't have bought a house six years out of college."

"Well, first of all, it was a *really* cheap house. Original owner died, family didn't want to keep it, it needed a lot of work. Also, I'm not making the payments – Ma is."

"But still. You need money to buy a house."

"Back then, you kind of didn't. I could have financed the whole thing. But yeah, I had some savings."

"Do tell. We're still a half-hour off LAX, at this rate." And there was nothing else to do since the driver could hear every word and see everything. Kelli was sitting as close to Vince as she could, hand in his and now with one leg over his knee.

"Nothing magic. I worked my way through

college, and got a couple of grants, so I didn't have any loans. Worked two jobs for a little while after that. Then I got hired on at a big bank that was a major mortgage lender and I was in their packaging group."

Kelli focused in. "Oh my lord, *you* crashed the economy."

Vince laughed. "Yep, that was all me."

"I read that those departments were, like, twenty-four hours seven days a week, for a while." That explained a lot.

"I worked about a million hours of overtime. Didn't have much of a life but I sure made money."

"When did you find time to dance?"

"As long as the days were, I held the line at working a maximum of six a week. So I always had one day off, and other days I would leave the office at six like a normal person, then come back at ten or whenever."

"So you went clubbing instead of getting some sleep?" Kelli had done a little of that in her time, but not much.

"Not all the time. Just enough to feel like I didn't live in a damn cubicle."

"I'm glad you're not doing that anymore."

"Believe me, so am I."

They were still God knew how long from the airport. She reached her other foot over to rub lightly along his ankle. "Too bad this isn't a limousine."

He was seriously regretting that it wasn't. "I'll make a note for next time." He glanced toward the driver, then thought *fuck it* and leaned over to kiss her. "If you're going to be naughty," he said softly, "so am I." He turned toward her and put his hand on her breast.

94

She giggled. The next time either of them noticed where they were, the driver was pulling up to the curb at their terminal.

Five days later, Kelli and Vince were on their way to an airport again, this time being driven by Kelli's sister Diana. The after-Thanksgiving traffic in Baltimore seemed negligible. "Mama thinks you've hit the jackpot, Kelli."

"Right? How funny was she when she got a look at Vince?"

"Your mom was very nice to me," Vince said sedately.

"Of course she was. I can't wait to call her up and get the uncensored version, though."

"I thought she was gonna faint when you played that show DVD, the first one," Diana said.

"She was kind of fanning herself, huh?" Kelli giggled. The women laughed. Vince just shook his head.

Diana looked in the rear-view mirror to catch Vince's eye. "Incidentally, Vince, you've given Steve a complex."

"How's that? He's a doctor, for God's sake."

"Yeah, but he didn't buy a house for *his* mother."

Kelli laughed. "Ooh yeah, he's going to be hearing about that for a while. And I heard Jay saying he wants to let his hair grow."

"Can you imagine? Eight years old and he wants to be El Matador, here."

"Oh hey, I like that. And just for the record, I do love the hair," Kelli said, twisting to look over her shoulder at Vince.

Diana asked, "Is this new? Because I like it."

"When I met him, it was practically a buzz cut. Or no, like the Caesar – remember that?"

"Looks good on very few, but I imagine he brought it off."

"I *am* still in this car, right?" Vince said, and the sisters laughed again. They mercifully changed the subject for the rest of the drive. He knew it had been nearly a year since Kelli went home, so he didn't mind the long round of hugs and goodbyes. It was so nice to be with someone who had a close family. His mamacita was going to love these people.

The return flight was packed, but they had seats in an exit row. After stowing their bags, Vince folded away the armrest between them and leaned over to kiss Kelli. "So you like the long hair, huh."

"Can't you tell from the way I've always got my hands in it?"

"Sharon told me to let it grow. And Vicky said something about it, a while back, but I thought she was just giving me shit."

"It suits you. Not that many guys can carry it off. It's usually the guys who really *shouldn't*, who even try. You see some guys in the salsa clubs with the ponytail, where it's like a comb-over ponytail, and it's just so sad."

Vince stifled a laugh; that probably wasn't as quiet as Kelli meant it to be. "Mmm. For the record, I like *your* hair too."

"Sometimes this curl drives me absolutely batshit crazy. I used to have it super-short. Like, next thing to shaved."

"I'll still think you're beautiful no matter what you

do with it, but I really dig this disco diva thing."

"And on that note, unless you want to sleep on the plane, I brought along some stuff to look at."

Vince smiled. "Disco stuff?"

"New Year's Eve stuff. There's a few dance parties around town. Unless you want to stay home." She gave him that option even though she couldn't imagine he was the guy who didn't like to go out for the change of year.

He didn't disappoint. "Hell no, let's party. Have to tell you about my terrible, horrible, no good, very bad New Year's Eve *last* year. That's a memory that needs to be wiped, stat."

Late that night, finally home and in bed, Kelli started snickering all over again. "Poor Vicente!" She started singing 'Just a Gigolo.'

"Knock it off, or I'll show you gigolo. You still owe me for the ride to LAX." He'd been grateful it was cold enough to justify the knee-length jacket.

She giggled and sang some more. Couldn't wait for him to collect. Squealed and laughed as he launched himself at her.

December 2011

Vince and Kelli were at the dance studio again the week after Thanksgiving, working on a mambo routine they'd started after Halloween. Dmitri was watching them run it through. When they finished, they turned to receive his opinion, then exchanged a glance. Their coach looked preoccupied, and also somewhat uncertain, which was very not the norm. Kelli made an inquiring sound. Dmitri said, "I have one question." Vince made an inviting gesture. "Do you wish to be best dancers you can be, or do you wish only to have fun?"

Vince blinked. "Whoa, where'd that come from?"

"Is serious. Either way is fine, you dance for you, not for me; but what I tell you must depend on your answer."

Kelli thought about that for a second. "You mean, you'd tell us one thing if we only want to have fun, but something else if ... the other thing?"

"Yes."

Kelli and Vince looked at each other again. She raised her eyebrows, he shrugged. She answered Dmitri. "I think we actually haven't quite figured that out."

"Then I tell you as if you dance for fun. You have excellent musicality. Your emotional connection is superb. You dance like you enjoy it very much. This makes you very enjoyable to watch."

Vince asked, "What would you say if it was the other thing?"

"You have some issues of technical quality, which if you fix them, you can be champions."

That was out of nowhere. Vince looked at Kelli again. "We haven't really talked about competition. Except for, like, the salsa things." And even then only in a 'maybe someday' kind of way. With everything else going on, Kelli had stepped back from her class in Santa Monica, and Vince hadn't returned to the subject of joining.

Dmitri was saying, "If you dance a perfect mambo, with show quality you already have, you win every time."

Kelli addressed Vince. "Do you want to talk about

98

this?"

"We can talk about it. We've just been kind of goofing around, really."

"If you work this hard to goof around, you are perfect students. Now, I have another session in half hour and must prepare. I give you information on what I wish you would do." Dmitri left them for a minute, going to his office and quickly returning to give Vince a brochure for a ballroom competition.

"Um, ballroom? I don't know all those dances."

"I give you this also." He handed over a homemade DVD marked Championship Rhythm. "Study, discuss, and we work again Tuesday evening."

"Thanks Dmitri!" Kelli said as he walked away, then turned to Vince. "First time we've gotten homework that wasn't just practice." They changed their shoes, collected their gear, and were heading out when Michelle arrived. Their paths intersected and they shared quick hugs. "Are you working with Dmitri tonight?" Kelli asked.

"Yes, we're taping our audition for this month's show."

"It's on our calendar," Vince said. "Can we watch?"

"Actually, could you stay and run the camera for me? That would be great."

"Ooh, a sneak peek. We can definitely stay for that," Kelli said.

"I'm a little nervous about it because we're not really using the pole. Well, I guess Dmitri is the pole? But it's Argentine tango." Michelle made an 'eek' face. "Never did it before."

Kelli patted her back. "You can do anything." She

meant it, too. Michelle had clips on her channel ranging from ballet en pointe to the aerial pole numbers.

They followed Michelle back to her favorite corner of the studio and set down their things. Vince took the camera and made sure it was ready to go, then glanced at Kelli. "I don't know much about Argentine tango, do you?"

"I went to see 'Forever Tango' one time. And I saw this guy, Julio Bocca? It was like ballet plus tango. It was super sexy. But basically no, I mean I've never done any."

"Then this'll be new for both of us. All I know is from 'Moulin Rouge.'"

"Then you'll recognize this music," Michelle said. She had her performance shoes on and was a few feet away, doing a quick warm-up at the barre mounted on the end wall. "I'm good, boss. Ready to go?"

"Ready." Dmitri took a position in the middle of the floor. The remaining students cleared away fast, giving him maximum space. Michelle walked toward him, stopping about a dozen feet away. Dmitri nodded to one of the other instructors, who started their music.

Vince wanted to make eye contact with Kelli approximately once every two seconds during the routine, but he didn't want to take his eyes off the dancers. Didn't want to jostle the camera. Couldn't believe what he was seeing. He knew Michelle and Dmitri were excellent at what they did. But he never expected a scorching-hot Argentine tango from the pair of them. And he never expected the strong desire, the *envy*, when he watched. He wanted to dance like that. Was it even possible for someone who never had a real lesson until he was in his twenties?

After handing off the camera and saying suitably

impressed things, they collected their gear and started the walk home. It was already dark, but the neighborhood was busy. As they passed a favorite restaurant, Vince turned to Kelli. "You hungry?"

"A little bit. I want to ditch the gear, though. Let's order for delivery."

"Genius. So what did you really think of that routine?" He glanced over. Neither of them had wanted to say much in the studio. Kelli opened her eyes wide and he laughed. "I know! I thought what we were doing was so hot!" Kelli snorted a laugh. "He's like twenty years older than me and he's throwing her around like it's nothing. I got a look at that music, it's called 'Tanguera.' Should I get it?"

"Um, yeah. We haven't got time to mess with it now, but honey, we're gonna have to find time later." She was so glad he brought it up. It really seemed like talking him into doing dance things was not going to be at all difficult. In fact, their challenge might be choosing *which* dance things. When they looked at the competition brochure after dinner, she didn't know if she wanted to jump in or run away. "Wow. This looks like a B.F.D. And it sounds like something that should be on ESPN. California Open."

"He can't seriously mean we would go for that one. It's only a couple of months off. And we have no idea what this is all about. Maybe we should talk to Vicky and Sharon, they know more about this ballroom stuff."

"Call 'em up. See if they want to have dinner on Friday."

Vince obediently picked up his phone, scrolled to the home number, and dialed. Sharon answered as he put the call on speaker. "Hey, Sharon. How's everything?"

"I've got another goddamned exam tomorrow and my brain is fried. You don't want to talk to me. Here's Vicky."

Vicky came on, laughing. "Hey, Vince. Or should I say Vicente?"

Kelli called across the room. "Vicente is *mine*."

Vicky laughed again. "Whatever!"

"If I can get a word in, you gals want to have dinner Friday?"

"Yeah, perfect. Tomorrow's her last final for the semester. You bring the beef and we'll cook it."

"Sounds great. Sevenish?"

"See you then."

Vince ended the call and smiled at Kelli. "Now that that's settled, do you want to do some homework?"

"Maybe we should. Because if we don't do the homework first, we probably won't do it at all."

"What I was thinking."

They loaded the DVD and settled down on the couch. There was no menu, so they scanned through the disc. "I'm not quite sure what we're watching here," Kelli said, puzzled.

"The girls could probably tell us. But you see those banners behind the dancers? They don't show up all the time."

"Where? Oh, there! Oh, okay. This is from a competition."

"A bunch of different ones, I think."

"Wait a second, that's Dmitri. Back it up."

"You're right. Let me re-start this section." He backed it up to the apparent beginning of the event, then pressed 'play' again. An announcer's voice was heard telling the dancers to cha-cha, please. Vince and Kelli watched without further conversation as five dances were performed. Then all of a sudden the disc went to a different event. Vince hit the stop button. "I hate home movies."

"Well, at least we figured out how to watch it." Kelli reached over for the competition brochure. "So that's what this is. Championship rhythm, five dances. Cha-cha, rumba, swing, bolero, mambo."

"What the hell is bolero?"

"That's the super-slow, melodramatic one."

"Have you done it before?"

"I've done all of them, for about a minute. But a long time ago."

"Is he seriously proposing we should start at that level? Championship? We're *beginners*."

We sure are, she thought. It was nice that Dmitri thought they could do it, but on the other hand this was a lot. They talked about it for a while longer without coming to a decision, and decided to table it in favor of fooling around. A bit later, Kelli looked at their tangled limbs in the light of a bedside candle and had another sort of wow moment. "You know, I didn't see many brown people in those competition videos."

Vince raised his head, frowning a little. "Those were all professionals, though, right? Maybe it's different at the amateur level."

"I'm obsessing. Never mind."

"Yeah, you're not supposed to be thinking at this point. I must be losing my touch." He changed his approach.

"No, you're not. But feel free to prove it. Ooh! *That* works!" She felt him laugh.

103

They were still discussing the competition question on their way to dinner Friday night. "I like the idea in the abstract," said Vince. "I mean, I like a challenge and we have fun dancing together and why not. On the other hand, I don't want it to be so much work that it feels like a job. Getting three routines to competition level in two months sounds like a lot of work."

"It still needs to be mostly fun."

"At least seventy-five percent fun."

"That sounds about right." They pulled up to the apartment complex, parked, and went up to the gate, loaded with a cooler bag and wine. Kelli dialed at the keypad.

Vicky answered on the intercom. "Izzat the Blue Angel?"

"And her little devil!" Kelli heard a laugh as the gate buzzed open.

Talk was general during dinner prep, and one bottle of wine was vanquished in celebrating the end of the semester. Then they adjourned to the table. "Miss Victoria has some news for you," said Sharon, after they were a few bites into their steaks.

"Do tell," Kelli invited.

"Okay." Vicki gestured with her knife. "You know Jim, the video guy?"

Vince nodded. "Did great work on those show DVDs."

"Which have sold really well, by the way. Especially the Halloween show because so many people couldn't get in. Next time people can book their tickets online, and there'll be a link to pre-order."

Kelli was impressed. "You're kind of smart, aren't

you?"

Sharon said, "She's thinking like an impresario these days. She got Randa – the gal who hangs around the Cabaret things? she's an entertainment attorney – to work up a letter about music rights and practically everybody has let the group use their stuff, for, like, a nickel."

Vicky laughed. "Anyway, Jim got a gig at the House of Blues on New Year's Eve. I don't know if you guys already had firm plans, but this year they're doing a variety show and the event planner asked Jim if he could recommend a dance act. And he recommended you."

"Whoa." Vince looked across the table at Kelli.

"Seriously?!"

"Out of all the acts he's seen this year, he said your 'Blue Angel' number was the most memorable. He played them the recording. It's yours to say yes or no."

"They know we're not professionals, right?"

"Well, that's part of the coolness here. They have a couple of big names but it's mostly local talent. And as you know, most local talent has a day job."

Vince and Kelli looked at each other. "I don't know whether to be flattered or horrified." He sat back.

"I would be horrified," Sharon said. "You should be flattered."

Kelli laughed. "Flattered, obviously, mi amor. I mean, I think it sounds like a blast. The House of Blues!"

"Out of all the bars on Sunset, that was *not* one where I expected to make a mark."

"So, you want to do it?" Vicky carved another bite off her steak.

"We're gonna have to *live* in the studio till then," Kelli said.

"Yeah, Dmitri can forget all about the California Open."

"So, let's do it?"

Vince smiled. "Fuck it. Let's do it."

Vicky grinned. "Awesome. I'll put you in touch with Randa. She'll make sure the contract is kosher."

"All I want is a couple of tickets for Ma," Vince said.

Kelli scolded, "Don't be silly. We also need Cristal in the dressing room, and a bowl of M&Ms with all the brown ones picked out."

They all cracked up. The Van Halen tour legend was – in Los Angeles – well understood. Then Sharon changed the subject. "Now that that's settled, what's this about the California Open?"

"Dmitri wants us to compete in Rhythm," said Kelli.

Vicky nodded. "This does not surprise me."

"But he's gonna have to cool his jets," said Vince.

"Maybe we can work on our technical issues at the same time we're brushing up Blue Angel." Then Kelli had to go off on a riff with Sharon about what, exactly, 'technical issues' could mean. She was hoarse from laughing by the time they left.

Dmitri showed no sign of disappointment when Kelli and Vince returned to the studio with their news. "Is good. We make plan. You will need to come more than once a week, yes?"

Kelli looked up from fastening her shoes. "Yes.

We're thinking three times a week."

Vince nodded. "How should we work this?"

"You remember the routine?"

"Pretty much."

"I suggest each session we run the routine, work one specific issue, run it again. You will be perfect."

"Okay. Where do we start?" Kelli stood next to Vince.

"We start with the posture. You have the music? Good. Places, please." They went through the routine, marking the tricks, finding only a few spots where one had to remind the other what to do. Dmitri set up a camera on a tripod. They recorded the second run-through, then Dmitri called them over to watch it. "Good. Now, the posture. Look here." He cued the recording to a point where they had taken a closed dance position. "You see? Here, the topline, it falls into the frame. Go, stand by the mirror. Sideways." Kelli and Vince stood in front of the mirror facing each other, sides to the glass. "Take your dance hold. There. Don't move but look at your shape."

"My shoulders are forward," said Kelli.

"My head is forward," said Vince.

"Good, you see it. Kelli, you look at Vince always like you want him to kiss you. That is perfect. But you curve your neck; your shoulders drop. Lift the chest, here," indicating her sternum, "and crown of head, here. Pull the neck up like ballerina."

"Wow, I'm two inches taller."

"And your frame is round and firm."

"Like my ass."

Vince laughed; Dmitri cracked a smile. "Now Vince. Same adjustment. Chest lifted, crown of head lifted. Look down your nose at her. Is dominant."

"Ooh, I like it." Kelli tried to look up at Vince without collapsing her neck. She lifted her chest just that little bit more, and her sightline rose. "It's like magic!"

Dmitri nodded. "Biggest part of your shape, always always always, on top. Fill the air, not the floor. Energy goes *up*."

"Oh, shoot! Is that what they mean by body flight?" Kelli caught Dmitri's approving look.

"Okay, so how do we hold this?" Vince said, cutting his eyes over without turning his head.

"You practice. Go back to lazy way."

Vince laughed. "Hey!" They let their frame fall back into its casual shape.

"Now fix." They adjusted. "Now mark the routine. Every time you close, every time you face each other, you fix." They walked through the routine, over and over again, skipping the tricks. "Again. You collapse, go up. Chest up, Kelli. Down your nose, Vince. Big, big! Better. Good. Good." He clapped twice, permission to leave the floor.

Vince collapsed into a chair. "Man, I'm exhausted."

"You do well. Thursday, we do again. Watch the show. You will see what needs work." Dmitri shook Vince's hand, kissed Kelli on the cheek, and went to prepare for his next session.

Vince and Kelli popped in the show DVD after dinner and watched the routine again. "Wow, he's right." Kelli was astonished.

"My foot, there. What the fuck."

"I threw away that line."

"What is my hand doing?!"

At the end they looked at each other and laughed. "Hey, it was good enough to get us the gig," Kelli said.

"I guess this is what they call learning to watch with a critical eye. We'll do better."

"You sound like El Kapitanski."

"Is good," Vince suggested, leaning over to put his mouth on her neck.

CHAPTER 8

By the weekend of the Cabaret's December show, the 'Blue Angel' routine had been completely reworked. Vince and Kelli gave themselves a night out to see Dmitri and Michelle perform. A few days later, they had Christmas brunch with Esmeralda, eating guava and cream cheese pastries from Porto's with their scrambled eggs and bacon. Opening their stockings and laughing about great minds thinking alike. Vince received gift cards for Amazon and for a designer specializing in men's dancewear, plus a small bottle of his favorite whiskey. Kelli was delighted with the Worldtone gift certificate and offered to share her massages. "Those are all for you, baby," he said. "I will help you drink that fancy-ass coffee, though." The pound of pure Kona beans was an impulse. He suspected it was the attached note saying 'we'll go see where these grow sometime' that she was really excited about. He couldn't wait to start talking about where to go for their honeymoon. His mother cornered him in her home office and tried to get him to tell her when he meant to propose. He said "Ten paciencia" and she smacked him lightly on the arm. "Soon," he added, very quietly, into her hair.

She squeezed him tight. "She is right for you."

"I know."

They were back at Shall We Dance the next day: D-Day minus five. They'd been in, on average, five days a week throughout the month. This time the studio was all but empty; they found Dmitri working alone, with concentration, in the middle of the floor. His action was very jazzy, but also Latin. The music was an

110

edit of Pink Martini's 'Bolero.' They hung back and watched until he finished. Kelli applauded. "Wow, Dmitri, what was that for?"

Dmitri was a little breathless. "Something I show to Michelle one day."

"That would never fit on the stage at Level," Vince observed.

"No, is for the ballroom. But now, time for you. I return." He went into the studio's bathroom, returning quickly with wet hair and in a fresh shirt.

Vince had cued the track for their rehearsal. "What should we work on tonight? We're warmed up and ready to go."

"Only dance, as if you are on stage. Places, please." They decided he meant dance it full-out, which seemed to be the case. After the first run-through Dmitri worked with them on a lift they'd changed the week before. Then he set up the video camera, and they did the routine again at full power. "Is good."

"Let's see." Vince and Kelli came up to the camera.

"You take it home with you. I give you nothing more now."

Kelli said, "What? We can't have nothing."

"Okay, one thing. Show me your bow." He turned on the camera again. They took their ending positions. Kelli pulled Vince to his feet and they did a simple bow before walking 'off' together. Then they turned to face Dmitri. "Mmm. How are you feeling when you take the bow?"

"Glad it's over," said Vince, and Kelli laughed.

"Yes, but." Dmitri didn't quite smile – he rarely did – but wore the expression they had come to think

111

of as his happy face. There was always something to improve, but they could tell when he was pleased. "You know, there is much acting. Especially a performance of this nature. Do not stop acting when it is over. Not until you are offstage."

Kelli wasn't sure she understood. "What do you mean, exactly?"

"Your exit is part of performance. You see? You must acknowledge the applause. There will be much applause." He made eye contact with each of them, to make sure they understood. "Acknowledge it, return it to them. You are pleased to have performed for them, you deserve the applause, and you thank them. Communicate all this."

They looked at each other doubtfully. Dmitri took Kelli's hand, led her to the middle of the floor, and demonstrated. Vince got it. "Oh!"

"You see? No apology, no little nod of the head. Big!" Dmitri returned Kelli to Vince's side. "My first teacher in the United States, he tells me most important thing. 'Attitude is Altitude.' Here I am, scrawny teenager with three words of English. He said, 'own the floor.' How tall am I?"

Vince was confused by the apparent non sequitur. "Six feet?"

"No. I am same height as you. You see?"

Vince looked at their reflection. "What the fuck?" He had honestly never noticed.

"Five feet ten inches. It is attitude that makes me look big. The *physical* attitude, yes? Show me your bow again."

Vince and Kelli went back out and Dmitri started the camera. They repeated the finishing pose, then Kelli pulled Vince to his feet. Copying what Dmitri had done, he presented her. They both extended their outside arms, palms up, and bowed. Vince gave her a turn to his other side and they both took an even deeper bow. Then, unhurried, they went 'off.'

Dmitri looked satisfied. "Good. Now you own the floor. Practice."

"And that's all for tonight?"

"What you have achieved is remarkable. I see you back here in two days but only to practice, yes? You have created beauty and I add nothing more. You are a credit to me and to the studio, but most importantly to yourselves."

"Oh, say that again," Kelli begged. "With more Ukrainian."

"You are a crrrrrrredit to me," said Dmitri, awarding that rare smile. This time, before they left, there was a group hug.

Kelli hadn't checked in with Alicia for a while. With family things and work things, they hadn't even managed a lunch since before Thanksgiving. Alicia had promised that she and Elliott would be coming to the big New Year's Eve show, but Kelli needed to touch base: *Hey girl how's things as an engaged person?*

Alicia wrote back without delay: *You'll know pretty soon I'll bet*

He's being cagey

LOL how's the big show coming along

I am SO SCARED but SO EXCITED

Did you change anything from Halloween?

Couple little things. Mostly we improved it. I hope.

113

Dmitri's been working us over

I feel ya. We started this month and OMG. He's all, if you want a wedding dance people will remember, start now

Have you even set the date??

NO

LOL

I kind of feel like we need to get this dance ironed out first!

Hee hee don't do that, you know the good venues go fast

Oh they do, do they. Have you been venue-shopping already?

For like a minute. Then I thought, ten to one we'll go do it in Baltimore, so I'm going to throw the whole thing at Mama and let her knock herself out

Girl you are smart. Still happy?

So happy. Thanks for introducing us. He is the BEST

I feel the same way about mine

That's how it should be. See you NYE! EEEEK!!

LOL see you then OXO

Finally – or much too soon – it was New Year's Eve. Vince and Kelli dressed in near-silence at home. They were due at the nightclub at eight-thirty and would perform at ten. Vince looked over at Kelli as he fastened his suspenders. "How are the nerves?"

"Oh holy hell. I didn't think I would be this shaky! The tech rehearsal was all hurry up and wait, and then that horrible gap with nothing to do but obsess."

"I know. I keep telling myself we've already done

this for an audience, and we've been practicing our asses off, and it's just for fun, but shit, piss, and fuck." Kelli snorted with laughter. "I almost wish Dmitri changed something on us this week so I'd have that to think about," Vince complained.

"Are you crazy?!"

He changed the subject. "You are head-bangingly gorgeous tonight, by the way."

"Oh, so *not* crazy. You like the new shoes?" Kelli preened, showing off her legs.

"I like everything about you."

"I like your haircut."

"Not quite as shaggy."

"Still enough for me to grab hold of."

"Why don't you do that?"

"Why don't I?" She grabbed him and they shared a deep, and prolonged, kiss. "Ooh, that's better." She looked in his eyes for a moment. "I really love you, you know."

"I love you, too." He kissed her again.

"Let's go knock 'em dead."

They arrived at the club perfectly on-time. Vince handed the car key over to the valet along with the parking voucher they'd been given and a five-dollar tip. With any luck, the car wouldn't end up alley-adjacent.

At the side entrance, their names were checked off a list by a burly security guard. Another guard inside escorted them to the performers' lounge, where a closed-circuit monitor showed them the stage.

They could hear the crowd already. A few other performers were there. They greeted people, found seats, and then noticed that, while there was no Cristal, there *was* a big bowl of M&Ms with all the brown ones picked out.

Vince stifled a laugh. "Props to Randa."

Kelli said, "Later for that. My teeth are all shiny clean. Is there a warm-up space?" They hadn't even seen this lounge during the tech run-through.

"Let's snoop around a little." They found a small empty room with a wood floor and full-length mirrors, then a pair of bathrooms, and then another security guard gave them the side-eye from his post at the control-room door and they turned around, snickering. "Well, we have everything we need," Vince said, trying to think of M&Ms and not the hum of the crowd out in the club. Trying not to remember that this was only the third time he'd performed. *This is loco. I am loco.*

When they returned, the lounge was surprisingly full. There were twelve acts on the schedule, and they were to dance at the end of the first block of six. They greeted the newly-arrived performers, then went ahead and changed into their dance shoes. Vince bounced on his toes. "Want to warm up just a little?"

"Just a little. I don't want to overdo it."

"Get sweaty?"

"Mm-hmm."

As they entered the practice room they realized that the first act, a blues-rock band, had started its three-song set. They relaxed into it and danced, freestyling along with the muted music, letting the familiar movement settle them down. After the set ended, they took some time to walk through their routine.

When they returned to the lounge, different people were milling around, and a production assistant was standing by to take them to the backstage area.

Kelli said "Oops!" then "Eeek! Is it time?!"

They followed the P.A. down the stairs and around a back corridor to the wings of the performance stage. Kelli was chanting under her breath; it sounded like 'dammit dammit dammit.'

They arrived in the wings. The number preceding theirs had just begun. Vince held on to Kelli's hand, suddenly calm. The P.A. said in an undertone, "Are you all set?"

Kelli murmured back, "If you call 'blind with terror' being all set."

Vince patted her on the ass and said softly, "It's okay, mi corazón. Nothing to worry about. I'm just going to throw you around a little, then you're going to kill me. And then I'm taking you home and fucking your brains out."

Kelli smiled brilliantly and answered very quietly but very sincerely. "Oh! Yes, *please*."

Vince winked at her. The P.A. was stifling laughter. Then their lead-in came offstage, and it was their turn. The MC announced, "Next, dancing to the Squirrel Nut Zippers' 'Blue Angel,' please welcome Vicente Connor and Kelli Lopez!"

Vince and Kelli looked at each other, then looked away. Summoning their characters, they walked out on the stage and danced. When they left the stage a few minutes later, neither of them could remember what they had just done. They heard the MC say, "Well, Jim and Katherine and the gang are gonna wish they'd been here to see that. Another round for Vicente and Kelli!" Vince and Kelli realized that they were being shooed back onstage for another bow. They ran out, looked at each other and smiled, did the 'own the floor' bow.

As they came off, the P.A. had her clipboard between her knees and was giving them the 'I'm not worthy' bow. Vince said, a little breathless, "How'd we do?"

Kelli added eagerly, "Was it okay? 'Cause I totally blacked out."

The P.A. assured them, "It was fucking awesome." The house lights and music had come up and the noise was tremendous.

"What do we do now?" Kelli was on a post-performance high.

"Up to you. You can hang out in the lounge, join your party in the house, or just take off. But there will be a little after-party if you want to stick around."

Vince looked at Kelli. "What do you want to do?"

"Everything?"

He laughed. "Okay, we'll do everything."

Through the corridor, up the stairs, and back to the lounge, feeling dazed and excited. They changed out of their dance shoes. Vince changed his shirt. Kelli sat with her feet in his lap as he fastened the buckles on her new sparkly stiletto-heeled sandals. "These *are* awesome shoes, by the way."

"I figured after the show, it was safe to be all about looks."

"They're giving me ideas." He ran his hand up her leg, dipping in behind her knee.

Mmm baby. She almost said that out loud. "You know how girls always go to the bathroom together?"

"Yeah, what's that all about, anyway."

"Probably not what I have in mind right now." She made it sound wicked. Slid her hand under the collar of his shirt, leaned forward to nuzzle his neck and nibble his ear.

"Maybe we should take a little stroll before we go downstairs." His hand went further up her leg. Hers was in his hair.

"Maybe we should." She stood up and pulled him to his feet. They moseyed down the hall and oh-so-casually stepped into the bathroom together. Vince locked the door. Pressed her against the wall, kissing her. Letting her feel his erection. "God, Vince."

"You do it to me every time, baby."

"Uhnn." She couldn't answer with his tongue in her mouth, so she put her hands to work. Pulling his shirt out of his pants, unfastening, unzipping. Plunging her hand into his briefs, half-laughing at the stifled sound he made when her fingers closed around him. "Want this," she tried to say. One of his hands was tugging her skirt up; the other was somewhere else, in his pocket? What was he doing? They didn't bother with those now. Vince put enough distance between them to tear the condom wrapper open. Moved her hand long enough to roll it on. "Baby?"

"I wanted to do this," he said against her neck. "If we got half a chance. Want to come inside you." He was sliding against her now.

She was so wet, so hungry. One leg hooked around his hip. Whimpering, waiting, clutching at him. "Do it."

"This way you won't be self-conscious about being squishy."

She half-laughed, half-moaned as he pushed inside her. She would've been. She'd've worried about standing up and finding a wet spot on her skirt. Jesus Mary and Joseph, how much did she love this man. "Oh *fuck* Vince." God, the feel of him, the strength, that growling sound. She was never going to get enough of this. She came before he did, holding on for dear life.

When they got back to the lounge, considerably more relaxed, they found a gift basket had been delivered. A gift bucket, rather – with an iced bottle of Cristal. Hanging from the neck of the bottle was a 45 rpm record of the Smash Mouth song 'All Star;' the sleeve was glued to a square of cardboard. On the back were written messages of congratulation.

Vince was pleased. "How cool is that?"

Kelli read the names on the card. "Elliott, Alicia, Vicky, Sharon, Michelle, Dmitri – did he come tonight?! – Patrick, Will, Randa, Esmeralda, Gabriel, Sherry – who is that? – and Adam. *Adam*? Is that your dad?!"

"Whoa, really? Let me see." He read the card. "I did leave him a voicemail, told him I'd have some tickets held for him, but I never thought he'd actually come. It's not exactly a short trip."

"It's so nice that he came."

"Yeah, it really is. He probably wanted to meet you."

"He probably wanted to see his son up on stage, mi amor."

"Yeah, maybe." Vince was smiling. "Ready to go downstairs? Get in place before act two starts."

"Yes, I'm feeling much more relaxed now."

"By the time I'm through with you, you're gonna be boneless."

"Ooh, promises, promises!" They collected their shoe bags and the gift to head downstairs. The next ten minutes were all greetings and congratulations, hugs

120

and kisses, yelling at each other to be heard over the crowd. It was surreal, Kelli decided about an hour later. She'd been in Baltimore for New Year's Eve 2010. A house party. Trying not to mind that she was there on her own, trying not to envy her siblings and even her parents because they had what she wanted. And now she had *all this*. These wonderful crazy friends, and this wonderful crazy man, and a wonderful crazy life where she got to dance on stage on Sunset Boulevard.

Vince held Kelli close because the dance floor was packed, and because he wanted to. Half-high on the thrill of performing (plus the champagne), nose full of the scent of warm woman, looking forward to the morning. He might have done the thing tonight, but why mix up the memories. This was the end of their first chapter. Tomorrow they'd start the next, with the new year. It was going to be great.

Long after midnight, Vince closed and locked the apartment door, dropped his shoe bag on the floor and set the empty Cristal bottle on the nearest surface. They were both exhausted. The first thing Kelli did when she reached the bedroom was pry off her shoes. "Oh lord, why can't cute useless shoes be as comfortable as dance shoes? I may have to take a rain check on that boneless thing."

Vince made a sound that meant 'oh no you won't.' After a minimal washing-up, he led Kelli to the bed and sat her down. Knelt by the side of the bed and started massaging her feet. She flopped onto her back. "Ooh, my goodness."

After a few minutes, during which Vince's attention had begun to migrate up her legs, he said, "How's the boneless thing coming along?"

"Not sure. Maybe you should join me up here and

check things out." She hitched herself up and he stretched out beside her, erection sliding hot against her skin. "Well, *you* certainly aren't boneless."

He laughed silently. "Maybe you could help me out with that." He pressed close, mouth on her throat and hand on her breast. Loving the feel of her, the scent of her, the sounds she made.

"I'll see what I can do," she murmured, skimming her hand down his body. Not too much later, he slung a leg over hers and braced himself over her. "Happy New Year," she said breathlessly, shifting underneath him, bringing a knee up and hooking her foot over his thigh. He smiled against her mouth and kissed her, sinking into her. *Happy New Year, baby*.

New Year's Day, 2012

It was late morning when they woke to the sound of a text notification on Vince's phone. He reached over to pick it up. "Fiesta at the mamacita's house at three o'clock. Dad and Sherry will be there."

"We could do that. But you might have to carry me," Kelli said lazily. "I'm still feeling mighty boneless."

"So am I."

She laughed. "That'll be the day!" They slid out of bed, took turns in the bathroom, and got the coffee going. Kelli threw on leggings and Vince's dress shirt from the night before. Vince rummaged in the closet for his gym pants. Kelli watched with approval as he came out, shirtless, carrying a hoodie. "I must say, you were always smokin' hot but your body looks incredible."

He pulled the hoodie over his head. "Probably the

most ripped I've ever been. Apparently throwing girls around is a workout."

"You sure have gotten good at it."

"It's been fun." He smiled suddenly. "Who woulda thought?" She couldn't decide whether to laugh or say 'I knew it would be,' so she kissed him instead.

They scavenged for breakfast, ate at the table by the window, then sat for a while in contented silence with supplemental coffee. Kelli leaned back with a sigh. "What a great year that was!"

"Think we can top that?"

"May have to do the competition thing just to keep the adrenalin going."

"Well, there was this wild idea I had," he said casually.

"Oh yeah?"

He pulled a ring box out of the pocket of his hoodie, flipped it open, and placed it on the table. Then he sat back, looking at Kelli with amusement. Her mouth had dropped open and her eyes were wide. *I love you so much*, he thought. "Shall we get married?"

"Oh!!"

Kelli thumped her empty coffee mug down on the table. Her hands hovered over the box for a moment, then she delicately removed the ring. It was a slightly domed band of gold, with four diamonds flush-set across the top. She slid it onto her ring finger and smiled at Vince through happy tears. "Yes, *please*."

PART TWO

CHAPTER 9

Thanksgiving Day, 2013

It was a trip making the call from one hour ahead of Baltimore time, instead of three hours behind. The first thing Diana (and everyone else back home) wanted to know was what Kelli and Vince were doing for dinner. Kelli made eye contact with Vince – currently lying with his head on her lap while she sat propped up against the headboard and approximately all the pillows – and stifled a laugh. "It's not actually Thanksgiving here, you know." She bit her lip at Vince's expression. "Uh-huh. Yeah. Not a holiday in Argentina. So we're probably going to do exactly what we did yesterday. The hotel sends up coffee and pastries. After a while we'll go out and find something to do, pick up a meal wherever we want, hang out in the sun. Yeah, it's summer here. No, we've been dancing every day but not at the same places. Well, it's all over. Seems like every street has somewhere to dance. We've been walking into classes. Walking into bars where people are practicing. Oh lord they stay up late here. We got in at three in the morning last night. I know! Re-setting to L.A. time is gonna be rough. No, none of our close friends have been here except Dmitri and Patrick. Well of course they're our friends, we've known them for two years. They got married this year too. Mm-hmm. No, they did it up in Washington. Guess it would have been too much of a big deal to try to do it at home. Well, Dmitri and Michelle had this really heavy competition schedule. Yeah, they just won the title." She couldn't quite keep the wistfulness from her tone; she would have loved to go to Ohio to cheer on their coach and friend. But the wedding was expensive, and neither of them really wanted to end the year in the red, so they couldn't do everything. Not going to the Ohio Star Ball meant a few extra days in Buenos Aires. "What? Do I want to do that?" Exchanging another glance with Vince. "I don't think so." It sounded a little like a question; they hadn't discussed ballroom competition with any seriousness. There were too many other things to do. "Well, yeah. We're still planning to do at least one Salsa Challenge event next year. Oh, and we're entering the L.A. Tango Championships in February. We went last time to see what it was all about, ended up taking six hours of workshops and then there was a milonga that went basically all night. Tired? Girl, please. I couldn't even *walk* the next day. Spreading it out over a week like this is better. Oh, it's gorgeous here. I don't know how it would be if we didn't both speak Spanish but it's great. Uh-huh. Honestly, even better than Puerto Rico. Oh, way better than Cabo. I mean, we had some good times in Cabo." Vince was laughing silently, no doubt remembering some of those good times. Kelli wound her fingers into his hair and tugged gently. He gave her a hot look. *Oh yes baby.* "Listen, everybody, I'm gonna let you go. Happy Thanksgiving. Uh-huh, going home Saturday. I'll send a text when we land." She rolled her eyes. You would think once a person got to be going-on-thirty-four that people would stop worrying, but no. "I love you too. Vicente says hi. Talk at ya soon. Bye." Kelli disconnected, blew out a breath, and dropped the phone on the nightstand. "God."

"All talking at once?"

"You know it. And now I need to pee."

Vince obligingly sat up so she could get off the bed and go take care of that. "Are you ready to get on with the day?"

125

She answered through the mostly-shut bathroom door. "No. You need to call Esme. And then we need to fool around." Vince thought about that order of business and decided to flip it. After all, they were way ahead of L.A. time. When Kelli left the bathroom she saw him sprawled out naked the way he was before, but with his cock in hand. He could tell she was about one word from cracking up, so all he did was raise an eyebrow. Kelli raised one back. "Oh, you think so?" She stood there with her hands on her hips, which conveniently held the unbelted robe open.

"Jesus, you're gorgeous," he said. "Want to help me out with this?"

"Help you out, huh." Kelli eyed him for another few seconds. *Speaking of gorgeous.* He'd been shaving before dinner lately, so he had the equivalent of five o'clock shadow instead of morning-after shadow. The hair (which he rarely bothered to put product in) was wildly tousled. The body was just fucking incredible. She took a couple steps with exaggerated sway, watching him watch her. She would never have guessed that she'd be in the best shape of her life at thirty-three. If dancing every day kept that look on her husband's face, she was never going to stop. "Why don't you tell me what I should wear today."

Vince loved this game. "For the next hour or so you should wear nothing." There she went, stifling a laugh. *God, I love you.* "Then maybe that other sundress Kenji made for you. The yellow one." Michelle's new husband – they'd been married only six months longer than Vince and Kelli – was a friend of Dmitri's and a professional designer. He made Kelli's wedding dress, and everything she'd performed in since their first Salsa Challenge event. With this trip serving as their delayed honeymoon, Vince suggested she should get some fun vacation clothes made. 'The yellow one' was a 1950s-style full-skirted dress in printed cotton, with a ruffled underskirt. She looked like a pin-up girl in it. Or out of it. He couldn't help stroking himself as she shucked off the robe and got on the bed with him. Stopping on her hands and knees, bending down for a kiss. "Mmm." He put one hand on her body, brushing across the hyper-sensitive skin between breast and underarm, over her ribs, around to the indent of her spine, and down to her bottom. Dipping in behind her thigh, teasing the way her mouth was teasing his. She made a restless sound and nipped at his lip. "So fucking hot," he murmured. His other hand was buried in her hair, and he didn't want to stop feeling that. He tugged on her thigh. Trying to bring her to him. "Come on, baby."

Kelli loved it when he was like this. Hungry, vocal, impatient. She let her knees go out to the sides, dropping her hips, rubbing against him. Oh Jesus that sound he made, when her wet slid along his hard. It was tempting to stay just like this. Get herself off without letting him in. He still had one hand in her hair, the other clamped on her ass. They were kissing open-mouthed, sloppy and a little bit toothy, while she worked herself. Starting to whimper as he started to growl. *Oh God baby you're amazing. Almost there I'm almost oh Jesus you're so yes there yes now YES.*

Vince felt her come. It was a full-body thing sometimes with Kelli, a ripple all along her spine to match the pulse of her hot wet center. A buck of the hips and a raspy moan. Sweat smeared between her breasts and his chest, irresistible slickness between their thighs. So much it dripped, running down along his balls. She was holding some of her weight on her elbows, gasping for breath. He got both hands on her hips and tipped her slightly, just enough to slide in. Surging up into her. "Oh fucking Jesus, Kelli, God I love you."

"I love you too." It was a faint, slurred mutter a few minutes later, when Kelli was on her back. Vince was still inside her. Still holding one of her legs up. Their other three legs were tangled some kind of way; his upper body was at an angle to hers and he was face-down in a pillow. She had the vague idea he'd landed there after coming with a shout people probably heard a block away. The thought made her laugh, which made him slide out. He grumbled a protest but rolled off to her side. She put together a few words. "I'm really liking this slow vacation morning sex thing."

Vince liked it too. Taking a whole ten days off together woke him up to the way their life was back in Los Angeles: always on the go. Going to work, going to class or a lesson, going out with friends. Competitions, performances, social things. None of it was stuff they wanted to do without, obviously. And maybe they just hadn't realized how great it would be to take a break, because neither of them had ever really done that. Until now, all their travel – aside from a couple of trips to Mexico – had been for competitions or family or, like the wedding, a combination of the two. Cabo almost didn't even count because both getaways had been so brief. Down there on Friday, back home on Sunday. "Maybe the next time we take a long weekend we should do a cruise."

"Ooh!" Kelli wriggled onto her side to see his face.

He was smiling. "What do you think? Once we get on the boat, everything's right there. One thing though."

"What."

"We should maybe pick one with no dance stuff." Kelli laughed. Vince wriggled close to kiss her. "Otherwise it'll be just like being at home."

128

"There's gotta be some other kind of cruises. Dance-free. But oh lord, it better not be one of those family cruises. Not till we've got our own kids. Otherwise we'll be hiding in the bar the whole time."

Another kiss. "Put that on the list of things to investigate." He sat up reluctantly, shoving his hair off his face, peeling his dick off his thigh with a wince. "Time to shower. And then call Ma."

Of course, as soon as they got back into their routine, the notion of 'taking time off' got pushed further and further down their to-do list. It was always tempting to do something with the Cabaret, because everyone said oh you should do one this month, and it was so easy now. An hour to do the choreography, three or four hours to get it ready, throwing together their costume, done. But early 2014 was devoted to working (semi-seriously) on a number for the Salsa Challenge, and (more seriously) on a routine for the duets competition at the Tango Championships.

Meanwhile, Kelli's work was its usual steady low-drama thing, while Vince's pace picked up considerably. The city was far enough out of the recent recession that everybody in the world seemed to be buying or selling houses. Elliott was doing some kind of showing every day and the mortgage-brokering side of things was nonstop.

Everyone else they knew was busy too. Their friends Mateo and Sam were both doing ballroom competition, in different divisions. Dmitri and Michelle were gunning for their second world title. Vicky and Sharon were training hard for the Gay Games. And every time they turned around, Tony was there with a camera.

Right around the time Vince and Kelli went to Baltimore to get married, Dmitri brought in Elena Hernandez as his studio manager. She was his professional Smooth partner for one season back in 2008, and rumor had it they didn't part on good terms, but everything seemed to be cool now. Elena's husband Tony was a filmmaker currently employed as the director of a docu-series called 'Live Work Dance.' They lived in the same building as Vince and Kelli; it didn't take long to get friendly.

At first the ever-present camera was mostly in service of Tony's series. But he started working on a private project, too. He was making a documentary about ballroom, beginning with Dmitri's season with Elena and now focusing on his campaign with Michelle. By late spring, Vince was thinking there should be another story arc. Mateo's competitive partnership wasn't going as well as everyone hoped. It seemed likely there'd be some kind of change soon. He and Kelli thought Mateo ought to be looking at Elena.

The perfect opportunity to ask about it came up a couple weeks before the Emerald Ball, California's biggest competition. Vince strolled into the Italian restaurant down the block from the dance studio, saw Mateo waiting at the host stand, and said, "Hey, good job at April Follies." They bumped fists. "Vicky told me the four of you had a blast. Getting takeout?"

"Well, I was going to, but I'd rather eat with you. Sam's at work."

"Yeah, let's get a table. Kelli's out with some girl friends." Not too much later, they were seated, with drinks on the way and menus in hand. "How's it going with Yolanda?"

Mateo rolled his eyes. "Bless her heart." Vince stifled a laugh. "Well, she comes from ballet, and just between you and me she's headed back there. If we don't make the final at Emerald she's calling it." His tone said that was exactly the outcome he expected.

"Oh shit. What're you going to do? Are you going to try and stay in it?" The professional Rising Star events in Mateo's American Rhythm division were what Vince thought of as accessible. There weren't a million competitors, which meant it was easy to get the judges to notice you. Unfortunately that also meant if you weren't doing well, everyone would see it.

Mateo swallowed some of his water, glanced around the restaurant as if to make sure nobody they knew was in there to hear, and said, "Elena and I tried out for Dmitri."

Vince's eyebrows shot up. "No kidding!"

"She's the perfect height for me, she knows the syllabus backward and forward, the Smooth experience she got with the boss gives her a real edge with bolero, and we get along." Mateo shrugged. The server arrived to take their orders. When that was done Mateo said, "I heard through the grapevine that back in the day, Dmitri tried to get you and Kelli to do Rhythm."

"He did." Vince smiled at the memory. "That was right before we got invited to do our thing at the House of Blues. So then we spent a month fixing everything we were doing wrong with that, and by the time we were done it was like eh. One dance at a time. I like being able to choose my own music."

"Oh God I know! You remember when Sam and I did our first thing with the Cabaret last fall? He tried out that choreography with Julia to some regular rumba music and he was like damn, that sucks." Vince laughed. "Anyway yeah. I don't see us making the final, which means Yolanda's gonna be leaving my ass. But Elena said, you know, why not."

131

"Kelli said Elena said for a long time she didn't think she'd want to compete again."

Mateo made a dismissive sound. "Kidding herself."

"What does Tony say about it?"

"He hasn't said much." A glance away, a wriggle that might have signaled discomfort. "I get a feeling he'd rather she didn't, but if she's going to, at least I'm gay."

"Mmm, yeah." Vince considered his friend for a minute. Mateo was extremely good-looking. Not that Tony was unsightly, but dancing together was intimate. Vince knew that Michelle's husband Kenji had some issues with her dance partnership, even though he and Dmitri had been friends for years. Not to mention Dmitri was nearly twenty years older than Michelle and also gay. "It's probably good he's got the boss and Michelle to look at as a model. Kenji and Patrick have their own ways of dealing with it." Patrick was Dmitri's number-one fan and supporter; Kenji signed up as a vendor so he could make the most out of accompanying Michelle to events.

"Patrick, my God, that man is a saint. I think the documentary's going to help Tony a lot. He'll have a good excuse to hang around all the time but also he'll have to keep some professional distance." Mateo registered Vince's skeptical expression. "No, really. Has he done any actual interviews with you yet?"

"No, not yet."

"He's good. He's all about context and psychology, plus he really knows his shit on the dance side. You should ask him about it sometime when you guys get together. Anyway, it seems like I've hardly seen you. What's been going on?"

"Everybody and their brother is buying and selling this year. I'm juggling deals ten hours a day." Their dinner was delivered. "Oh damn this smells good. Mmph." Mateo didn't answer; he was already digging into his vegetable lasagna.

June 2014

"I've been feeling so guilty about missing your big win at Emerald Ball," Kelli said as she leaned in for a hug.

Alicia made a dismissive sound and squeezed her. "Sit your ass down. We both understood. It was kind of a miracle Elliott even got there, and believe me he knows about working on a closing. Tell you something else." She waited for Kelli to glance at the menu and set it aside. They'd both eaten at this place so often they really only needed to verify that their favorites were still on the menu. When Kelli looked up, Alicia went on. "I think E was glad Vince wasn't there. He's always a little bit nervous about dancing but especially in front of you guys."

"Aw." Kelli made a sad face. "Not you too, I hope."

"I'm nervous about dancing *period*. Having friends close by to talk me off the ledge is a good thing."

"So you gonna do it again? Or keep doing it?" A sip of water as she registered the approach of a server.

"Eh." There was a pause to give their orders. Once food was on the way, Alicia drank some of her Arnold Palmer. "Mmm. Tangy. Good. To be honest probably not. We liked getting that little trophy, and God knows working up to the event sure helped me get back in shape after Elizabeth, but once she's toddling? Once she's, like, mobile?" Kelli snorted out a laugh. "Yeah. I'm thinking no. We're going to have our hands full. So

133

maybe some lessons here and there, like if there's a special occasion and we want to brush it up. Maybe a social here and there for a date. But probably not competition again. That's your jam."

Kelli made a dismissive sound. "Hardly! That's *his* jam."

"Really?" This was interesting.

"I mean I like it, sure. It's a kick to see how you stack up against other dancers. But it's a fuck of a lot of money, as you know." Alicia made an 'oh yeah' face. Kelli made a 'for real' face back at her. "We've always done way more with the Cabaret than competition. And then there's this absolute batshit crazy thing that man is involved in now." Kelli told her friend all about the Beowulf-based dance concert. "Our friend Mateo and his boyfriend Sam are doing a lot of choreo for the troupe, and Vince is in the troupe. It's all these battles. It's war, no lie. They're having the first full-cast meeting and rehearsal in a week or so and from then till the thing closes he's gonna be some new combination of bruise colors."

Alicia was grinning. "Anybody else in it that I know?"

"Vicky."

"For *real*?"

"She's the only woman in the troupe. But the star of the thing is this six-foot-tall woman from England. I've seen a couple things of hers that I found on YouTube so I'm super curious how it's going to come together. But tell me about you!" Food was delivered and they got most of the way through their meal while discussing the cascade of personal changes related to eight-month-old Elizabeth. Once the leftovers were taken away to be packed up, Kelli leaned back in her chair with a sigh. "Still glad you got pregnant right away?"

"Oh, totally. She'll be starting school the year I turn forty-two. I keep hearing how the forties are the best decade of a woman's life. I'll be ready for it." She gave that a wicked little twist. "How about you?"

Kelli knew what she meant. "Next year. Like you say. Once you have little kids, that's your life. We want to do it right, like you guys. And we want more than one. So we're taking another year to dance our asses off, and then we'll start trying. Or stop not trying." Alicia cracked up. Their leftovers came back. They consulted silently about dessert; Kelli turned to the server and asked for one tiramisu and two forks. "Okay, got that rolling. So listen, I'm going to be sending you a thing when I get back to the office. The real-estate guys are bringing in a lateral with a big book of business, and unlike some firms I could name they do not just pile more work on the people they have, so we're looking to add a support desk."

Alicia instantly went into legal-recruiter mode. "Great! I've got a few people who are looking for new roles, so maybe we can match something up."

"Anybody fresh?"

"One guy. Really fresh. He just moved out here from Minneapolis. Only had one law job before, and not for very long, but he's got good recommendations and decent skills. Plus he's super nice."

"What did he do before law? I mean, I'm assuming it's on the resumé."

"Well, don't get too excited, but he was a dancer."

Kelli blinked. They already had one other dancer at her office, a woman Kelli's age who'd done a few things with the Cabaret. "Was?"

135

"Twelve years with a company. Retired unwillingly due to injury."

"Oh, shit, the poor guy. Twelve years! He must be the real deal."

"I think so, yeah. I'll send you his profile for sure."

"What's the hardest part of the hard sell." There was always something. This guy wasn't a job-hopper (yet) but the lack of experience was going to weigh against him. If there was anything else, it might not even be worthwhile bringing him in for an interview.

"No college."

"Oh *shit*." But if he didn't go to college then he might have gone into the company job right out of high school, which meant he was not too old to be a beginner in this field. Kelli thought she could work with that.

"He's very articulate, he reads, and he can type. I know you like to hire for personality, and seriously? He's *super* nice. You keep telling me the balance is off at your place," she said persuasively as the tiramisu landed.

Kelli dug into it. "Mmph. Could use a guy on this desk," she said after she swallowed. "He's not too good-looking, is he?"

"Uh." Alicia dodged that with a bite of dessert. Kelli rolled her eyes. They didn't say anything else till the tiramisu was gone. "He doesn't look like Vince, but nobody's going to think he's unsightly."

Kelli inhaled some water, coughed, and laughed for a few seconds. "Is he with all the recruiters? Am I going to get twelve copies of his resumé?"

"He's with at least three. He told me one of them's trying to pitch him to entertainment companies, but he's got a place on the Westside here, so he's not too thrilled at the prospect of driving over to the Valley."

"Ooh, that's good for us though. Send it over. And anyone else you've got."

Two weeks, four phone interviews, and a prelim with a second candidate later, Kelli walked Mike Borodin out to reception to get his parking validated. "Thanks for coming in." She offered her hand. He shook it lightly, with the pleasant non-smile she thought must be his default expression. It was somewhat bemused, as if things kept happening too fast. Judging from the little he'd said about his accident – the words 'head injury' had been spoken – he wasn't quite fully recovered. If they brought him on, and if he was okay talking about it, she'd find out more. At the moment she was happy to recommend him for a second interview with the office administrator, and to tell the head of the real-estate group about him. She watched him go, thinking *not unsightly, huh*, and exchanged a speaking glance with the receptionist, who fanned herself and made a 'wow' face. Kelli stifled a laugh and headed back to her office.

The next day, the senior partner in the real-estate group frowned at the resumé. "No college?"

Kelli stifled a sigh. "I know, Tom. But he did well on the assessments, and honestly? You're not going to find a worker more disciplined than a professional dancer."

He dropped the resumé on his desk and leaned back, staring at her. "Sell me."

That was unexpected. "Well, first of all, you know Paula. She is not the warmest fuzziest person but she gets the work done, she puts in extra hours when necessary without whining, and the work product is good. This guy," she tapped the paper that gave such a limited picture, "strikes me as the same kind of worker. Plus he has an easy way about him. Meaning not someone who's going to let you guys walk all over him, but someone easy to get along with. The thing about a dancer?" She paused, waiting to see if Tom wanted to hear more. He nodded. "Every day starts with basics. A guy who's worked for this long in a company knows all about how important it is to do things right. He's not going to blow off steps one to whatever of the workflow. He's going to be methodical, he's going to practice until he gets it right, and here's a thing I really think you ought to consider." Another pause, another nod. Tom was letting her say a lot more than she expected; it was kind of great. "He's not going to take it personally if you correct him. As long as you're not a jerk about it."

Tom laughed. "Okay, fine. Bring him in for round two. What about this other person."

"She's fine." Kelli shrugged. "She could get the job done. I wouldn't think it was a mistake to hire her. But she's going to be more expensive, and she's got a lot of years in an actual brokerage. She might have some preconceived notions about how things should be done."

"Good points. Bring her back too and make sure I get to meet both of them."

"You got it."

"Thanks, Kelli."

"Thanks Tom!" She got out of there, a little bit blown away. That was the first time she'd really gone to bat for a candidate, and she'd half-expected to be shown the door before she got a word out. Maybe she should have been more assertive before. Or maybe Tom was paying attention to the rest of her hires. Not one of them had been a disappointment. As soon as she was in her tiny office (no window, barely big enough for two people to have a private chat, which was sometimes necessary when you worked in HR) she grabbed her phone and sent a text. *Hey baby guess what? I just got LISTENED TO BY A LAWYER*

A minute later, Vince's reply landed: *That's my girl. This your dancer candidate?*

Yup. We'll see what happens!

CHAPTER 10

August 2014

Kelli stabbed the meat thermometer into the roast, drizzled marinade over the vegetables, and heaved the pan into the oven. Set the timer, turned on the exhaust fan, and said, "There. Now we can sit around and gossip till they get home."

Sharon poured her a glass of wine. "I remember one time I heard Patrick call himself a ballroom widow. I was all, aww, poor baby. Now I'm like, yep." She picked up her ice water and followed Kelli into the living room. "Which is ridiculous after what we just did."

"That was so awesome. I would have so loved to be there." Kelli set her glass down on the end table, then curled up on the couch. "It was fun, right?"

"Oh *shit* yeah it was fun." Sharon was grinning. "Being there with Sam and Mateo was great. Plus Dmitri and Patrick supporting us. I think I would have been freaking out nonstop if we were there alone. I mean, hello, Gay Games. It's not quite the Olympics but it's the fucking Olympics!"

Kelli laughed into her glass and changed the subject. "You gonna tell me why you're not drinking wine today?"

Sharon made an apologetic face. "It wasn't about not telling *you*, specifically." Kelli made an 'I get it' face. Sharon rolled her neck. "It was kind of like, let's wait till the wheels are turning because everybody's going to be all up in our business once the word gets out."

"I can be discreet." When she had to be.

"I know you can. So the story is, we're trying to get pregnant." Kelli squealed with suspicions-confirmed glee. Sharon laughed. "First round was this week."

"That's so exciting!! Are you using an anonymous donor? I'm, hold on." She swallowed some wine, set the glass down, wondered for a second if this was even a thing she should say. "Vince would've done it for you."

Sharon reached across the couch and patted Kelli's hand. "I know. And believe me, he was high on the list. Because the answer is no, our donor is not anonymous, but again until we really have something to report we're trying to keep that a little bit quiet. It would be so disappointing for everybody if it doesn't take."

"I get it, I really do. One of the paralegals at my office got pregnant last year. They'd been trying for a while, had a miscarriage once. She didn't tell anybody until she was into her second trimester. You're not going to wait that long, are you?"

"Me? No. I cannot keep a secret, and Vicky is worse. Sam and Mateo know. Obviously our donor and his partner know. It's only a matter of time till everybody knows." Sharon didn't look troubled about that. "Anyway yes, thank you, we did consider asking you guys. Because when we talked about it, I'm the one who wants to be pregnant, but I want our baby to look like *our* baby, so we were kind of wracking our brains going who do we know who's got dark hair like Vicky, on the tall side, with all the smarts and talent and everything." Kelli was giggling. "Well come on! We don't want some good-looking idiot." Kelli laughed out

141

loud. Sharon was grinning again. "This person's going to be in our life for eighteen years."

"At least." Kelli wiped her eyes, composed herself, took another sip of wine. "But you didn't choose Vince."

"Well, because you two are going to have your own kids. And knowing us, twenty years down the line one of your kids will want to marry our kid, so." They both cackled. After a minute Sharon said, "How about you?"

Kelli blew out a breath. "Next year sometime. I feel like that's as long as I could wait and still have good odds. I'll be thirty-five."

"Yeah. We definitely didn't want to wait much longer. Once the clock went off it was like, okay, let's make it happen. But then we had the damn Games to get out of the way. After working up to that for so long, I wasn't going to fuck it up with morning sickness."

"Mm-hmm." Kelli wriggled her back, re-settled into the couch, and thought about things. "I did not expect our dance year to get hijacked by fucking Beowulf."

Sharon laughed again. "God, I know! You've hardly even done the Cabaret this year, and then there goes Vince into the super troupe and he's no good to you for months. It's going to rock, though."

"Uh-huh. I'm envious. I mean, I don't want to be *in* it because *damn*. But I'm annoyed that he's loving something so much, and I'm not involved." She shrugged. It felt petty, but if anyone would understand it was Sharon. "Dance is our thing."

"Totally get that. It's not quite that way for us. I mean, I like dancing, and I especially like dancing with Vicky, but it's more something I do because she's doing it. If that makes sense."

"Totally does."

"She's made plenty of changes for me, anyway." They were both quiet for a moment.

Kelli was wondering, again, if she should say something. Curiosity got the better of her. "I remember you said you both used to date men."

"Mm-hmm." Sharon gazed at Kelli for a moment as if deciding whether to elaborate. "You ever heard of the Kinsey scale?"

"Like the Kinsey report?"

"Right. So there's this scale from zero to six. Zero is fully heterosexual, and six is fully homosexual. I'm like a four, maybe even five. I'm mostly attracted to women. Vicky's about a two."

"Oh. Oh! Huh." Kelli thought about it. "I might be like a one." Sharon laughed. Kelli made a face. "I mean I appreciate women, most of my close friends are women, and I definitely recognize when a woman is attractive. But I've never been attracted *to* women. Not in a sex way."

"It's a fine distinction," Sharon agreed. "But so the reality is, and maybe I *am* pregnant because are my filters off or what? The reality is I very much doubt Vicky would be with just any woman. I think she's with me for love. That doesn't necessarily mean I'm going to do it for her forever."

Kelli stared at her, appalled. "But, what?"

Sharon shrugged. These were not new thoughts, so she wasn't upset. "We've already talked about it a little. There are times when one or the other of us is like, a dick would be good here." Kelli collapsed laughing. Sharon watched her for a minute, sipping water, amused.

143

"Oh. Oh my lord." Kelli pressed her hands to her face for a second, laughed again, fanned herself. "But what are you going to do?"

"Toys only go so far. The fact is, she spent a lot of years fucking people bigger than she is. She is tall and strong and tough. I'm none of that. I told her, if there comes a time when you need to be manhandled, you tell me and we'll figure it out. I want her for life, so it's up to me to make sure she gets what she needs."

"Wow. *Wow*. You are such a fucking grown-up."

Sharon looked pleased. "Yeah. Well, I work in litigation, you know? And I see in living color, every damn day, how an ounce of prevention could've made a million-dollar difference."

Kelli reached for her glass again. "I'd better give some thought to that. I mean, I haven't been bitching at Vince about all the time going into this crazy show. But like once we have kids. We're not going to be doing what we've been doing. I talked about that with Alicia a couple months ago. I'm going to be the primary caregiver, and I'm fine with that, but that means a lot of hours are not going to be available for dancing. And I shouldn't expect him to give it up. Not when he's getting so good. Not when he loves it so much." Her glass was empty.

"He loves you a lot. A *lot*," Sharon emphasized. "You both do everything you can to make each other happy. I seriously doubt he'd ever be tempted by another woman, not the way he is with you. But if you can always give him dancing, your odds will be even better."

"Jesus." Kelli stood up, went to get herself a glass of water, then came back for Sharon's. Handed her a refill, leaned on the back of the couch, and stared at her.

"What?"

"Who was the last man you were with?"

"Bob. Robert. Bless his heart."

Her tone made Kelli smile. "Tell me."

"Met him at the gym. This was right after Vicky bounced her deadbeat off the wall and started dating again. Robert is a sports agent."

"Oh fuck, *sports*."

Sharon snickered. "Exactly. Nice guy, honestly, but there was no zing and we had nothing to talk about. The sex was, like, lamentable." Kelli laughed again. "But he asked me to marry him! Super fast! I was like, what? Kept the ring for a minute because it was really kind of awesome, but then I gave it back and told him I was in love with somebody else, which I was."

"Vicky."

"Right. So then Vicky and I are down at Disneyland for Dapper Day, the first one. And who do we see strolling along but Robert. With his boyfriend."

Kelli blinked. "Are you fucking with me?"

"No! God's honest truth! They met the very day I told Robert no. Got married last year, out at the beach. We were invited. His husband is Jade Derecha, he's a stylist down at that salon." Sharon pointed in a general direction. Kelli just shook her head; she went to a place in East Hollywood that knew Black hair. "So that was a trip. Anyway Jade does my hair now. We're not all BFFs but they're in the decent people we know and get along with category."

And of course the last man Vicky was with was Vince. If she and Sharon didn't come to Vince as a sperm donor, they surely wouldn't ask for anything else.

They were talking office politics when their tired, sweaty, hungry warriors staggered into the apartment. Vince let Vicky take a shower first, because he was a gentleman, handing her one of his tee shirts and a pair of yoga pants. By the time he was clean too, the roast was ready to carve.

Elena's husband Tony might have tried to cover 'Green Darkness' for his series anyway, but the fact that the troupe was rehearsing at Shall We Dance made it a sure thing. He was in there constantly with his camera, doing interviews and taking footage. Once Mateo and Elena started training in earnest, Vince saw Tony almost every time he was in the studio himself.

Thus it was no surprise at all to see him there the day after tech rehearsal, one week before the first performance. If he had things to say about the way the troupe numbers had evolved, he kept it to himself. Mateo and Sam had been working on this stuff for months. Vince still wasn't sure how they managed to do it at the same time they were prepping for the Gay Games.

Tony left them alone until they were done with their rehearsal. All of them were flat on their backs on the floor, gasping up at the ceiling. "Ow," Vicky said faintly.

"Ow is right." Vince didn't even want to sit up. "I thought it would be no big deal by now." There was some tired, hysterical giggling from the others. He took a deep breath, wondered how he would find the strength to walk home, and heard the street door open. Heard Tony say something to somebody. Turned his head, frowning, lifting up a little to see what was going on. "Oh my God."

Mateo lifted his head too. "Is that food?"

Sam said, "I think it's food." He sniffed. "From the Mexican place."

There was a brief gabble, probably the way people sounded when they witnessed a miracle, as the eight troupe dancers creaked into semi-upright positions. Tony brought over the bags, set them on the floor in the middle of the haphazard circle, then went to get bottles of water for everybody. For the next ten minutes the only sounds were the crinkle of bags, some growling over who got which burrito, and yummy noises.

"Oh my Jesus." Vicky lay down again, reversed herself, stretched out a foot to hook the leg of a chair, and dragged it over. Then she dragged herself up onto the seat. "Holy cats. Who did that?"

"Your director," Tony said, sounding amused. "When I asked if I could film this rehearsal she said she would provide sustenance."

"I suppose you want to talk to us now." Mateo didn't sound like he minded. He got to his feet and collected chairs for the others.

Tony retrieved one for himself. "If you don't mind? I've spoken with the stars, the designers, and the director. We've discussed the possible career implications. And I've spoken with Mateo and Vicky about other things. But this is such a unique project, my producers have asked to hear from all the dancers."

Another gabble, this one composed of variations on "Fine with me" and "Let me send a text" and "Can't stay long."

"Excellent, thank you." Tony brought his tripod over, loaded a fresh SD card into the camera, and switched it on. "First please introduce yourselves, and

147

tell us why you chose to join the troupe. Mateo, you will begin?"

Mateo gave him an amused look. "You know I'm a camera whore. I'm Mateo de la Cruz. I'm an architectural draftsman, I compete professionally in American Rhythm and I teach Rhythm and Latin here at Shall We Dance in WeHo."

"And you're completely insane," Vicky said. At least four of the others laughed.

"Maybe?" Mateo shrugged, unoffended. "Our Beowulf, Red Warner, approached me to join the troupe back in, what, May?" Sam nodded. "And he gave me the playlist, and I started noodling around with it."

"And the next thing you know, he's choreographing all the paso stuff for the whole show." Sam was smiling. "Sam Lee. I compete in pro-am Latin with Julia Hart. Used to be an MMA fighter, now I run a tux shop. Mateo and I just won a bronze medal in Latin at the Gay Games. We were there with her." He pointed at Vicky.

She wriggled on the cushioned folding chair. "Vicky Russo. My girlfriend and I did *not* win a medal at the Gay Games. We went in Standard and didn't even make the final, but whatever. I only started dancing four years ago."

"We have already spoken of this." Tony was smiling. "You've come a long way."

"Thanks, yes. Anyway I'm a patent paralegal and I wanted to do this because I saw what Mateo and Sam were doing. Also once I found out the star was a woman I was like, yeah."

Tony made a move, inviting the next person to speak. "Uh, I'm Sean Esparza? I'm a student here at

Shall We Dance. Amateur dancer. When Mateo said the troupe material was going to be based on paso I wanted to do it. Once I graduate from college I probably won't get a chance to do anything like this."

"Same and same," said the next guy. "I'm Gary Franklin, another of Dmitri's students. Sean and Michael and I all do pro-am Latin with Julia."

The third student nodded. "And the paso stuff was way cool, but once they started adding jazz and flamenco and fight styles and shit we were like damn." All the others snickered. "I'm Michael Cooper. Used to do ballroom with the USC team but since I graduated from law school it's only been a little bit of pro-am here and there. It seemed like this was a chance to do something really challenging to kind of cap off my dance career."

"You don't think you'll keep dancing?" Vince was smiling. "It's tough when you have an office job, I know."

Michael half-shrugged, half-smiled. "One of these days my girlfriend is going to ask for more of my time." A chorus of comprehension from the others. "And she's not interested in ballroom dancing. You're lucky that way."

"I am lucky," Vince agreed. "My wife and I connected over dancing and it's still one of our favorite things to do together. Uh, I'm Vince Connor and I'm a mortgage broker. I've been friends with Sam since we both worked at the Men's Wearhouse, and friends with Mateo since he started training at Shall We Dance. Pretty much the minute they said hey there's this show I was like yes please." Vicky laughed; Sam was smiling. Vince did a half-shrug, half-smile thing. "Kelli and I compete in salsa and tango, plus we've done a few shows with the Underground Cabaret."

"A few," Tony said dryly. "And our final dancer?" The most well-known person in the cast, aside from longtime stuntman and fight choreographer Red Warner.

"Ray Daniels. I'm an actor. I was a musical-theater boy growing up, did a ton of work as a dance extra before landing my role on '10-31.' I compete in professional Rising Star Latin with my girlfriend Julia Hart. We've done some work with the Underground Cabaret and when this thing started coming together it was, well." He paused, looked around the circle. "Projects like this don't come around very often, not even for people in a company. I understand it started out as a play but after Mary Bassey was cast as Grendel and his mother, it turned into a dance concert."

"Because why wouldn't it." Vicky made a 'what else could they do' face.

"So none of you are full-time professional dancers," Tony said. "How many hours have you put into this show?"

Everybody made some kind of sound. The result was a combination of laughter and groaning. Vince stepped into the following pause. "We've met as a group twelve times, counting today. The show is ten numbers and we're only in five, but there was other material we've done on video for the production. Altogether I'd estimate that as a troupe we've put in fifty solid hours since the first weekend in July. Individually or in smaller groups, couldn't guess. I've worked with some combination of Vicky, Ray, Mateo and Sam at least five times." Vicky was nodding. "Mateo and I have worked with Michael, Sean, and Gary three or four times." A nod from Michael. "And based on personal experience, I'm guessing Mateo and

Sam put in nearly fifty hours building the choreo before any of the rest of us even saw it."

"All on top of full-time jobs," Tony said. "A once in a lifetime experience?"

Vicky said, "Jesus, I hope not. This has totally kicked my ass but it's been so much *fun*."

"What I was about to say." Vince was grinning at her. "Ten out of ten, would do again. It's been fantastic digging so deep into storytelling, and getting to know all these people so well." He and Ray did a fist bump.

"So if there were to be another show like this, you would want to be considered?"

Vince gave Tony a look. "I'd be jumping up and down going, pick me!" The others all laughed. "But I sure hope if there's a next one, it's something Kelli would do too."

CHAPTER 11

Vince was still thinking that after closing night, when he could finally get back to dancing with his wife. The Underground Cabaret show for Halloween was a can't-miss. He and Kelli threw together a tango-flavored rumba set to 'Red Right Hand,' joining a lineup of movie-inspired routines. "You know," he said after dress rehearsal, watching Kelli lick pepperoni grease off her fingers, "we could do this exact same choreography to some other music for next month."

"For Andalusia?" They hadn't discussed submitting a routine for the November edition of Mating Dance. Kelli cocked her head. "You wanted to do something in December, too, right?"

"Mm-hmm. And we have to start working on a new routine for the Tango Championships. But if we could get three for three to close out the year it would kind of make up for missing out on some other things this summer, wouldn't it?"

Her toes curled a little at his expression. "You know, mi corazón, I don't actually think I missed out on anything this summer. Watching you have that experience was almost as good as having it myself, which by the way I did not want to do. That was some crazy shit." He inhaled some water, coughed, laughed for a few seconds. "But since we're talking about what to do next year, maybe this is the right time to confirm something. I'm stopping the pill after the tango event, right?"

Vince's heart lit up. He actually hadn't been sure she still wanted to. "I'm ready. You're ready?"

"Baby, I'm so ready. I've *been* ready. I was just trying to squeeze in a little more dancing with you because, you know."

Somehow he was holding her hand. "I'm always going to want to dance with you." She squeezed his fingers, didn't let go. "Are you pissed that Vicky and Sharon are going to have a baby before we do?"

Kelli cracked up. "So pissed! Oh my God! But I guess it's only fair. They've been together longer than we have. And we got married first."

"They could have gotten married last year too," he pointed out.

"Honey, please. Vicky's parents were still all, you know, maybe this is just a phase. It's no wonder they decided to do it guerrilla-style out here." It was going to be a very small affair: Vicky and Sharon, Vince and Kelli, and Sharon's parents, with their mutual friend Rory as celebrant and her girlfriend Dana distracting security at Urban Light.

"Next time they go to Brooklyn they're gonna get their asses handed to them. There'll be a mushroom cloud of Russo complaints." They were both snickering. Vince thought about weddings for a moment. "This'll be the first one we've gotten to go to since Elliott and Alicia."

Kelli turned her head, gazing across the room at Mateo and Sam. "Speaking of which. When are they finally going to do it?" Vince shook his head. "Sam ever talk about it?"

"Nope. They're good the way they are, I guess."

"Hmph." Kelli was pretty sure Mateo wanted to be married. It was something everybody had to take at their own pace, though. Like getting pregnant. She had no regrets about waiting, because they'd done so many great things, but she was ready. And Vince never stopped being awesome, so she was sure he was going to be a fantastic dad. Six more months to be fancy-free.

153

Get closer, she thought. As if he'd heard her, he scooted his chair toward hers.

August 2015

Kelli leaned against the back of the loveseat, letting her head rest on Vince's arm. Her legs were across his lap; he was slouched into the corner of the seat, gazing at her. *Maybe tonight*, she thought idly, half-smiling at the look on his face, half-conscious of Andy Martin moving around taking more pictures. It was late to be doing promo photos for this production, but he'd been out on a road trip with his boyfriend Victor for weeks. The production team pulled some old stuff out of the Cabaret archive for advance press. Rumor had it opening night was already close to sold out.

She was feeling kind of indulgent about the pictures anyhow. This right here was the perfect time to take pictures for this show. Plus, before that road trip, Andy and Victor sent up a smoke signal about looking for a place to buy together. The Cabaret grapevine waved it down to Vince, who passed it to Elliott, who was now working on closing the deal. It would be a nice fat commission for him.

Every month since March when she didn't turn up pregnant she'd been half-relieved. It was going to change their lives in so many ways. But the other half was nervous and disappointed, because what if they waited too long? Maybe now that 'Gaucho' was almost over her body would chill the fuck out and get busy. Or warm the fuck up and start cooking.

They'd been working on the tango show for a solid five months. It was probably the best dance experience they'd ever have together, which meant she couldn't regret it. Things were so polished in this dress rehearsal. Red and Mary were great. Sam and Mateo were great. The troupe – including Vicky and Ray again, but also including director Alison Jarvet and Dmitri – was terrific. And Kelli thought she might be excused for thinking she and Vince were awesome. Their duet number, set to 'Palomita Blanca,' was possibly her favorite thing they'd ever done.

"It's kind of amazing how things have changed here," she said.

Vince caressed her leg. "At Chrome?" The club owner had done a huge renovation and re-branding in 2012.

"Mm-hmm."

"Still mostly a bar."

She made a dismissive sound. "The one and only bar in Los Angeles to host full-on theatrical dance productions."

"Last year was a big risk. This year, not so much." The tango-based shows from the Underground Cabaret had been successful all along. Plus, Red Warner was much higher profile now than the year before, having booked a major movie role right after 'Green Darkness.' Ray was also high profile, a fan favorite on his cop show. The rest of the cast had a strong enough following that marketing 'Gaucho' was mostly a matter of posting TICKETS ON SALE NOW. They all agreed that this show was a career highlight.

After Alison called it for the day, troupe members Mike Borodin and Paula Ross asked to make a personal video onstage. They danced to Sam's solo music. Vince wouldn't come right out and say it was dreamy, but he could think that to himself. Dreamy, and sexy. Maybe because Mike and Paula just got engaged. He remembered how that felt. "How'd you like that freestyle?" He studied Kelli's sleepy, warm expression. A woman ready to go to bed. It was only midafternoon, but he was ready too.

She moved her head slightly, in a way he knew meant 'come closer.' He leaned in. She murmured, "Let's go home and make a baby." He shifted again and kissed her. "Mmm."

God, I love you. "Let's go home."

Two weeks after 'Gaucho' closed, Tony asked for a one-on-one interview with Kelli. She wasn't feeling all that well, but there was a pattern to the general crappiness, and she couldn't help thinking 'now or never,' so they made a date. She went downstairs to his apartment, declined a coffee with what she hoped was not an obvious spasm of revulsion, accepted a glass of water. His camera tripod stood near his task chair. Once she was settled he took a seat. "We can begin?"

"I'm still not sure about doing this, honestly," Kelli confessed. "I have things to say but I'm not convinced I should say them." She was sitting on Tony's couch, a few feet away from his task chair. Her legs were crossed almost casually, but her arms were crossed too, at the wrists, resting on her knee. Tony had seen body language like that many times. It wasn't the outright rejection of arms crossed at the chest; it was more like shielding.

It was Tony's job to put the subject at ease, to provide a safe place for them to speak. This time he knew he had to get personal. "Remember, anything you do not want to have seen can be erased. This project, I can do what I like. It's mine, it's my therapy. When Elena said she wanted to try competition again, it felt like a knife in my heart." Kelli's startled reaction told

Tony that Elena hadn't shared too much. "Even after she said she wanted to dance with Mateo. Could he ever be a threat to me? No. He's like a brother to her. But I wished to be everything to her. And it was unjust!" He threw his hands up, shaking his head. "I have my work. I'm with other women almost every day, beautiful dancers."

Abruptly Kelli understood why Tony was opening with this. "The jealousy factor. That thing last year was really the first thing Vince did without me since his very first number with the Cabaret."

"May we speak of this? You've known Michelle and Dmitri so long. You know Elena and Mateo."

"Sure, okay. I wasn't a hundred percent on why you wanted to talk to me without Vince in the room. So you're looking for a different perspective on the challenges of these partnerships."

"Yes, exactly."

"And I'm guessing you want my take on this will they, won't they. Vince and Michelle." Tony performed a complicated gesture that combined apology and eagerness. Kelli huffed out a laugh. It was so not a sure thing, they were barely talking about it as if it *might* be a thing. Michelle and Kenji had spent most of the year traveling, indulging in some serious quality time to make up for the years she was on campaign with Dmitri. But she'd dropped a hint to Vince about not being quite ready to hang up her competition shoes. And Vince had immediately told Kelli, because no matter what happened, she needed to know.

She sighed. While this wasn't the thing she most wanted to talk about, there might come a day when a record of her feelings at this stage would be helpful.

"Fine, turn on the camera." She consciously relaxed, making herself as comfortable as possible, grateful that the apartment didn't smell like any of the foods that set off her not-just-morning sickness.

Tony led her through some basic history, asking for her view of the studio environment and chemistry since she and Vince started dancing there. How it changed when Dmitri and Michelle began their competition partnership; how it changed again when Elena joined the staff. And then a swift recap of her own performance and competition history with Vince. "You've done so many things," Tony said with clear admiration. "The two of you are stars of the Cabaret."

She waved that off, blushing. "We just really love it, you know? Dancing together like that is our thing."

"And even if he trains in Smooth, it will be different."

"Exactly. Ballroom competition, even a show dance, is not the same as doing one of our little personal numbers. It is never intimate. So that's why it really doesn't bother me. I mean that part of it. I will be jealous of the time he's giving her, but it's not *personal*, you know?" She checked in with Tony, saw his nod of comprehension. "The thing is, I don't want to do that. I don't want to compete at that level. It's been a while since we even talked about going pro. I have security needs." Another nod. "If one of us has a full-time job with benefits, we're going to be a lot more secure. Especially with having kids. He's still acting like maybe he won't do this but between you and me I think it's pretty much a done deal. He loves competition. He's ambitious. She's a champion." Kelli shrugged. "And they've danced together before, they're good together."

"He is very like Dmitri."

She sat forward a little. "Yes! Well, most of his real dance training came from Dmitri. If they go ahead, they might even start with some of Michelle and Dmitri's old routines, see how those work for Vince's body."

"You have already talked about this."

"Oh yeah. Honestly the person I'm worried about is Kenji. I don't know how well he'll cope once the new thing starts."

"If Vince were not so," Tony made an eloquent gesture, "it would be easier?"

Kelli laughed. Her man was definitely *so*. "Dmitri is a handsome man, but he's almost twenty years older than Michelle, and there was never any question of a sexual connection there. Vicente is too good-looking," she admitted. "And too young, and too straight." Now they both laughed, but Kelli sighed. "I'm really afraid their friendship won't survive. Vicente and Kenji. We'll have to figure out some way to make the whole situation less threatening."

"But this fear, you don't feel it for you and Michelle."

Kelli shook her head. "I know she loves Kenji. She's not considering this because she wants to mess that up. It's because she has a window of opportunity, and she's still coasting on some momentum from the last campaign. By the time a better potential partner comes along, it might be too late for her. She is my friend." A pause, as much to collect herself as for emphasis. "And I want her to have another chance."

"He is lucky to have you," Tony told her sincerely.

Kelli waved that off. "If we were twenty-five things might be different. I'd like to think we're grown-ups now."

159

He nodded, smiling, then considered her for a moment. "I wonder if I could show you an interview with Kenji. You have time?"

"I have time." She still felt okay. That was no guarantee these days; if Tony thought she needed to see something, she might not get a better chance.

He didn't waste time ejecting the SD card with her interview, slipping it into a labeled sleeve, then going over to his computer suite. "The history of these partnerships is much more complex than I suspected. Elena's competition season with Dmitri, seeing some of their rehearsals," he shook his head. "It taught me why he runs Shall We Dance as he does."

"He's very particular," Kelli agreed. "But it's not just about good manners. It's about being open-hearted and loving with each other."

"Yes, exactly. Elena told me once, she thought he might not have hired her if she and I were not already in love."

"Huh." That was interesting. But probably correct: Dmitri wanted people who were capable of commitment. Kelli waited while Tony brought up the file he wanted, pulling it onto his biggest screen so she could see comfortably from the couch.

He turned to look at her. "Michelle has been a very interesting subject. When I spoke to Kenji I wanted his view on how she went from being a theatrical dancer, working with a burlesque company, to champion ballroom dancer." He clicked something and pushed back from the desk.

"It was that first number she did with Vince," Kenji said to the camera. "That's one of the things making this difficult for me. I've always felt that if she had not done that number, the Cabaret might not have taken the direction it did. The shows they do now, the reviews they get. There was nothing like that before Vince. Have you seen it?"

"No, not yet." Tony's voice, offscreen.

Kenji said, "Ask Michelle to get you the video. If you look at the history, it's completely unlike anything the Cabaret put on stage before. It was the first time I saw her dance."

"Were you there with her?"

"No, I didn't even know her at the time. I knew Dmitri, because of our connection through the church. We'd worked together before on costume. I went to that show because I'd costumed one of the other performers and she gave me a flyer. I was only there out of curiosity. Didn't expect much. Most of the show was entertaining, but nothing special. Then that song started, and Vince came onstage, and almost everyone in the room sat up straight. Including me."

"He has a presence."

Kenji almost laughed. "You can call it that. The charisma was undeniable. Then Michelle came out, and she looked simply incredible in this costume that on anyone else might have looked silly. And she's a brilliant dancer, very intelligent about how she uses the stage or her props, with excellent technique. But their connection was so," he paused for a moment, looked away, then back at the camera, "so hot. It really looked as though the minute that performance was over, they were going to be, you know, in the green room."

"Did you try to meet her then?"

"No, I went home and took a cold shower." Tony laughed. Kenji smiled and said, "I found out later that Vince was already involved with Kelli. Michelle was single when she came to me for her first ballgown."

161

"So when I see this performance, what will I think?"

"You'll think what I can never seem to avoid thinking. That if Kelli had not been in the picture, I would never have met Michelle. Dmitri might not even have met her."

After a pause, Tony said, "But there was the ballgown. How did that come to pass?"

"Vince and Kelli started working with Dmitri. Michelle met Dmitri through them. He talked to her, in a noncommittal way, about having her do some teaching - pole dance - at the studio. It was trendy at the time. But then she asked him to do a routine with her. She would have asked Vince again, I'm sure, but he was doing this thing with Kelli for the House of Blues. Anyway, the number with Michelle and Dmitri turned into a theater-arts Argentine tango that was a sensation. She had never done tango before. After that he asked her to train in ballroom."

"I see."

Kenji said, "You will." After a moment he added, "I still have trouble watching that video. I like Vince a lot. I appreciate him as a dancer and as a friend. I try very hard to be rational about the situation. He can't help being sexy. That's simply not me. We have a complete relationship, Michelle and I. But when I walk into a room, most people don't notice. Everyone notices Vince."

Tony reached over and clicked again, then turned to look at Kelli. She was wide-eyed. "I never knew he felt that way," she said. "He was a fashion model! He's the hotness! When I went to see him that first time to get my dress for 'I Love Paris,' and Michelle came with me? She wanted to climb him like a tree!"

Tony laughed. "She said you encouraged him to ask her out."

Kelli snorted. "Yeah, and even then she kind of had to help him along. Wow, that is, *wow*. It never occurred to me a guy who looks like that could think he isn't sexy. Believe me, people notice when he walks in. There are people who keep track of his schedule so they can be at the studio when he's bringing something. Not saying Mateo," she added, which made Tony laugh again. "My lord. I haven't seen that number for a while. You've seen it now?"

"Yes, Michelle sent it to me. And I understood."

"You have it? Can I see it?"

"Of course." Tony turned back to the computer, retrieved the file and clicked.

Kelli tried to watch as if she'd never seen it before. As if she didn't know these people, and wasn't right there in the audience. This was the second night of performance, less than twenty-four hours from the first time she and Vince went to bed.

His entrance was casual, unstudied, sexy. Everything about his posture, his movement, his expression said 'here to get laid.' The dance in full was inventive and funny, but mostly seductive. It was almost impossible to tell that Vince and Michelle hadn't, in fact, kissed during the dance; it seemed that they must have, but they hadn't.

When the clip ended, Kelli huffed out a breath. "Yeah, okay. What did Michelle tell you about it?"

"She said, I think everybody in the club wanted to get in Vince's pants after that." Kelli laughed. Tony went on, "But she said it looked hotter than it felt. Let me remember. There were all those props. The coat, the

163

dance pole, the bar and stools, steps behind the bar. They had lyrics to hit, and every beat was choreographed. She said it was much more produced than it looks. There was not a second when they weren't very aware that it was a performance. There was too much going on to get distracted. And she said that was Vince's first time doing anything on a stage. I couldn't quite believe it."

"None of us could. He was really nervous."

Tony smiled. "What do you think it is about him, that makes him sexy?"

Kelli thought for a second; it was hard to verbalize, because if you just talked about the physical things you missed so much. "Well, obviously, he's good-looking. Great body, well proportioned. The way he moves is very integrated. But it's, I think, about the way he looks at you. He's got those bedroom eyes, and he'll look at your mouth as if he's imagining kissing you. That is, I have to say, well-nigh irresistible." She glanced over at the screen, frozen on the ending pose. "Run it back a little bit. To where they're using the pole?"

Tony turned around, slowly dragged the recording in reverse until she made a sound. They both studied the image on screen. Michelle was crouched at the base of the dance pole that was mounted on the stage back then. The leopard-print trench coat hung open over her black bikini. Vince was in mid-air, one hand braced on the pole, body at a forty-five degree angle to the stage, one leg kicking up and over. He looked like a martial artist, or like Gene Kelly. A second later he would land on the stage by Michelle, pull her up in that almost-kiss, then strip the coat off. "Mmm?"

"Yeah. It's no wonder Kenji had trouble watching this." Kelli sighed. "We'll think of something. That is not ballroom. Ballroom will not be like that. I mean, thank God they're not talking about doing Rhythm or Latin." Tony choked back a laugh. "Seriously!" She shook her head, took a sip of water, consulted her interior. It was time to go back upstairs so she could lie down. "I'll need to head back home."

"Of course. Thank you so much for your time today. How do you feel?"

Kelli grimaced. "Eh. Could be worse." He gave her a hand up from the couch, kissed her on each cheek, thanked her again. She gave him a wave at the door and turned toward the elevator.

CHAPTER 12

January 2016

Michelle's partnership with Vince was still not a done deal, but the inner circle of Shall We Dance regulars were all betting they would move forward. Michelle was still too young, and too clearly capable of remaining at the top of the rankings, to call it quits. And Vince was too obviously a close-to-ideal partner: the same height as Dmitri; in the same studio; young, athletic, and indisputably talented.

On the other hand, Kelli would tell anybody who asked that she felt like crap, and everybody knew why. She hadn't been in the studio since the week after 'Gaucho' wrapped, and Vince was there much less often. Tony caught up with him after a follow-up interview with Mateo. "Is all well?" he asked. "We've barely seen you." They weren't intimate friends, but up until October they'd seen a lot of each other.

Vince sighed. "Kelli's still sick, it's been extreme. That morning sickness that never quits. There are other issues, too. Her doctor says she might have to go on bed rest." He meant to stop there, but the words kept spilling out. "We're probably going to move in with my mom. She's started fixing up her house just in case. She works part-time and I know she'll give it up like a shot if we need her."

"That's wise," Tony said. "If Elena had not been so well, I would have wanted someone with her. How are you doing?"

"About how you'd expect. Trying not to think about all the things that could go horribly wrong. So much is already wrong." He glanced away for a moment. Tony knew that this kind of tangential story would be great for his film, but he didn't want to ask. It was too private, and the potential for disaster was too high. Vince looked back at him. "Once we move down to Westchester I'm never going to be here during the day, except on weekends. It's a good thing Michelle has so much else going on here, and with the Cabaret."

"She would have wanted to start training, eh?"

"I'm betting. And you know if she says 'let's go' I'd be a fool to say no. It's going to make a hole in your project, huh?"

Tony shook his head. "Non ti preocupare. I am busy with the series anyway. I'm following Elena and Mateo. And I'll interview Michelle about her transition to coaching. She has so many students already. Also, she says she may work with Alison on the showcases this spring." The Underground Cabaret had recently undergone a further evolution, moving away from a steady schedule of alternating Cabaret and Mating Dance shows. Now Chrome would play host to three straight theatrical dance presentations: one-night student showcases in April and May, and then a large-scale professional dance concert to play three Sundays in a row in August. The 2016 project was still in the works but there was some discussion of basing it on martial arts.

Vince said, "We might not even see those. Kelli's due in June. Her doctor doesn't think she'll make it that long."

Tony impulsively touched Vince, a hand on his arm. "We will pray for you, for your family."

"Thanks, Tony." Vince smiled, putting his hand over Tony's for a moment. "I don't mind talking about this, you know. It helps to talk about it. Come up to the apartment

167

sometime soon, we can do a little thing. I'll show you the tape from our big show at the House of Blues."

"Yes, all right. I have so much back story for Michelle, it should be balanced with yours." They shook hands, and Tony went away. Vince sent a text to Kelli: *Hey beautiful, Tony's going to come up fairly soon to talk about our Story*

She was - incredibly - still working almost full-time, but she kept her phone on all the time now. *LOL capital S Story?*

Movie magic baby

You should play him the tape from our wedding party

Bring Me Sunshine, you always do, yeah good idea

I'm heading home soon, feels like I could eat

Want something from the Italian place? He knew by now what the likely triggers were.

Yes please

I'll meet you at home. I love you

I love you too XOX

A couple weeks later, Tony and Elena came upstairs to join Vince and Kelli for dinner. Tony brought one of his cameras, just in case Vince felt like talking. Kelli was having a good day, in terms of food, so that was the priority. "I am *so hungry* every minute that I'm not actually feeling like I'm about to puke," she confessed. "I wonder sometimes if I didn't have this bullshit condition, would I have gained a hundred pounds."

"I got pretty round, and I only had the one," Elena said. "But I'm shorter than you, too. It looked like more than it was."

"You looked cute," Kelli said, grinning. "All the way through."

Tony was smiling. "Yes, she did."

"Whew." Kelli sat back, regarding her empty plate with satisfaction. She wriggled a little, then relaxed. "Fair warning, I may nod off. Don't take it personally. Why don't you get that video set up, honey."

"Let me chuck this stuff in the dishwasher. No, you all take a load off. I had an easy day today." Vince cleared the table, put away leftovers, and generally tidied up while the others chatted. Then he turned Kelli's chair around (she was more comfortable in an armchair than on the couch these days) and brought her ottoman over. Only then did he switch on the TV, connect his laptop, and cue up the video. "Okay. So this was the first routine Kelli and I did together. I thought I'd show you the version we did at the nightclub, and then the version we did at House of Blues. Dmitri put us through the wringer in between."

"We were getting coached three times a week," Kelli said. "So much pain. That's when I started calling him El Kapitanski."

Elena said, "Mateo calls him that now. I don't think anyone else dares to."

"Mateo gets away with a lot." Vince was smiling. He started the video. They all watched without comment. He glanced at Kelli's face at the end; she was looking at him. "That was the most fun I ever had dancing. Until we did the next thing."

"Then every new thing was the most fun," Kelli agreed. "We'll get back to it someday. When I don't feel like puking."

Vince nodded. "Okay, so I'm sure you could see all the things that weren't perfect about that. Now you get to

169

see how much of it Dmitri fixed." He started the next video.

"Holy smokes," Elena said at the end. "How long did you have to re-work it?"

"About a month." Vince hadn't watched the two videos side by side for a long time. He was a little impressed himself. "Seeing them like this, I guess I get why Michelle thought I might be worth training for ballroom. Why I might be able to pick it up."

"You can totally pick it up," Kelli said. "And you're going to be raising the temperature in that ballroom, that's for sure." She and Elena both giggled. Tony and Vince exchanged an amused glance.

Tony was feeling grateful that Elena's partner was Mateo, and not Vince. He couldn't blame any woman for feeling the heat. He said, "What made you choose that music?"

"The Halloween theme for the Cabaret show. We were originally looking at the song 'Hell!' because we were thinking of doing mambo. But 'Blue Angel' is on the same album and it connected to a story we'd heard."

"And it fit the theme every bit as well," Kelli said. "I still love that piece. I can't quite believe we did that our first time out. And then the video guy hooked us up with the House of Blues. It was *bizarre*."

Elena changed the subject. "When you were planning your wedding, how many different songs did you consider for a wedding dance?"

Kelli laughed. "Oh my God, *all* the songs. That was two years from when we met, more or less. Basically all we did, those two years, was dance. Vince never stops thinking about music. And we hardly even did any swing by that time, we were deep in Argentine tango plus doing the Salsa Challenge competitions, but when he found 'Bring Me Sunshine' it was all, okay. Everybody we know is going to love that."

"Some friend of a friend on Facebook turned me on to that," Vince said. "Posted the video and I was like, who are these guys and why haven't I heard of them. The Jive Aces? I should know who they are." He shrugged. "Anyway. Kelli had the wedding dress design working already. We knew it was going to have a tear-away skirt. So we built that into the dance."

"It was hilarious." Kelli was giggling. "My parents had no idea. My sisters, my mom, they were shrieking when he pulled it off. All the guys were whistling."

"We did that one twice, too. We did it at the actual wedding reception, and then we did it here at the studio when Dmitri threw that party for us. Which was right before you started there, Elena. You want to see it?" Vince collected nods from his guests, and located that video. "My buddy Elliott recorded it that time."

Kelli was giggling again at the end. "That was so much fun. It's so not your usual wedding dance."

"I love it," Elena said. "We didn't have a party like that. Neither did Tony's brother and his wife. Next time we go to Italy, honey, let's have a party. We can all do crazy wedding dances." Tony was laughing. "Okay, though. We can't keep Kelli up all night. Can Tony do a little back story or would you like us to get out of here?"

"We can do some back story," Vince said after a glance at Kelli.

"I might go lie down," she said. "But stay as long as you want."

Elena stood up. "Let me come and rub your legs." She went over to Kelli and helped her out of the chair. "Not being able to stretch the same way is a pain, isn't it?"

"Girl, please. If I could stretch *at all* it would make such a difference." Both women went through to the bedroom.

Tony glanced at Vince again. Vince had his eyes closed. After a second he took a deep breath and opened them. "Another five months of this," he said softly. "How did you cope?"

"We were so fortunate. Elena wasn't sick. She danced almost every day, at least a little. She could stretch without feeling ill. We could, you know." Tony sketched a shrug. He couldn't finish the sentence, couldn't say 'we could make love' because – though he hadn't even thought of it before – it was fairly clear that Vince and Kelli couldn't.

"Never again." Vince was completely serious. "We both want these babies, but this is it. Before we were like, maybe three. Three would be fun. Then they said twins, and she was already so sick all the time. Ugh." He shook himself. "Okay. Get yourself rolling." He waited for Tony to set up the tripod, attach the camera, and start it. "So those things, the 'Blue Angel' and the wedding dance, were mostly for fun. Dmitri told us if we worked that hard only to have fun, we were the best students ever. But we wanted to be good, you know? We both want to be good. The first time we won at the Salsa Challenge, that was dope. Doing a theater-arts thing at the Tango Championships," he shook his head. "We did not feel bad about taking second to Red and Mary. We both wanted to get back out there, mind you. But then Alison had 'Gaucho' going, and that was an even better opportunity to really dig in and improve, without having to carry the whole thing. It was such a great cast. Alison had jazz elements in the choreography. We all did our own duets, basically, and then she helped us re-combine them. Kelli and I learned a lot of vocabulary. Dmitri was in the troupe for that, too. He was like, now that I'm not on the road with Michelle, I have time."

"I was surprised," Tony admitted. "For a dancer of his stature to go into an ensemble role."

Vince smiled. "Dmitri is not an egomaniac. He's extremely confident about what he can do, about his skills. That's not the same thing as thinking he has nothing left to learn. He is the best possible role model for me as a dancer."

"But for 'Gaucho,' you went to Mike Borodin."

"You've seen Mike's performance of 'Rock Star.'" It wasn't a question. Tony nodded. That particular dance had been recorded in a studio, not on a stage, but nearly everyone associated with the Cabaret had seen it. It was a hard, hostile, violent jazz piece set to music by N.E.R.D. "I knew that music because Tanith used it for 'Green Darkness,' the Beowulf thing that Red and Mary starred in. They came to me for a little Argentine tango coaching on one of the numbers, so I got the whole playlist ahead of time and me being me, added it all to the library. That whole 'Blue Crush' soundtrack is fantastic. Anyway, Mike. He gets character. He could have been an actor."

"Michelle said that about you."

"No, really?" Vince smiled. "When was that?"

"We spoke about the first routine you did with the Cabaret. She said you were very nervous."

"Fucking *terrified*. I was looking for the exit."

"It didn't show."

"Yeah, thank God. So the storyline of 'Gaucho' was this ménage scenario." He checked in with Tony, visually confirming that some background would be

173

good because the documentary viewer wouldn't know. "Three couples. Mateo's character broke everybody up, there were all these recombinations. I had to lead Mateo, and follow Red and Sam. In a serious way, in character, which I hadn't done before. And I was tripping, because all of those were, in a way, seductions. The whole idea was that the men were using each other for physical comfort. Whether that went all the way to sex was for the audience to decide, but the implication was there." Tony nodded comprehension. "I was teaching Mike and Paula then so I yelled for help. They'd both done same-sex performances before. Mike told me about this thing he did for a Pride event, fully homoerotic. And you know he's as straight as I am, so clearly he was the right guy to ask. Kelli and I met up with him and Paula, and they gave us the beat down."

Tony laughed under his breath. "They taught you how to access the character."

"Exactly. For my follow parts, it was easier. All I basically had to telegraph was willingness. Submission, maybe, in a kind of band of brothers way. Does that make sense? Like, I'm here for you. I will add my strength to yours, and we'll work this out. I've thought about this a lot since then," he added. "It wasn't simply pretending to be attracted to Sam or Red. More like, friendship without limits. Which was something I hadn't experienced. My best friend is Elliott, and we bro hug. You know, the handshake and then the free arm around the shoulders but the other arms are in between because God forbid you get too close." Tony laughed. Vince was smiling again. "But then I had to take the other side to Mateo, and he still hasn't quite forgiven us. I was supposed to dance a duet with him, and it was that seduction thing on his side, but with a

174

lot of rage on mine. I'm not the rage guy, so I really hadn't even thought of that for my character in the show. We all went into that rehearsal and the other guys were forewarned, but Alison wouldn't let me warn Mateo. So I go into this whole 'you took my true love and you may be pretty but I will end you' mode, and he had no idea it was coming. I felt like I was kicking a puppy."

Tony remembered his thoughts when he and Elena saw the dress rehearsal. He understood completely. Vince and Mateo were friends; to produce that performance had to have hurt both sides. "Your affect in that dance was venomous."

"That's exactly the word I found for it."

"By the time it was on stage, you were both performing. His reaction was critical, to set the character."

"Absolutely critical. Because Mateo in real life is not a homewrecker. He's a flirt, but only if he knows it won't mess somebody up. In the show, he was negligent. He didn't care if somebody got messed up. That's why Alison didn't want me to warn him in rehearsal. She wanted him to really feel how it would be if someone took him seriously, and resented it in a potentially dangerous way, so he could access that."

"And since then, your dancing has changed?"

"Well, that remains to be seen. Because Kelli and I haven't done anything since. We got pregnant toward the end of 'Gaucho,' and she was sick right away. Dmitri said my dancing would change. And I can't imagine having that toolbox open and not using it again, when the time comes. So now, when I listen to music, I think about the character and not only the movement. Some songs, like 'Blue Angel,' the story is right there on top. Others you have to dig a little deeper."

"When will you decide?"

"If the Michelle thing is happening? After. After Kelli and I are squared away. Once this whole thing is over, and she's feeling better, and I'm not worried all the time. Michelle understands."

"Of course she does." Tony thought that was enough. All of the talk about character was deeply interesting, though he might use only a small part of it. Ballroom wasn't known for producing eloquent performances. Even on Dancing with the Stars, the most narrative was typically seen in contemporary or Broadway-style numbers. But the art was evolving. By the time Vince and Michelle took the floor, things might be different.

Elena may have heard the end of the conversation. She came out from the bedroom. "Kelli dozed off. Did you get what you need?"

"I did," Tony said, "and Vince was distracted for a while."

"Which is what I needed. Thanks for coming over."

"Can I help clean up?" Elena was poised to move into the kitchen. Vince shook his head with a smile. "Okay. Get some rest. We'll see you soon." They exchanged hugs and handshakes, and Vince closed the door behind them. He wasn't used to talking so much; it was tiring. Maybe it would help him sleep.

"This is the first Valentine's Day since I've been with this man when we haven't gone out to do something fun and romantic," Kelly told Alicia. "And frankly, I'm pissed off about it."

"Oh, honey." Alicia patted her hand. "You still feel awful, huh."

Half a nod, half a shrug. "The nausea isn't quite so all the time, but it's everything else now. My OB says I can't keep working." Spider veins – she dreaded dealing with those later – fatigue, blood-sugar issues, and scariest of all were the blood-pressure issues. The sympathy on Alicia's face was enough to get her going. Kelli sniffed, swiped at her eyes. "We're moving in with Esmeralda. She fixed up the guest room for us and turned her office into a nursery. She's the best mother-in-law on planet Earth."

"I'm so sorry you're going through this."

Kelli was too. Sorry and frustrated and resentful. No other woman she knew had this kind of trouble. Of course, none of them had twins, either, but still. "On the plus side, we'll get our two in one fell swoop and save some time."

Alicia stifled a laugh. "That's definitely a plus. Thanks for inviting us over tonight, by the way. Last year when we went out we thought, was it always this crowded and loud? Did we think it was romantic because we were supposed to?"

"Nice quiet dinner at home instead."

"Better yet, *not* at home. I mean, I'll offer to help with the dishes but I know Vince won't let me."

"He says he likes doing the domestic stuff right now. It makes him feel," Kelli hesitated, then forged ahead. "Like he can help."

"Oh, bless his heart."

"Yeah." Kelli swiped at her eyes again.

Meanwhile, out in the kitchen, Vince was throwing some frozen peas in the microwave. "Ten minutes to stroganoff," he said. "I never knew there were so many ways to deploy noodles."

"I lived on box mac 'n' cheese in high school," Elliott offered. "And ramen in college."

"God, didn't we all. Ramen, pizza, and taco truck." They both laughed a little. "I was down in Westchester last weekend doing another thing."

"What thing?"

"Ma's patio. Met these neighbors of hers, really nice people. Had to check them out, of course." That was a tangent, but he followed it, because every conversation came back to what was happening with the love of his life and every distraction was welcome. "Anyway this guy is a lottery winner. Actually they both are, that's how they met, at a counseling place. But he's a builder. So first he helped me clean out the garage, and holy shit was there shit." Elliott laughed. "For real. Then he helped me turn the patio into more usable space. Put up a better roof, screened it in, stuff like that. It'll be a good escape room for everybody."

"Great idea. Capture some more square footage so you all don't feel crammed in there. How long has your mom lived alone?"

"Going on twenty years. She says this will be better, and even if it isn't she'd still want to do it because this way she'll never have to ask if she can come and see the babies."

"Aww." It escaped him, but it made Vince laugh. The microwave beeped. "Guess that's our cue." Elliott stood back to let the man of the house deal with final assembly. Checked the table was all set, then went down the hall to retrieve their women. "Come on ladies. Master Chef is plating."

"God, he's the best," Kelli said. "How did I get so lucky."

Out in the kitchen, Vince heard her and swallowed hard. Swiped a hand over his eyes, glad he was alone. Took a deep breath and poured the wine. When Kelli could drink again, he owed her the best bottle they could afford.

CHAPTER 13

March 2016

Kelli was supposed to be on bed rest, and because she felt marginally less crappy when she stayed in bed, she mostly did. But she was so bored she actually missed her job. She picked up her phone again, debating. Couldn't text Vince; she'd already pestered him once today, and she knew when he saw her name pop up he immediately went to 'oh shit is she okay.' So she decided to pester Michelle instead: *Hey girl greetings from jail in Westchester. Esmeralda is the best MIL in the world and she sure did a nice job with these rooms but HOLY HELL DO I NEED A THING TO DO*

Michelle wrote back within the hour: *Poor baby I'll bet you do!*

Why did I not learn to fucking knit?! I'm way too irritable to try it now, you do not want me to have sharp pointy things

LOL How many books have you read?

It's been three weeks and the number is twelve. Eleven fun romance novels and one thing from somebody's book club that I was like, why would anyone choose to read this

All tragedy all the time?

So much tragedy, ugh. Skimmed to the end to see if it got any better and it didn't. Would have thrown that bitch across the room if it had been an actual paperback. Do you have a minute or am I busting into a coaching session?

I have plenty of time for you, want me to call?

Yes please! A minute later the voice line rang. "Hi Michelle. Tell me all."

"Well, *all* would be that Elena and Mateo are seriously gunning for Emerald Ball. She says if they don't win Rising Star there it's going to be Occupy Ballroom."

"Jeez, I guess. That'll be a whole year, and they started out in fourth place! What gives?"

"I don't want to say it's because they're brown, but I'm afraid it might be because they're brown. And they have their own style. I personally think it's a great style, it's very authentic." Michelle sounded equal parts doubtful and frustrated. "There have been a couple non-white champions. But they had white partners."

"Maybe it's just taking the judging panels a while to get used to them. To take them seriously. It might even be more that Mateo is out. Ballroom guys tend to not be. And you know he's at the events with Sam, and they kiss."

Michelle made an enlightened sound. "Holy crap, maybe you're right. I never thought of that, and I should have. It's so *normal* here under our little rainbow." Kelli giggled. "But damn! Yeah! Dmitri never kissed Patrick in the ballroom, not until that very last time out. Patrick told me those two trophies were on the table and it was like, now I finally can. God, it's so stupid."

"We can all go picket if they don't win. They're here, he's queer, get used to it." Michelle laughed. Kelli said, "What about you? Did Alison rope you into working on the showcases?"

"Yes she did. Basically I volunteered. I needed something to do. I was underfoot all the time at home. At first Kenji was like, hey baby. I was gettin' it." Kelli snort-laughed. "Then he was like, um, I have clothes to make. He's doing the launch this month." Kenji was live-streaming a fashion show with his new dancewear line; Kelli would have loved to be in it, or at least to be there. She made a frustrated sound and Michelle said, "I know, honey. We'll miss you. So I try to stay out of his way during regular working hours. Most of the time I'm here at the studio. I'm doing about four coaching sessions a day on average. Dmitri says he'll do a number with me for the Cabaret show in June. But we haven't started on that so yes. I needed a job. Alison handed off the whole submission-management process."

"What kinds of things have come in?"

"Everything from hip-hop and tap to pointe, solos to small groups. The Chrome people are really going out on a limb with this. Everyone has to be over twenty-one, for the obvious reason. And it's the first time, so everybody is like, we are suspicious."

Kelli snickered. "I bet! They're all like, seriously? You're putting on this show and we don't have to pay you? What's the catch."

"Exactly. Alison put out the word to all the studios and collegiate dance programs in the tri-county area. She got back a lot of uh what? You know they always have their own showcases. So she said, this is a juried showcase – which it is, it's Alison and all us principals looking at the submissions – for an adult audience, which will include company scouts and others looking to hire. She was able to point to the people that Cirque and other production companies have taken out of the Cabaret. There's all that great video content from the pro shows. I mean, even the career boost for Red."

"That was non-trivial," Kelli said. "The guy was always working, but he was not a movie star until after 'Green Darkness.' So a good response?"

"Almost too good. Once the word trickled down to the students, oh my God. We've already cast both showcases. Filling the slots was not a problem."

"How many did you go with? The biggest show so far was your 'Blue' show. God, four years ago, the big re-opening. That was the shit."

Michelle laughed. "It was! It was awesome. You know, sometimes I forget how long we've been doing this. That was fourteen numbers. We asked Tyrone if he thought the audience could take more. We're marketing it to people who would be new to the venue. He said go ahead and do it how the hiring people will expect. We said, that means probably twenty separate performances. At least eighty minutes, is that too much. And he kind of cringed."

"Oh lord." Kelli giggled. The owner of Chrome was solidly behind the Underground Cabaret, but the place was still a bar. "Poor Tyrone. That does sound like a lot."

"It was a lot. And we want this to work for him, so we all voted for quality rather than size. So it's sixteen. Two acts, eight performances on each side of the intermission. Between the two dates we'll have four of the best in each style, plus a few groups."

"Well that seems fair." Kelli wriggled around a little. "God this situation is, well, it's literally a pain in my ass." Michelle stifled a laugh. "Go ahead and laugh. If I were not positive these are going to be perfect babies I would be all, what have we done."

"Everything checking out?"

"So far, everything's fine with them. I am the weak link here. So I will stay in my bed on my sore ass and live for the day they are on the outside." Kelli sighed. "And for the day, not long after that I hope, when I can have a glass of wine. Because *damn*." Michelle laughed. "Okay, I'll let you go. It sounds like those showcases are going to be great. I wish I could get there. I might send Vince with Esmeralda, they both need to get out more."

"Only if you have someone good to stay with you," Michelle said.

"Oh, I do. We met some neighbors, they are super nice. She makes paella. You should bring Kenji for dinner after the fashion show." That was an inspiration.

Michelle heard Kelli's voice brighten. She and Vince had lived in walking distance from the studio for a long time; it must be a little lonely down there. "I will do that. You take care of yourself."

"I will. Ciao for now." Kelli disconnected and set the phone down. She gave the TV remote a look of revulsion, gave her e-reader a look of hatred, gave the sunny blue sky outside her window a look of pitiful yearning, and laughed at herself. *Couple more months. You can do it girl.*

May 2016

Vince's cell phone buzzed while he was in the middle of a business call. The text read *Vicente vamos al hospital you should come. Kelli es fuerte. Besos.* "Oh shit," he said out loud. Heard a questioning, possibly-offended squawk at the other end of the office line. "Sorry, I'll have to continue this later. My wife is on her way to the hospital. Have to go. Email you. Thanks, bye." He hung up the office phone, stood, texted a quick *On my way* to his mother and wished very intensely that Elliott was in the office. Did he have everything he needed? Shrugging into his suit jacket. Powering down the computer. Walking fast across the

184

suite to the manager's office to tell them he was leaving. Another text while he was waiting for the elevator, this one to a select group: *Kelli's in transit to the hospital. Will advise when I have news. Light candles for us OX.* Then it was down to his car. Had to drive carefully. At least it wasn't rush hour. With any luck, he'd be down there in less than forty minutes.

By the time he parked, there were three more texts from Esmeralda. He wasn't to go to the ER, it was this other building. Ask at this desk for this doctor. This was the status. They were expecting him. "A friend may be coming down to wait with me," he said. "Is there a waiting room?"

"Yes, down the hall here. Any friends should check in with me. It's good you have people coming."

"Why? Is something wrong?" Something aside from the obvious, that it was weeks till Kelli's due date and she was bleeding.

The person behind the desk tried to be reassuring. "Your wife is in good hands, Mr. Connor. We'll take care of her. I think your mother is down the hall?"

Oh Jesus yes. "Right. Thanks." Vince turned away. Evidently Esmeralda had heard him; she stepped out of the waiting room before he got there. "Ma."

She grabbed him, hugged him tight. "Don't worry, m'hijo. She was swearing when they told me to go wait."

That almost made him laugh. He eased back, couldn't help noticing how worried she looked. *What are you not telling me.* "What have they told you?"

"Eh, not much. It will be a while."

"Are they inducing?"

She made a helpless gesture. "I think they want to wait and see."

Obviously she didn't agree with that. They were far enough along that he would have thought delivery was the obvious solution. Vince had never felt so helpless in his life. "Have you eaten?"

"I brought some snacks." Another gesture, at the cooler bag beside one of the chairs in the waiting room. Nobody else was in there. "Only little things though."

"I'm going to rally the troops. Whoever can come down, I'll ask them to bring us something."

"Like when you moved? Good idea." She patted his chest. "If as many people come for this, you're gonna need a bigger room." He kissed the top of her head and got on the phone.

It was another three hours before the medical team decided to proceed with a Caesarian. By then Vince had been up to see Kelli twice. He was with her for the final consult and told her the waiting room was full of friends: Esmeralda's neighbors Linda and Diego, Vicky, Sam, and Elliott. His phone had been blowing up all afternoon. Kelli's parents were on their way from Baltimore; they'd be staying with Linda. Vince felt the near-continuous buzz in his pocket, looked around the empty surgical waiting room, and thought *I can't do this*. He went out, told the person at the nearest desk that he'd be down in the main waiting room, and headed for the stairs.

Vicky and Elliott both stood when he joined the group. "What's up?"

"Caesarian. They told me I could wait up by surgery, but I didn't want to be alone up there." Hugs, much-needed, and murmurs of reassurance from everybody.

It was another long, anxious hour before the surgical duty nurse came down. "Mr. Connor?"

"Here," said Vince.

"Your wife is in recovery. Everybody's okay. You can come up and be with her now."

There was a chorus of relieved exclamations, and a few quick hugs. "Can my mother come?"

"Yes, but only one person in the room at a time."

Twenty minutes later, deeply grateful that Kelli was the only witness to him completely losing his shit, Vince took a selfie with the twins, in their bassinet between their parents. Kelli looked exhausted but happy. He composed a text to go with the picture: *Thank you all so much for coming. Kelli is okay. The twins are going to the NICU but they're only a few weeks early so the doctor says don't worry. I know, I'm going to worry anyway. Kelli can have visitors tomorrow. Till then here are Thing 1 and Thing 2.*

"Did you call them Thing One and Thing Two?" Kelli sounded drowsy.

"Mm-hmm." He leaned over to kiss her again. "Thought I'd give you the fun of introducing everybody to Carlos Primero and Celia Madrigal."

"Huh." Something close to a laugh. "You staying?"

"Until they throw me out. The mamacita will take care of the troops."

Kelli woke up to a dark room. Vince was slumped in a chair beside her bed, sound asleep. She was profoundly uncomfortable. Couldn't tell if it was active pain; her whole system was so fucked up nothing was working right, including nerve endings. She hated ringing for a nurse, but she needed to hear about the babies. And maybe they could tell her what was up with her.

Vince heard a low-pitched conversation, registered his physical state – stiff, cramped, thirsty, and in need of a piss – and squirmed around in the chair. Made eye contact with Kelli, who was talking to a nurse. "Everything okay?"

"Just checking me out. Carlos and Celia are fine, they say."

He nodded, hauling himself off the chair. "I'm gonna do a thing." Amazingly, Kelli's face lit up with a smile. He wanted to kiss her, or at least touch her, but there was a blood-pressure cuff in play and later for that. Across the room to the attached bathroom, taking care of business, wondering when she would be able to go home. Wondering if she still wanted him to stay. He had plenty to do, with about a thousand texts and emails to answer. Well, his mother would be back in the morning, and by then they'd have more information. Maybe he could go down to the NICU and take another look at the babies. Maybe they'd even let him hold them. He could get another picture, to show Kelli when he got back to her room. *Thank God she's all right.*

Tony met with Vince a month after the twins were born. It was the first time Vince had come into West Hollywood since early May. He looked even less rested than he had early in the year, but the worry was gone. "What an ordeal," he said, before the camera was turned on. "It was awful for Kelli. She put on the happy face as much as she could."

"She is well now?"

"Getting there. Her whole metabolism got seriously fucked. And they can call a C-section 'routine' all they want, but that scar is *huge*. From here to here." He drew the line on his own midsection. Tony shuddered. "Yeah, exactly. So Dmitri told me Rory's friend Tomás was going to be in town, and he's a genuine Argentine tanguero, and would I mind if Tomás taught at Shall We Dance over the summer. I was like dude, please. Give him all my students, with my blessing. I didn't have that many to begin with but I did not need to be responsible to anybody else for a while there. Still not. I'm not going back in till Tomás has to go back to Las Vegas. Haven't even met him. I hand-waved the whole situation." Tony was snickering. "Have you seen him in action?"

"I have. I was in to interview Mateo. We talked about 'Gaucho.' You were right, he has not forgiven." Vince laughed. "And we talked about their win at Emerald Ball, and the new pro show, with all the martial arts. That will be," Tony shook his head, "pazzo. Sam and Mary are the stars, there are battles. Anyway yes, I saw Señor Calderón. He is very tall, very severe-looking, but patient and, hmm, courtly. Old world. Your students love him."

"Good. Dmitri said he was satisfied." Vince lifted his chin, indicating the camera. "I have been deputized to bring back mass quantities of lasagna and tiramisu. Want to get that rolling?"

Tony turned on the camera. "So. Mr. Connor, congratulations. We will expect to see Celia and Carlos on the dance floor very soon, along with you and your lovely wife Kelli. I spoke with Michelle before she and Kenji left for their vacation. She told me that you've been talking."

"We have. She said, when we get back, I'd like to meet and really hash this out. See if we can work together. She's had a lot of time off now, and she's restless. I knew she would be. I'm lucky she waited for me."

"She told me she would only look outside the studio if you said no."

Vince smiled. "If she saw me right this second she might re-think that. I'm so out of shape. Not getting enough sleep, not eating right, not getting my workouts."

"I remember," said Tony. "Those first few months, the adjustment is difficult."

"And that's with my mother right there to help us. We would be totally screwed without her. So I've had all this time to think about it, and talk about it with my wife. Kelli says she is completely behind it. She knows I love competition. She says even when she's fit again she wouldn't want to do ballroom, because you have to do four or five dances. So we'll go back to tango. I honestly can't wait. Our neighbors asked for coaching. They're my only students right now. Kelli comes along and watches and gives advice."

"That must be fun and frustrating for her."

"Both, exactly. And I know once Michelle and I start working it'll be tricky. Finding that balance. I'll be commuting, so my days will already be longer. We will never have as much time for each other, ever again, until the kids are grown and gone. We're already kind of looking at each other going, how can we do this. How can we keep hold of each other. Adding in a ballroom partnership with somebody else, eh." Vince took a moment. Tony let it rest. "What it comes down to is, I want to try it. I want to see if I can do it. Because if I can do it, then I could legitimately have a full-time dance career, instead of a full-time job as a mortgage broker and another job as a part-time instructor."

Tony completely understood. "Elena says this only works because she is employed by the studio and

Mateo is so close. She's here all the time, he comes in when he can, and they can work."

"That's where Michelle and I will be. She'll be here, I'll come when I can. And we'll both have to be careful with our people."

"But Kelli supports you."

"She absolutely does. I love her so much. Everyone wants that person, you know, who's there for you no matter what. Like you are for Elena. I told Kelli to keep a scorecard. Keep track of how much I owe her."

Tony smiled. "Did she say she would?"

"No, she said don't be ridiculous. So I'll have to keep score myself."

Bringing Kelli home a couple days after the surgery was good. Having two weeks with her before the babies came home was great. It would have been perfect if she hadn't still been feeling so crappy. And there were so many adjustments, so many new things. She was pumping; they were fine-tuning the nursery; Vince was running errands all over, or else staying home with Kelli so his mother could run around. They were getting on each other's nerves a little. Esmeralda said it was only to be expected. Alicia and Sharon said the same thing. It still felt like he must be doing something wrong.

Six weeks in, Michelle came down to Westchester to take Kelli to the salon. There had been a bit of friction about that, because Kelli wanted to go see her usual stylist but wasn't comfortable driving yet. The place was a long way from where they lived now. Once she made the plan with Michelle, Vince shut up about it. She'd be out in the world for at least four hours, which was a record since bed rest (or house arrest, depending on who you were talking to) started.

Vince took the twins out to the patio, settling in for a few hours of relative peace. They were easy at this stage, requiring only the occasional diaper change, feeding, or cleaning. He was stretched out on the new recliner, crib within reach, eyes closed. Wondering if he would ever fully relax again. If this would all stop feeling so scary at some point.

"Vicente, quieres algo?"

"Mmm? You making coffee?

Esmeralda laughed under her breath. "I'll bring you some." Ten minutes later she was sitting out there with him, relaxing on the wicker settee. She had some music playing inside; sounded like Perez Prado. It was a good half-hour before either of them spoke. They might not have then, except his phone rang.

Vince set down his mostly-empty mug and picked up the phone. "Hey Dad. Everything's good. Kelli's gone out for the day with one of her girlfriends. Going to the salon. She's been all, this hair is out of control. Should make her feel better. Yeah. How's Sherry like her new job?" He listened for a while. "That's good. And what about you?" Adam had recently taken a position as an expeditor in a major online retailer's shipping hub. Everyone was relieved that he wasn't doing the long-haul driving anymore. Vince listened to the updates, smiling. Glanced at his mother. "Did you get the pictures of Carlos and Celia?" He laughed. "Yeah. They're so squishy-looking. Cracks me up all the time. Listen, I wanted to ask if you thought you guys could get away at Thanksgiving. Yeah. Well, there's this apartment unit upstairs from Ma's garage.

It's not much but it's free. I could fix it up a little. Mm-hmm, I'm taking some leave so I've got time. You think so? Great. Just us plus our neighbors Diego and Linda. I'm teaching them tango. Small party, yeah. No, you don't have to bring anything. Well, I mean, if Sherry wants to make a pie I'm pretty sure we'll eat it." He listened to his father laugh, watched his mother roll her eyes. "Okay great. Thanks for calling. Talk to you soon." He disconnected and set the phone down.

"It's good they're coming," Esmeralda said. "That upstairs unit es un desastre."

CHAPTER 14

August 2016

For a number of reasons, Vince and Kelli weren't planning to get up to Chrome for the latest pro show. But because everyone knew them and missed them, they were invited to the dress rehearsal. They weren't the only non-performers there. Longtime Cabaret members Rory and Dana were stage-managing. Dmitri – who'd provided rehearsal space for months – was there with Patrick. Several of the cast members had guests. Kelli was able to catch up with a lot of people she hadn't seen for months. "Oh my Lord this is great," she murmured to Vince during the break. Rory and Dana were busy reviewing the Act 1 tape with director Alison Jarvet, and everybody else was roaming around chattering. "I have missed this so much."

"We'll get back to it," Vince promised.

"Do you wish you were in this one?" He gave her an are-you-kidding look and she laughed. "Okay yeah, it's pretty nuts, but you did some similar stuff in 'Green Darkness.' All that shit with the spears."

"Similar, okay. Not on the same level. Every one of these guys could break my neck." Kelli was snickering, thinking through the list. Several of the men in the cast were actual martial artists. Two of them – Vince's friends Ray and Mike – were highly-trained theatrical dancers. Another, a new guy, was an award-winning b-boy. Vince filled in the last blank. "And most of them are taller than me. So no. Tango yes, anytime, with any of them. Sparring? That flying shit? No."

"You had fun at that tanguero photo shoot."

194

"That was excellent," he said. "Also very motivational. Andy's face when I took my shirt off, oh my God." Kelli laughed out loud. "Diego and I were both, can we be excused. Ray was totally mocking me. I said shut up, TV star, your whole job is about working out."

"What did he say?"

"He said if you do that shit with Michelle, yours will be too." The partnership discussions weren't exactly common knowledge, but Ray lived with Dmitri's colleague Julia.

"Truer words." Kelli regarded her husband for a moment. "You're going to do it, though, right?"

"I'm a little freaked," he admitted. "It's a lot. I have to talk to Dmitri."

"Go find Julia and send her over here to talk to me. You go talk to Dmitri. Act 2 isn't getting started for a while, from the look of things."

"Okay." He leaned over and kissed her. "I love you."

"I love you too."

Patrick was glaring at his phone, typing something, and completely ignoring the room when Vince fetched up beside him and Dmitri at the bar. "What's up?"

"He has new client with tax situation," Dmitri said. "Is good to see you here."

"It's great to be here. This show is bananas." Dmitri almost laughed. "Kelli was asking me if I wanted to be in it, and I was like, that's a solid No. You too?"

"I as well," Dmitri agreed.

"Do you have a minute to talk about this whole smooth ballroom thing?"

"Of course."

Vince dove right in. "I'm having this anticipatory anxiety about it. I talked to Michelle again and it seems like she's sure I can do it. Kelli and I have done all those dances before, so it's not as if I'm starting from nothing. And we've been working with you for so long. I figured if you thought I would suck at it, you would have said something long ago."

Dmitri nodded. "I would have. You should not worry."

"What's going to be hardest?" Vince was thinking the answer would be 'Viennese waltz' or 'foxtrot.'

Instead Dmitri said, "Time."

"You took her out in two months. That's not what Michelle expects, is it?" Because Vince honestly didn't think that was possible. Not with the commute, and the babies, and his job.

Dmitri studied him for a few seconds, perhaps seeing all that. "If you begin in November, I recommend a full year."

Vince was astonished. First at the November start date, and then at the rest of it. "Seriously?"

"I can begin developing routines with Michelle. We will study your competitors. There will be innovation since we competed. When you begin, it will be technique first. Then choreography. Then repetition and refinement. You will re-work the routines."

"I will?"

"The two of you." Dmitri almost smiled. "You are my student, but you have ideas. Good ideas."

Vince accepted that. The prospect of having a full year made the whole project seem do-able. "Kenji won't mind having another year before she hits the road again, will he."

"No. Is good?"

"Is good. Thanks, boss. You know I want to do this right. I want to be a good partner for Michelle, and I want to show up for the studio. For you." It was as close as he'd come to stating how much Dmitri meant to him. Probably as close as he could get without making them both horribly uncomfortable. *I'm such a guy*, Vince thought.

Dmitri did something unexpected then. He reached over and put his hand on the back of Vince's neck, squeezed gently, and leaned in close. "You will be the champions," he said quietly. "I know it." He let go and sat back, ever so slightly smiling at Vince's expression.

Do not cry, Vince was thinking. He didn't say anything for a minute. While he was trying to think of what he could possibly say without losing his shit, Dmitri turned to the bartender. The club wasn't open to the public during dress rehearsals, but the management had long since concluded that adult beverages were both welcome and, occasionally, necessary. A moment later there were two shots on the bar: vodka for Dmitri, tequila for Vince. Dmitri handed him the tequila. They tapped their glasses together and drank. Vince set down the glass and said, "Let's make it so." Dmitri nodded as if satisfied. Vince wanted to hug him, but that would probably be a disaster. So he nodded too, and went back to Kelli.

"What happened over there?" she said. Act 2 was about to get started. "You look a little shell-shocked."

"Well, two things." But before he said what they were, Vince kissed his wife again. "He says a full year to train, starting in November."

"A *year*?" Kelli squeaked a little. It was a long time, and not even starting until the twins were six months old. More time with Vince than she'd expected. It was fantastic. "What's the other thing?"

"He says we'll be the champions." Vince leaned back in his seat, amused at her expression now. Big-eyed and amazed and excited. "He may be tripping."

Kelli laughed. "Oh honey no. That man does not trip. Holy shit!" She squeaked again. Vince caught her hand and kissed it. Then Act 2 was underway and they settled back to watch. It was even crazier than the first half. They made what-the-hell faces at each other in the finale number, when nine of the dancers did some huge ballet-looking jump as a relay, one right after the other. "Holy shit," Kelli said again, under her breath. "No wonder she called it 'The Great Wave.'"

Vince was thinking the same thing. "And there's another reason it's a good thing I'm not in this one. My leg would snap right off." Kelli snorted. "Oh, I'll bet Paula's pissed. I'll bet Red is pissed." Those two weren't in the relay.

"His leg would have snapped right off," Kelli said. "But I'll bet you twenty bucks by this time next year, Paula's doing that trick. Whatever the hell it was."

November 2016

Neither Vince nor Michelle had been in the studio much during the summer; he and Kelli were adjusting to their twins, and Michelle took a long vacation with Kenji. She and Dmitri did a disco number for the Cabaret's June show, then she was gone for all of July and August. That fact alone had alerted the studio regulars to the likelihood that a new title campaign was about to begin. Nobody knew when the new

198

partnership would begin training in earnest, or when they intended to make their debut. If Vince and Kelli had still been living upstairs from Tony and Elena, or if they were still in the studio with anything close to their previous frequency, Tony probably could have deduced the timeframe for the campaign. As it was, he texted Vince when the fourth-quarter calendar went up: *My friend, Dmitri has confirmed to the studio that you will train with Michelle. When do you begin?*

Vince was prepared for this. Michelle had agreed he could talk to Tony about the whole thing. He replied *Hi Tony, long prep time while I phase out of the brokerage. California Star 2017 is the target. You know I can't look unprepared*

Quite so. May we meet soon for an interview?

Bring Elena & Gio down to Westchester. Ma will cook, then we can be patriarchal jerks and leave the babies with the women while we talk

Tony laughed. *We can make amends later.* A little back and forth was required to arrive at a mutually agreeable date, but the dinner and interview took place the first Saturday in November.

Elena and Kelli dominated the conversation during dinner, talking about 'The Great Wave' and the two most recent Cabaret nights at Chrome. "I was so jealous the whole time at 'Milonga,'" Kelli confessed. "Vince is working with this couple in the neighborhood and they've been out to compete a couple of times, but we haven't done any dancing yet. I'm still kind of healing." She made a face. Her doctor had warned her that complete recovery from the difficult pregnancy and the Caesarian delivery would take the better part of a year. "At least I could enjoy the Halloween show without being all envious."

"I feel the same way," Elena said. "The Mating Dance shows are what I want to do. The others," she shook her head, rolling her eyes. Kelli snickered. All of the Underground Cabaret shows were dance-heavy, but their self-branded presentations featured circus arts and burlesque as well. There was a lot of very athletic near-nudity. The Mating Dance shows, on the other hand, were all about partner dancing. "Mateo and I are doing 'Jump Jive and Wail' for November."

"Oh my God, even though you're going to Ohio?!"

Elena nodded, making an 'eek' face. "We're entering the show dance event, and that's our routine. We entered Rising Star since we didn't go to Ohio last year."

"But you've won three times already. If you win in Ohio, you'll go to Open Professional from here on out, right?"

"That's the plan. It's kind of amazing."

"It's fantastic. But that's a good segue, isn't it. I know these guys want to get on with their business." Kelli stood up and started helping Esmeralda clear the table. Elena pitched in while Tony and Vince went to set up on the back patio for their interview.

"This space has been a lifesaver," Vince said. "Before Kelli and I moved in, Diego and I did a little work out here to make it more of an actual room. It was a big adjustment for Ma, having us here, and then all those babies. This is the place any of us can go when we want to hang up the Do Not Disturb sign for a minute."

Tony laughed under his breath. Two babies could seem like a lot. "Your student, he went with you this summer to the tanguero photo shoot. Dmitri mentioned it."

"God, that was fun. Tomás blew my mind with that cabaret routine he taught us. Diego's too, he was like what the what. Good sport, though. Andy's got the pictures up, we're all going to see them tomorrow." And they'd be great, if they were anything like the ones from 'Gaucho.' Vince had a framed print, of a picture taken when they were eye-fucking each other on the loveseat after dress rehearsal, hanging over their bed.

"We'll go too." Tony had the camera ready. "So, we spoke earlier about all the work you've done with tango. With Kelli, and in 'Gaucho' last year. Did the photo shoot bring back memories?"

"It really did. Kelli and I started learning Argentine tango after seeing that routine Dmitri and Michelle did five years ago, right before he started training her for ballroom. We did our first tango performance a year after that. My students Diego and Linda, they said they wanted to learn tango because it seemed more grown-up than salsa. I don't know if that's exactly why Kelli and I like it so much."

"Part of it, perhaps? The music, it's more subtle."

Vince nodded agreement. "Yeah, exactly. It's not as much about percussion and the beat. For me and Kelli, it was a great way to explore interpretation."

"And then it became about character."

"For the pro show, definitely. That would have been a totally different show if we hadn't gone to Mike and Paula for help."

"How will that affect your approach to ballroom?" Tony was genuinely curious. Vince had an instinctive, rather than analytical, way of creating movement. "You've always worked with specific pieces of music, yes?"

"I have. Michelle told me, you can't get too attached to music. You never know what they're going to play in a competition. It might be something you hate. She said, if I never hear 'Dark Waltz' again it will be too soon." Tony huffed out a laugh. Vince was smiling. "I hate that one too. But yeah, she gave me all this music and said learn it, love it, live it, even if you can't stand it. And oh my God, some of these alleged tangos are *garbage*."

Tony laughed. "When do you begin?"

"Right after 'Swing It.' I'm already working with Dmitri a little bit on solo technique. Thank God we started with him back in the day, he already cleaned up some of my crap, but you know how different the technique is for Smooth. He's got me at the frickin' barre."

"May I tape you there sometime? I think the viewer would find it interesting." Tony was certain that even true dance lovers might not comprehend the scope of work that went into championship-level ballroom dancing.

"Sure. I'll ping you when I'm going to be working there."

"You said you'll take a full year to train for your debut. You wished to be prepared."

"Well." Vince gave Tony a sideways look. "Michelle and Dmitri won the championship two years in a row. If I go into competition with her as my partner, and with Dmitri as my coach, without shooting for perfection? How much of an asshole would I be? It's not only about my ego. You know, oh, I have to look good. It's about being a good enough partner that Michelle can still be the phenomenal dancer she is."

"You were a good partner for her from the beginning," Tony said.

"The Big Bad Voodoo Daddy number. She said so. I look at it now and all I can see is the things I could do better if we did it again."

That didn't surprise Tony. Most serious dancers were very self-critical. "Would you ever return to that routine?"

"Eh." Vince looked unsure. "I doubt it. I don't think it would accomplish anything for me career-wise, and I'm pretty sure it would be hard on Kenji. Maybe on Kelli, too. She knows I love her, but that was an intentionally sexy piece. If I'm doing something like that again, I want to do it with my wife."

"You could re-create it," Tony suggested. "Do new choreography." Vince seemed to be considering it. "But once you are deep into ballroom, you may have new ideas."

"Kelli and I have never done a show foxtrot, or a waltz," Vince said, smiling. "Unless you count 'Palomita Blanca.' And I kind of don't, because that was still Argentine tango."

"If you could do a foxtrot with Kelli, what music would you choose?" There were so many wonderful songs.

Vince shook his head. "Ask me when I know if I can do foxtrot at all."

"So did you bring Tony up to date?" Kelli said later, when they were alone. Vince was sitting on the end of the bed, absent-mindedly stretching with one ankle hooked over the other knee, watching her. She was wearing one of her sleep shirts with fuzzy slippers; he was in flannel pajama bottoms. They used to sleep naked, but since the babies, one or the other of them was reliably leaving the bedroom at some point during the night. They rarely even saw each other naked anymore.

I miss your body, mi corazón, he thought, but answered the question. "Pretty much. He knows it's

203

going to be a lot of boring stuff between now and this time next year."

Kelli made a dismissive sound. "It's not boring. It's like the behind-the-scenes stuff they put up for Dancing with the Stars. Everyone likes to see how the routines come together."

"Yeah, I guess. When you and I start back, what would you want to work on first?"

Kelli was startled. Pleased that he said 'when' and not 'if,' but surprised the thought was even in his mind. There was so much about them that wasn't what it was. Still good, but not how it used to be. "Honey, I don't know if you should even be thinking about that. You're about to get the matrix download for ballroom."

He smiled, but didn't drop it. "Yeah, I know. But you and me and dancing, that's a thing. I don't want to lose that. Remember the tango championship?" The most technical, most challenging of their competition routines.

"I'll never forget it." She didn't know what to tell him. Her body was so changed. She still carried extra weight, the surgical scar was still tender, her blood pressure still fluctuated. And she was so tired. She wouldn't change a thing, those babies were a hundred percent worth it, but in that moment the last thing she wanted to think about was putting together any kind of performance. They hadn't even been out social dancing. "Maybe we could start off slow. Go to the socials. Let me get myself back in shape."

"I like your shape." He meant it, but he could tell his reassurance wasn't what she wanted. She wanted to be Before Kelli. That he'd so quickly gotten back to Before Vince had to chafe. "If I could have carried those babies for you, I would have."

"I know, honey." She sat beside him, let him put his arm around her, accepted and returned a kiss. Held him close for a few minutes, but in the way that subtly let him know a kiss was all there would be tonight. She went to check on the babies again, and then to wash up. He went to wash up in his turn, spending a little quality time with his hand, so he wouldn't go to bed craving her.

Eventually they turned out the light. Eventually they slept. In between, both of them were thinking *how do we get back to before.*

CHAPTER 15

December 2016

Vince was sitting in the studio office with Michelle, side by side in the two guest chairs. It had been another productive evening. He'd mastered the basics of American Smooth, and now Michelle was teaching him the more advanced technique they'd be using in competition. The plan – to take a full year to get him ready – was looking like a good one. Vince knew he'd be held to a higher standard, because of his partner and his coach. It was a daunting prospect even though he wanted to do it. He knew, by this time, that dancing was what he wanted to do most in life. But only if his wife was in it with him, and something was wrong. So they had to fix this before it really went off the rails.

Kelli wouldn't admit that anything was the matter, but Vince could tell. It wasn't the babies; it wasn't the living situation. He didn't think it had anything to do with her job. She was glad to be back at work and didn't even seem to mind the commute. So the only other likely contender for 'cause of trouble' was him. More specifically, him and Michelle. "You and I have hardly started," he told her, "but something's up. Is Kenji okay with it?"

"He seems to be," she said, a little doubtfully. "So far. It's different this time, though. Dmitri, well." She made an eloquent gesture. Dmitri may have taken up a lot of Michelle's time, but he was not in the class of men who might have tried, or even been tempted, to take anything else.

"Yeah. I was afraid of that. How do you think we should handle it? Because you know I think you're

206

gorgeous, and if I'd never met Kelli I definitely would have made a play. But I did meet Kelli, and I love her more than life, and I know you feel the same way about Kenji. So help me out here. You're a woman, what would you want? Or need, I guess?" He studied her face while she considered the question.

Michelle sat forward, inspired. "How long has it been since you went on a date?" Vince's eyebrows went up with surprise and she almost laughed. She could tell he didn't need any other prompting.

"My God," he said. "We've been together more than five years, how could I not have thought of that?"

"Well, relationships change, right? First you're dating, then you're living together, then you're married. You're dancing together all that time, getting better and better, winning awards, looking amazing. Then after a really high year of dancing, you get pregnant, and it's eight and a half months of misery and anxiety and really, outright fear. Plus having to uproot yourselves, and since then it's not enough sleep, and not much privacy, and basically no dancing. And her poor little body's been through the mill. Then you turn around and start dancing with me instead of with her, and all I ever do is dance, and I look like this." It wasn't a boast. Michelle still had a perfect body.

"Jesus, no wonder half of all marriages end in divorce. It's probably the half that have men in them." Vince wiped a hand over his face as Michelle laughed. "We talked about it a little. About dancing. She said, maybe we could start at the socials. I assumed we'd do that this month but I haven't said anything else about it. She probably figured I forgot. And I almost fucking *did*." He sighed. "You realize this means less time for the training. If this, then not that."

"Yeah, I get it," she said. "It's probably just as well, though. Because I need to do more quality time with Kenji, too. It's easy for me to forget he needs that, because he hardly ever says so. And you're going to get this faster than you think. Remember how good you got at Argentine tango with hardly any coaching."

Vince shook his head. "I understood it. I don't understand this shit yet. And it's four dances, not one."

"Don't worry. Just dream of the day Dmitri says we can start working on a show dance. Because you know it has to be tango, and you know you're going to kill it." She patted his leg. "Anyway, I think we're done here for the day. So maybe you should look at the calendar, send me the updated version, and then go take care of your wife." She leaned over to kiss his cheek. "And I will go take care of my husband." She stood up and went out. A few minutes later he heard the back door of the studio close behind her.

Vince took her advice. First he sent a text to Kelli: *On my way home soon. Sorry so late. Love you, miss you, really want to kiss you*. He went through the Google calendar he and Michelle shared, ruthlessly deleting every Friday night from the practice schedule. He added the Shall We Dance socials, so he couldn't possibly forget (and neither could Michelle). Getting to all of them wouldn't be possible, but getting to one per month had to be. Then he looked at the tentative schedule for the Underground Cabaret in 2017. *We can do something*, he thought. *And she needs to try out for the pro show, whatever it is*. He turned every other Sunday afternoon into a practice session for him and Kelli. He would ask his Westchester students, Diego and Linda, if they would lend their home practice room; he thought they would probably say yes. Finally he sent another text, to his mother: *Hey mamacita, I want to romance Kelli a little bit over the next few months. Date night every other Friday. You get the alternating Fridays to go out with one of your gigolos, okay?*

He got a text back with a speed that said Esmeralda was probably on the couch with the twins, watching TV while they napped (or not): *Good idea! It is time we all got out a little!*

Be home soon. Gracias por todo mama. Te amo

Te amo tambien. Vince put away the phone and got himself ready to go. At least at this time of night, getting from West Hollywood to Westchester didn't take too long. When he arrived, Esmeralda had already put the twins to bed; she and Kelli were having a cup of tea in the breakfast nook. "Hey pretty ladies," Vince said, giving each of them a kiss. "I had a little come to Jesus with Michelle."

Kelli asked, "Was there a problem tonight?"

"Well, I realized that the most important woman in my life - sorry Ma - was not on my calendar nearly enough, and I have changed that. So, mi corazón, can I take you on a date this Friday?" The look on Kelli's face told him this was exactly the right thing to do, and not a moment too soon. "That looks like yes, is that yes?" He kissed her again.

"That's yes," she said when she could. "Where are we going?"

He didn't answer directly. "How late can I keep her out, Ma?"

Esmeralda pretended to think about this. "Have her home in time for breakfast." Kelli laughed, and a few minutes later she and Vince retreated to their semi-private rooms.

"I'm sorry," Vince said quietly, after they were in bed.

"What for?" She sounded surprised.

"I let things get away from me a little bit there. You know you really are the most important person in the world to me, right?" Kelli turned toward him, resting her head on his shoulder and draping an arm over his chest. He folded his arm over her back and kissed her forehead. "I sent Michelle an updated calendar. All Friday nights off. You and me, every other Friday, so Ma can have date nights too. All the socials are on the calendar. And every other Sunday, a dance date for you and me, so we can get back to doing what we do. Is that good?"

"That's great," Kelli said. She was petting his chest absently. "I didn't want to ask. This whole ballroom thing is such a big change for you. I know it's going to be a lot of work, but you and Michelle are going to be champions."

"I don't give a damn unless you're happy." He shifted, touched her face, kissed her. "My darling beautiful wife." Her mouth opened under his, and the kiss got hotter. "Mmm." Vince turned a little more and pressed close, holding her body tight against his. Their formerly robust sex life had never recovered since the pregnancy, since the C-section. It had been weeks since either of them initiated anything, and he was hungry. Her breath was fast; he thought she was hungry too. He ran a hand down her side, then under her sleep shirt and between her legs. *Oh yes*, he thought, and kept his hand there because she made a muffled sound that said she liked it. He kissed her again, moving against her a little because he couldn't stand it, and then she turned onto her back and raised a knee. He slid a finger inside her.

"Oh," she said, "yes. More." He slung a leg over hers and moved half on top of her, kissing her face and her neck. Then he moved down and put his mouth on her. "God, Vince!" she breathed. He listened, felt her rhythm start, brushed his fingers down her leg to the sensitive skin behind her knee. She raised her leg and hooked her foot over his back, hips moving against his mouth. He looked up; she was biting her lip, whimpering, eyes tightly closed. *Go now, before you kill me*, he thought, and must have done just the right thing because she bucked against him and stopped breathing for a few seconds. He felt her pulse and licked her one more time, then moved up.

"Can I," he said, because he was still afraid of hurting her. She didn't answer with words, simply put her hands on his hips and pulled him down. He sank into her slowly, carefully, and was rewarded when she arched against him. He kissed her again, holding most of his weight off of her, and then she pulled him closer, hooking that foot over his thigh, her head pressed back into the pillow. They moved together for long delicious minutes until all at once she curled up against him, stifling a cry with her mouth on his throat, and he lost control. "Jesus!" It felt so, so good. She held him tight when he went still, turning with him so that they lay locked together on their sides, holding him inside her as long as she could.

"I think I'm working again," she said after a few minutes. He laughed against her skin. "That felt really good. As good as ever."

"I agree."

"What should I wear?"

He moved his head back a bit, so he could see her face. "On Friday? Something to dance in."

"I'll have to shop. None of my old things fit right now."

He stroked his hand down her back and kissed her neck. "How about your shoes?"

"The shoes fit." He could tell she was smiling.

"Good. I love you."

"I love you, too." She pushed him over, so she could rest her head on his shoulder again. He pulled the covers up, and a few minutes later they were both asleep.

Vince woke at dawn, aware of a hand on him. He lay still for a minute. He knew she could tell he was awake. "If you keep doing that," he said softly, "I'm going to pounce on you again. Or, you know, you could lose that shirt and pounce on me."

"I'm self-conscious. I don't look the same."

"You're still beautiful. Still my gorgeous Kelli. Still the only woman I want. I love you so much." Maybe that was the right thing to say; she took her hand off him and moved over, straddling him, hands planted beside his head. He put his hands on her body, stroking down to the hem of the shirt, and pushed it up. She pulled it over her head as he moved one hand so his thumb could play with her. She was wet against him; he moved his hips almost without meaning to, and she raised up enough to take him in. "Oh my lord," he said, and she laughed a little, leaning down to kiss him.

"I like how I make you pray," she said against his mouth, and started a new rhythm. "Mmm, Vicente, mi amor." She reared up and threw her head back, and the line of her throat was as perfect as ever. He watched her in the dim light as she worked them both, filling his hands with her breasts, stroking with the tips of his fingers over the outer curves where he knew she liked to be touched. "How did we live without this," she said breathlessly.

I don't know, he thought. He sat up so he could kiss her, and the change of angle made her squeak, then sigh, then lean back on her hands. "So beautiful," he said, and wrapped an arm around her, pulling her close and tipping them over so he could move the way he needed to. She was coming almost as soon as he sank deep, both legs wrapped around him, biting her lip to stifle her moan. He made it last as long as he could because he'd missed this, he'd missed her, so much.

A minute or two later, he moved again. "Was that as loud as it sounded inside my head?" Kelli started giggling. "It was, wasn't it." He was laughing too, trying to be quiet, although what was the point. His mother was on the other side of the house, and the twins were just going to have to get used to it. "God, I love you," he said, and kissed his wife one more time.

"So what did you say to Vince, because damn," Kelli said to Michelle on the phone later that day. She was sitting in her office at work, still feeling the afterglow from that morning encounter.

"Did he talk to you about the new calendar? He sent it to me barely a half hour after we talked."

"He did that before he came home, I think. He got in and went straight to can we go on a date this Friday. So what did you say?"

"He said, Kelli's not happy, if it were you what would you need. So I thought for a minute and then said how long has it been since you went on a date. And he basically smacked his forehead and said Shit!" Kelli cracked up. Michelle listened, smiling. "And then I went home and asked Kenji out."

"How'd that go?"

"Let's just say it's a good thing nobody else was around. I think we might have shocked the cats." Kelli laughed some more. Michelle said, "So you know he texted me. Vince did. He said thanks."

"I'm saying thanks, too. It was a good night. And a good morning. Are you sure it's okay, though?"

"Uh, what?"

"Taking all the Fridays off the schedule. Taking every other Sunday off. Is it going to screw up your training?"

Michelle made a *pfft* noise. "No. You know how good he is. He's freaking out because it's a lot of new stuff, and he feels like he's got to be as good as Dmitri straight out of the gate, which is nuts. Honestly, I think spending less time on it is going to make us more productive. Because he's going to be happy, instead of worried."

"Will it be good for you too?"

"Definitely." Michelle checked the time. "I've got to get over to the studio. Are we okay?"

"Well, sure," Kelli said, confused. "Why wouldn't we be?"

Michelle laughed under her breath. "You're such an angel. I'll see you soon."

"Bye." Kelli put her phone down, stretched her back, wriggled in her seat. This felt like those early days, when she and Vince couldn't be in the same room without sexing each other. All warm and a little squishy, a little sore, but in the best possible way. That reminded her it was time to check in with Alicia. And then she'd get back to work.

Kelli was practically buzzing with excitement when they got out of the car. Vicky and Sharon had moved to this amazing Mid City duplex – called the

Faux Chateau – on Labor Day Weekend, but she and Vince hadn't been inside yet. She'd only been to the property once before, when they came to see Andy Martin's 'Tangueros' photographs. His studio was upstairs from the garage, separated from the duplex by an entertainment-friendly backyard.

Vicky was out on the patio, doing something with the gas grill, when they went through the gate. "Hey! How was the drive?"

The real answer was 'shitty as usual' but Kelli said, "We're so used to it now. I have to tell you, I considered bringing the kids for exactly two minutes. Then Esme said leave them here so we did." Vicky laughed. "You look great! How've you been?"

"I'm good," Vicky said. "Continually amazed and confused about the dancing crap. Job is fine. Hecking *love* living here."

Vince almost laughed. "Hecking?"

"We're trying not to use the F word. Simka is picking up vocabulary at an alarming rate."

"Got it." He glanced at Kelli, snug against his side in the circle of his arm. "We should probably keep that in mind." She was giggling. He kissed her face. "As you can see, I brought wine."

"Making you even more welcome than you already were. Go on inside." Vicky gestured at their kitchen door. "Hand those over to Sharon and give yourselves a tour."

"What've you got going?" Kelli looked past her. "Oh, grilled veggies, yum!" Zucchini and onions and big portobello caps. Lined up along the back of the grill were what had to be baking potatoes, wrapped in foil.

Vicky didn't really have a hand free, but she bent down to press her cheek against Kelli's. "It's really good to see you."

215

"You too." Kelli patted Vicky's back, then let Vince lead her into the house. "Jesus, I just had an envygasm."

Sharon giggled in a very smug way from the far end of kitchen. "It's kind of nice, huh. Wait till you see the master bath."

"Oh my lord. Nina Simone! Hey baby! Look at you!" Kelli crouched down to greet the toddler, who was staring at her suspiciously. "We have met before but you were a teeny tiny tadpole. I'm Kelli. I've known your mommies since before they had you. Yes! Before the world began!" Vince and Sharon were both snickering. "Hello Prospero. Hello Miranda. What pretty kitties." She petted the cats absently, half-listening to Vince and Sharon chat, studying the 'taking care of business' space on the other side of the kitchen door. A tiny room was tucked under the stairs, perfect for stashing a baby when people were over.

Before long, she was wandering through the apartment, holding Vince's hand. The downstairs was public space, dominated by a spacious, casual-glam living-dining room. At the front of the building was a guest bedroom, separated from the living space by a full bath and adjacent closet. She glanced at Vince. "Someday I predict Simka will be in here." It didn't look entirely un-used, though, so she guessed one or the other of their friends used it as a retreat from time to time. Queen-sized bed, recliner and reading lamp, nightstands. No need for a dresser because of that well-designed closet. Big bay window overlooking the shallow front yard. *Yes, okay, envy.* She shook it off. "This is a heck of a place," she said softly as they went up the stairs.

The master suite featured a huge walk-in closet on the street side and a palatial bathroom on the other. On the far side of the bathroom was a screened-in sunroom, with an exit door to the stairs that led down to the backyard. It wasn't as big as their patio in Westchester, but being up high, with the city view screened by a pepper tree, made it feel luxurious. "I would be out here all the damn time," Vince said.

Vicky heard him from the patio. "We are."

Since the stairs were right there, Vince opened the door and they went out that way. "Is it the same on the TV-star side?"

"Flipped layout, but yeah. When they bought the place last year, they came to us and said what do you think. Sharon was like, well, since you ask." Kelli laughed. "It was *such* a mess."

"I heard about it," Vince said. "Ever since the Power is On party." Which they'd missed, because Kelli felt too crappy to go, and he didn't want to go without her.

"A year ago." Vicky shook her head, watching the grill. "Andy managed the reno. Sharon worked with her dad and Mateo on the floor plans. All summer we kept going, let's get in there, but doing it before 'The Great Wave' was just not happening."

"Trying to do anything once you have a baby is four times as complex," Kelli said. "We heard you, we understood you, but we did not truly believe you."

Vicky and Vince both laughed. He said, "Elliott said he couldn't believe they actually wanted to fix it up, instead of tear it down, but he's glad they did."

"God, me too. It's gorgeous now. Of course the things on either side look even worse in comparison, but we avert our eyes." Vicky prodded a potato, then lifted the veggies off the grill onto a plate, handing it to

Vince. "Take that inside? Tell Sharon these spuds are almost done. Thanks." Once he was through the door she looked at Kelli. "Really okay?"

"Really okay," Kelli said. "Had a rough few months there, I won't lie. Thank you for coming down that day at the hospital."

"You already thanked me." She studied the grill for a moment. "We were so scared."

"So was I. So was he. I know he looks at those babies sometimes and thinks, you better be glad she's okay. He loves them like crazy," Kelli hastened to add. "He's great with them. But yeah. He was scared."

Vicky nodded. "And everything's good with Esmeralda?"

"She is literally the best. There are days when I wish we had the place to ourselves, and then the next thing I know she's like I'll be out for however long, and it's like she can read my mind. Vince fixed up this apartment, did he tell you?" Vicky made an interested sound. "Studio over the garage. Used to be a rental unit. His dad and stepmom stayed there at Thanksgiving. Maybe one day we can really do it up."

"Income property?" Transferring the potatoes to a bowl, turning off the grill.

Kelli made a sound of disagreement as they walked inside. "Princess tower." Vicky laughed. So then Kelli had to tell Sharon and Vince what was so funny, and before long they were at the table, eating and drinking like old times. On the drive home, Kelli reclined her seat (because her midsection was still not so comfortable with seat belts) and gazed at her handsome husband. "I'm glad you kept them as friends."

"*We* kept them," he corrected. "If you weren't the way you are, it might not've worked."

"The way I am?"

He glanced over for a second. "Perfect."

Look who's talking, she thought. "I love you too." She turned her head to gaze at him. "Which part of that apartment made you most jealous?" He laughed. She was grinning too, but deadly serious. "I can't decide between the kitchen or the bathroom. When the kids get old enough to want their own rooms, we're moving up above the garage, right?"

"Ma may want that," he warned her, smiling. "Maybe even before then."

"Well okay, I guess that's fair. Either way, there's gonna be some extreme makeover home edition going on."

"You plan it and we'll build it, baby." He was watching the road, but he felt her pat his thigh. She left her hand there.

CHAPTER 16

January 2017

Vince was at the gym, in the weight room, when he heard his phone buzz. Between the training he was doing with Michelle, his own business, his mother and Kelli, and the always-in-mind twins, it was never turned off these days. A text notification usually meant 'call back' or 'FYI' but he was ready for a break anyway, so he set down the barbell, pulled the phone out of his bag, and brought up the message. "Fuck!" he said out loud, and sat down on the weight bench. The text was from Michelle, but it wasn't about training.

The message read *Vince terrible news accident at studio Ray was hit by a car. Julia Paula & Mike were outside too. Everyone else is all right well more or less but all have been taken to the hospital. We don't know how bad it was but honestly looked very bad. Didn't want you to get back here without a warning*

He wrote back immediately. *Thanks Michelle you and Dmitri really okay? Anybody still there?*

We're still here. Police were doing statements. Dmitri could use a hand if you have time

Dmitri was his friend, mentor, second father. Vince would always have time. *Be right there.* He put the phone away, put his weights back on the rack, and went to the shower room. He was trying not to wonder, trying not to worry. Ray had been his friend for more than three years. He and Julia had been married for only a month.

Vince got back to Shall We Dance within twenty minutes. As he walked down the street he could see that the front of the studio was heavily damaged; the big windows were shattered, the brickwork was crunched, and there was police tape all over the place. There was also a large dark stain on the sidewalk right in front, inside a ring of traffic cones wrapped with more police tape. Seeing that felt like walking into a brick wall, with bricks made of ice. He didn't go closer. Instead he went around to the rear entrance, and found that door still unlocked. He put his keys back in his pocket as he went inside. All of the students were gone. "Michelle? Dmitri?"

Michelle came out of the office. "The boss is on the phone with the hardware store. He has to board up the windows. Patrick's on his way, he's going to take Dmitri over to Granny Miriam's to spend some time with Simka."

When the news got out that Dmitri was Vicky and Sharon's donor, everyone said 'what' and then 'of course.' Vince knew his daughter was like a tranquilizer for the studio boss. "Is he doing all right? Are you doing all right?" Michelle looked like she could use a hug, so Vince gave her one. She held on tight. He kissed her forehead. "Is Kenji coming for you?"

"Yeah," she said, sniffling a little. "He'll be over soon. I didn't want to leave Dmitri alone. He's, well, you know how he is. We haven't heard from anybody. We don't know what's happening. Paula said the SUV just plowed into him, it's so awful," she said in a rush, and started crying. Vince held her for a few minutes, hating the mental images his brain was supplying.

He stayed at the studio, occasionally talking with Dmitri and Michelle, until Kenji arrived to take her home. He was still there, out in the main room because

221

he could tell Dmitri needed some space, when Patrick arrived a few minutes later. They usually smiled when they saw each other; not today. "Hey Patrick," he said quietly. "Dmitri's in the office."

"Were you here?"

"No, I was at the gym. Michelle texted me. We don't really know … the status." Patrick nodded, patted Vince on the shoulder, and went into the office.

Vince heard him say, "Sweetheart," and then the door was closed. Vince walked slowly around the studio, straightening chairs, emptying abandoned water bottles and pitching them into the recycling bin, turning off the music system. There hadn't been any music playing. He imagined that whatever had been playing when the crash happened would be seared into everyone's brain. He'd already told Dmitri that he would stay to meet the delivery, and make sure the windows were secure. When Patrick took Dmitri out a few minutes later, they didn't speak, only nodded. Vince didn't think of asking about Elena until they were gone. He sent a message to Tony: *Over at the studio. Was Elena here this afternoon?*

A reply came back immediately: *No thank God she was with Mateo at Kenji's fitting new costumes. Are you all right?*

I was at the gym. Not exactly all right. Can't believe this happened. I'm staying to meet the hardware store guys. Tell Elena the studio is closed tomorrow and don't even look at the front

Understood, thank you. Take care

You too. Vince would have thought the hardware guys would be here by now. Then he looked at the time again and realized how little had actually passed. He texted Kelli to reassure her that he was okay, and that he'd be home later. Wondered when they would find out what happened to Ray.

The answer came the next day, close to noon, via a group text from Julia's daughter. Vince was at home, because he hadn't wanted to go to his office. He was alone with the twins, because Kelli was at work and his mother had taken advantage of him being home to go and do a consult for an interior-design project. He set down the phone and stared into space. *Not Ray*, he thought, *not that guy, they just got married, it's not fair*. Wiped his face. Sat with the babies and waited for them to give him something to do.

Ray had been an up-and-coming actor, so the news was all over the internet by midafternoon. Vince wanted to call Ray's wife Julia, but her daughter had said 'no calls,' and he knew it was for his own benefit that he wanted to talk to her anyway. She didn't need to hear how he felt. There was another group text later on, this one from Vince's friend Mike. He and Paula had been walking out right behind Julia and Ray. Neither of them were injured, but Mike had been nearly killed in a traffic accident five years before; Vince couldn't imagine that he wasn't completely shell-shocked. And Ray was Mike's friend too. Vince did a little bit of caretaking with the twins, settled them back down, and then went to the bedroom to call.

"Hi Vince." Mike's voice sounded husky, as if he'd been talking a lot that day.

Or crying, thought Vince. "Mike. I'm so sorry. How are you doing?"

"Not great. We're drinking a lot."

"I'm going to do some of that when Kelli and the mamacita get home. On baby duty right now. I'm glad you're not alone."

223

"Me too. Paula's taking care of me."

"Good. Anything I can do? For either of you?"

"Not really. It's just … ."

"A really shitty day." Vince heard something, a non-verbal acknowledgement. "Call me if you need anything. I'll see you soon."

"Yeah. Thanks for calling." Mike disconnected.

He'd been through a lot, and Vince knew he was tough, but there was no way to tough this out. No way to not be gutted by the loss of a friend, or not to think 'what if.' Vince pulled up another number and sent a message to Elliott: *Hey buddy, wanted to check in. You and Alicia and Lizzie good?*

A reply came fast: *Vince hi glad you checked in I was about to call, heard about that godawful mess at the studio. So so sorry. We're all good. How are you holding up?*

Never thought we could lose someone, you know? Not so young

The universe preparing us for old age maybe. Hi here's a taste of the shit yet to come

It's shit all right. Let's get together soon

Definitely. We need some quality time, I miss you

Once Vince returned from leave there hadn't been much face time outside work. He knew that last bit was something Elliott would only have written in circumstances like this. *I miss you too. Glad you are and were and will be my friend*

Always and ever and let us never refer to these messages

God no. Love to Alicia

And to Kelli. See you soon. Vince would not have said that the exchange made him feel better, exactly, but once he'd wiped his eyes again, and the tightness in his throat had eased, he was able to spend a mostly-steady hour answering messages from students and from friends connected to the studio. There were a lot of them. Then his mother got home, and took his mind off the tragedy by chattering about her new design job, and by the time Kelli returned he felt almost normal. He could tell from her worried eyes that Kelli knew he'd had a bad day. "We all had a bad day," he told her after dinner. "I'm lucky I have you, and Ma, and the babies. Talked to Mike, ugh."

"Oh lord I know. I talked to Paula. I didn't tell her what it was like at the office today. They're really only close with Susan and me, but everybody knew what happened, and it was kind of grim. I talked to Michelle again too. Did you talk to Dmitri?"

"For a minute. Studio's closed until Saturday. I might call Vicky in a bit. Ray helped her so much with that trick last summer."

Kelli rubbed his back. "That's the problem with a community like ours," she said quietly. "If something happens, we all feel it. I wouldn't change it, though." It had helped them, the year before. Helped Vince, especially, to have friends with him at the hospital.

"No." That was all he could say. Kelli changed the subject, suggesting they all pile into the living room for a movie. She cued up 'Ant Man,' figuring it would meet the current need. Had to pause it about halfway through, when Vince's phone chimed. "It's Vicky. I could call her back."

"No, go talk to her. This can wait." She watched him leave the room as he connected.

"Hi Vicky," he said. "How are you doing?"

"I'm here to ask you that question. We're okay, we're here with Andy and all the critters drinking whisky."

"All of you?"

"The adult humans are drinking whisky. I'm guessing you've had a very lousy twenty-four hours."

"Yeah. I was at the gym yesterday when the accident happened. Michelle pinged me, I walked back and," his voice caught and he had to take a moment. "There's blood all over the sidewalk."

"Jesus, Vince."

"Did you hear what actually happened?"

"When I talked to Mike. He had to put me on with Paula for a minute. He's wrecked."

"Yeah, I know."

"Paula said they were all going out, Julia was in front. Ray saw the SUV coming and just, like, threw Julia back at Mike, and then wham. So completely awful."

"I can't stop picturing it. It was so clear that the car only stopped because it hit the wall. I should never have gone to the front. Wasn't thinking." His voice was unsteady.

"I wouldn't have thought of that either. Thank God it's a strong old building and nobody inside was hurt. I wish I could hug you right now." Her voice squeaked a little. "Actually I wish I could dump you on the couch in the love pile we've got going. But I guess you've got your own love pile."

"Yeah, kind of. But I appreciate it. Next time I see you, you can hug me."

"I always hug you," she said. "You sure you're okay?"

He really wasn't. "The only good thing about this is, it wasn't you. I don't know if." He had to stop talking.

There was not-quite-silence for nearly a minute before Vicky said, "Fuck, Vince, did you have to say that? You know I hate to cry."

"I hate it too." He took a deep breath. "I've got to get back to my love pile. Take care of each other. I love you." They'd been friends for seven years. He'd never told her that before. The thought of going another day without saying it was intolerable.

"I love you too." Vicky disconnected.

Vince went to the bathroom and splashed some water on his face, did some more deep breathing, and finally went back out to the living room. His mother looked at him anxiously. Kelli had a shot of tequila waiting for him. "How'd you know I wanted that?"

"Lucky guess." She watched him drink it, then un-paused the movie. He leaned in to kiss her, then lay down with his head on her lap. She wrapped her arm over his chest. Exchanged a glance with Esmeralda. Knew they were both thinking *thank God he wasn't there when it happened.*

March 2017

Nobody was the same after the accident. It seemed everyone was a little more careful with each other. When the studio re-opened, all the students and teachers were back – except for Julia – because everyone had a show or a competition or simply a personal goal. At first everyone was quiet, and nobody was hugging. It took about a week for the regulars to feel like they might be able to laugh, and about three to stop choking when they did. The Cabaret's February show went on as usual, without Ray and Julia.

Tony talked to most of the performers, as he did regularly. Many had already been featured in the docu-series. He went with his wife and Mateo to their first few Open Professional Rhythm events. He spoke to Vince and Michelle about their own training. The conversation also, almost of necessity, touched on what had happened at the studio. "Michelle, you were friends with Julia for a long time. Have you been in touch since she left?"

"Yes." Michelle didn't really want to talk about this, but she knew why it was important. "She apologized for leaving us like that. Apologized! I was like, Julia, honey. We miss you like crazy, but we don't blame you at all. It was weeks before anybody could go in that front door. Dmitri hasn't even set up the café tables he usually puts out there. He's interviewing for a new Latin specialist. In the meantime, he's overworking himself and going quietly crazy. And then *he* apologized."

Tony made a confused face. Vince answered the unspoken question. "He apologized because he doesn't have time for coaching us right now. I was like, dude. Of all the things you should *not* be worrying about, our deal is top of the list. I said, how about this. We'll keep running all the routines, but we won't really work anything except tango this month, because I like that one best for maybe obvious reasons, and we'll do a show number for 'Casino.' We'll put it together with the routine you choreographed as the base, and maybe if you get a minute you can look at it for us and tweak it. Then after you get a new person, it's bound to happen soon, we'll move on to the next dance. It's not like Michelle doesn't know what she's doing."

"Dmitri wants to work on all of them at once," Michelle said. "That was all right for me, but I was mainlining this shit. I was in here every day, doing every class. It was literally all I did aside from work, eat, and sleep. Vince has a lot more demands on his mental process. I think we might get better results if we work them separately. The technique for each dance is different."

Vince said, "Thank you. I keep saying that."

"Perhaps you could expand on that," Tony suggested.

"Well, okay. The smooth waltz now, the body shape and the way you, like, *deploy* different actions when you're not in hold, is a lot like ballet. Right, Michelle?"

"Correct. Everything in the upper body is port de bras. That carries over into the American-style Viennese waltz, too."

"Right. But in the slow waltz, you have the really pronounced rise and fall, which you don't have as much in the Viennese waltz."

"Because of the tempo," Tony interjected.

"Exactly." Vince was gaining confidence as he talked, as if saying these things out loud was confirming that he actually understood them. "Then you go to foxtrot, and all of a sudden you're working more with a jazz vocabulary. It's very Broadway now. Depending on the music it can go more bluesy, which I dig, or more kind of Fred Astaire. Dmitri's style was very Fred Astaire. I might be more Gene Kelly." Michelle was nodding. "So our challenge there is to get me some kind of grounding in jazz. Because of course Michelle's been doing that all her life but the closest I've come is what I did in those two pro shows. And don't get me started on ballet. Jesus, that barre." Michelle snorted. "Shut up. I used to think I was pretty flexible, you know, for a guy."

229

Michelle laughed out loud. "You've been working in this studio with Mateo, and Sam, and Dmitri, and Mike, and –"

"Oh don't even. Mike is a freak. Anyway, deficit identified, attempting to rectify. But then, *then*, there's tango. American style has next to nothing to do with Argentine style." Vince was animated now. "It's like they took International style, which I hate, and softened it up a little, and now they try to add Latin actions and Argentine embellishments, and it's a fucking mess. Oops, sorry."

Tony was stifling laughter. He shook his head, making a 'don't worry' gesture. Michelle said, "Vince has a point. American-style tango is kind of a mess. There are elements that do not exist in the other three dances, and the timing is completely different. The frame is different, the use of the feet is different. I don't even know why you like that best right now."

"You liked it too," Vince pointed out. "Maybe because Dmitri started you out with that show dance." He focused on Tony. "I'm hoping that doing a show dance will help me get in the groove with it."

"If it does, will you try that for the other three dances?"

Vince and Michelle stared at each other for a moment; they hadn't thought of that. "Huh," he said. "Maybe?"

"That's a good idea," she said. "You love to perform. So do I. It could make the whole thing less of a grind. Because actually," she added, directing it to Tony, "we already talked about entering the show-dance event right out of the gate. Dmitri was a little doubtful, but if we pull off this routine for 'Casino,' he'll come around."

"We'd probably have to do them at the socials," Vince said. "After 'Casino' there's not really any Cabaret thing where we could break these in."

"Well, maybe the pro show." Michelle was still staring at Vince. Now she transferred her gaze to Tony. "We are way off track."

"Not at all," he said. "It's good to hear the strategy. The way you might choose to attack these different challenges. If you did a show dance of each style, through June. If that helped, as you say, get in the groove."

He didn't actually state a question, but Vince answered anyway. "If we did that, we'd have four months still to work on them. And we'd have something to look at that would tell us what does and doesn't work for us, on the floor. I do my best to copy Dmitri, but I have a different body and different movement, so it's a whole different experience for Michelle."

"It's not *worse*, though. You need to accept that," Michelle said. "Different isn't necessarily bad. And," she began, then stopped and looked around. Nobody was listening. Everyone in the studio was so used to Tony and his interviews that they tuned the whole thing out. Michelle lowered her voice a little anyway. "The fact is, Vince is twenty years younger than Dmitri. He doesn't have to work quite as hard to keep his weight down. He's strong, is what I'm saying." Vince was blushing a little. "That means his movement is going to read differently on the floor even if the shape of it is identical to Dmitri's."

"And will that change your approach to show dances? You did some very difficult, very challenging aerial work with Dmitri."

"Dmitri's lift technique is amazing. He got that pas de deux training when he was young. Vince is playing catch-up there. But the flip side of that is, he never tried to do it before he was strong enough to do it. I see how they put weight on those teenage boys, who are still growing, and I think, ugh." Michelle grimaced. "Not only weight, but force. A moving body is not the same as a static weight."

"I've never been injured," Vince said. "Not even a sprained ankle. Dmitri's been hurt a lot."

Tony nodded. "We spoke of that, a little. He said there was a near miss, before your spotlight dance, after the second championship."

"A bobble," Michelle said. "It's not like he almost dropped me. But yeah. One tiny off-balance moment, and his shoulder was messed up for a couple of weeks. Patrick was like, goddammit."

"What else will you do to prepare for the show dance?"

Vince answered that one too. "I'm in the gym pretty much every day, and I'm working with Mike again. Not on character this time, but on tricks. I've had trick envy ever since he and Paula did 'One For My Baby.' You saw that, right?" Tony nodded. "Remember that hands-free cartwheel thing he did? Couldn't even hear him land it? So much envy." Michelle was giggling. "Everything else in the damn routine I thought hey, I could do that. Then he goes and throws that and I'm like, goddammit. That's the first one I wanted to learn. So of course, before I could even attempt that, I had to learn to do a regular cartwheel." Michelle laughed out loud. "Because of course, this one can do that trick too. *And* she does it in high heels."

"If we put that shit in a show dance," she said. "If we both did it? People would go *nuts*." Both men could tell she liked that idea.

"We should do the double one, the Benji Schwimmer one," Vince said. "The pinwheel thing. That would be *sick*. That would be so not strictly ballroom. They'd be all, No New Steps!" They both cracked up.

CHAPTER 17

Michelle and Vince chose 'Gimme Shelter' for their show dance music, to fit the 'Casino' theme. Dmitri reviewed their choreography during an after-hours closed rehearsal, nodded, and didn't suggest any changes. "Okay, what." Vince couldn't believe it. "There has to be something."

Dmitri shook his head. "Is good. Good balance of show elements. Good use of the competition routine. After performance, you must bring the routine back to full size." The Chrome stage was not as big as a competition dance floor.

Vince sighed. "That is my absolute weakest point. All those years doing dances that don't travel. I'm running, though," he said. "At the gym. I try to run with smooth footwork."

"Is good," he said again, with something close to a smile. "Run at Viennese waltz tempo." Vince laughed and nodded. Before starting home that night, he texted Kelli: *The boss did not change anything for Casino. WTAF*

She replied immediately with a row of crying-laughing emojis. Then a supplement: *Do you like it?*

It's not as awesome as dancing with you but it does not suck. Speaking of dancing with you, Alison claims she's going to do a first-look at the summer pro show next month. You're going to try out, right?

Eeek!

Come on, you know it won't be martial arts again. Remember how much fun Gaucho was. So much fun, all those hours rehearsing hadn't even felt like work.

Are you going to try out? Will you have time??

Story is it's ballroom heavy. Michelle said we could. Vince added the clincher: *Dmitri said we could*

OMG well OK if Dmitri said you could. Yikes I'd better get my tushie in the gym

LOL and let's do some long walks on the beach. Get some sun on Carlos and Celia in their dune buggy. Vince had been delighted to find the beach-accessible stroller.

You're so cute. Heading home now?

Out the door in 3 2 1

Love you baby

Love you too

At the 'Casino' wrap party, Kelli plopped down beside Michelle on one of Chrome's lounge loveseats and said, "You two are going to kick so much ass." Michelle giggled. "How's Kenji doing?"

"He likes this routine. And the calendar management is working for him. Is it still good for you?"

"Oh sure. We have plenty of time to do our thing. Esmeralda's enjoying it too. Now that the little monsters can boogie a little, we turn them loose in the backyard and practice on the patio till they get tired. Esme can go out with one of her gigolos or one of her girl friends, we all get quality time. We started working on something."

Michelle instantly understood that meant a dance, and was thrilled to hear it. "You did?! That's great! What? And what for?"

"We thought about bringing back 'Palomita Blanca.' No new choreography." Their duet piece from 'Gaucho' was still one of Kelli's all-time favorites.

"For 'Milonga?' Because that would be fantastic. That was such a pretty routine. No wonder Vince hasn't been bitching about American style so much."

Kelli snorted. "Was he bitching?"

"Oh my God." Michelle rolled her eyes.

Kelli laughed. "Well I guess if throwing him a little Argentine here and there keeps him happy, that'll make your life easier."

"It sure will."

"It was Paula's suggestion. Back in January. At the time I thought hey yeah, and then I thought ugh, because the last time that was on the stage Ray and Julia did it."

"Oh," Michelle said, remembering. "That was right after Mike and Paula got married. Oh my God, they did it too. They danced that at their wedding, I saw the video."

"Mike and Paula knew every number in that show. They are not normal." Kelli was trying to lighten it up, and she was successful. "Anyway, now that we have a little distance, I brought it up to Vince and he said he'd like to. So even if Alison doesn't cast me in her summer thing I have a reason to get my ass in shape."

"Your ass is a very nice shape. And I'll be astonished if Alison doesn't cast you. I'm so glad you want to be in it."

"I want to dance with Vince. I'm glad he's doing this with you, I really am, because I do *not* want to do what you guys are doing. But man, even a couple of hours working on a dance again is like, mmm. Yes honey. This is our thing. This is us."

Michelle patted her. "I know what you mean. Kenji only even learned to dance for me, so when we get to do it it's like aahh." Kelli smiled, nodding. "Did he tell you what we're doing next?"

"Viennese waltz, right? For the studio social?" Michelle made a sound of assent. Kelli said, "Is it going to have lifts like this one? Oh lord. He gets so ripped when he's doing lifts. He took off his shirt the other day and I was like, Esme, could you keep an eye on the critters because there is something I have to do here." They were both still giggling when Vince found them.

It felt like approximately a million years since 'Gaucho,' so Kelli was ambivalent about auditioning for the summer show, even though Vince told her he wanted her to. Then he told her he'd understand if she didn't feel ready. That sparked a text to Diana: *You know that feeling when your guy really sees you and is giving you an out on something you're scared to do and you know he loves you either way but you're totally pissed off that he's not all get your ass out there and do that thing you want to do?*

About a minute later, which was surprising given this was happening in the middle of a workday even with the time difference, Diana's reply rolled in: *What are you being a chicken about?*

Kelli laughed to herself, glad her sister could still read her mind. *Summer pro show*

Like the tango one? You loved doing that!

Kelli switched modes and called. Diana picked up instantly. "Hey girl. Yes I loved doing that. It was two years ago and I looked like a pin-up girl and things are different now."

Diana made a growly sound. "Things may *feel* different, but are they really?"

"Huh." That was actually a good question. Kelli stood, closed her office door, and sat down again. The truth was, the important things were not different. The ambition and desire were still there. Dancing was still a complete joy, and dancing with Vince was the next best thing to sex. It was arguably better than sex because they could do it for hours, interrupted only by the kind of baby maintenance that felt like a real imposition when you were trying to fool around. She said all that to Diana, waited patiently through the resulting fit of giggles, then said, "Well, you know. Jay's pretty self-sufficient by now but the little monsters are not."

"Lord help us yes. He's starting high school this fall."

"He is not! Oh my Jesus are we that old?!" They both cracked up.

Then Diana said, "So you want him to push you?"

"I kind of do. That's not fair, is it."

"Mmm. What do you know about the show? I mean, last time it was one thing but then it kind of changed after a couple months."

"It changed a lot. The director swapped in different music, it was a scramble." Kelli leaned back in her chair, asking herself why she didn't talk to her big sister more often. *Well, because there's not enough time in the world to keep up with everybody.* True, but she felt guilty anyway. "I want you to know I am totally blowing off work to talk to you."

"Good, me too. So what's up."

"There was a first-look meeting a couple weeks ago. We have a song list. I know where Vince wants me. The director wants to see a current video, which kind of stings but on the other hand I haven't been out there for a long time. Linda took one for us last Sunday when we were over at their place practicing."

After a moment: "And you hate it?"

"No, actually I don't. I'm trying to be objective about it."

"Well, so is this tango again?"

"Two numbers, both groups. One of them is a tango. The other one's a cha-cha and rumba segue."

"That's where they blend the styles?"

Kelli smiled. Diana had picked up a lot of the jargon over the years. "Right. So this is, like, best-case scenario for getting back in the dance groove. Not a duet number where the whole world is looking at us. Not a competition. Not super technical. I mean, I'm guessing. If everybody who was at the meeting is in the cast then the choreography could get a little challenging because damn." Diana laughed again. "Some real heavy hitters, girl. Dmitri, his new Latin guy, Michelle, Vicky. Sam and Mateo. That big red-headed actor is back with his wife, they're doing a duet in the tango act."

"How many acts?"

"This thing is huge! Four acts! Sixteen numbers!" She kept her volume down, but she couldn't keep the exclamation marks out of her tone. "Mike and Paula, those people who work in my office?"

"The contemporary pair."

Contemporary and everything else, Kelli thought. There were a lot of incredible dancers associated with the studio and with the Cabaret, but Mike had turned out to be, well. 'World class' might be an exaggeration, but only a slight one. That he'd quickly bonded with Paula had amazed exactly nobody. "They're doing six numbers."

"Out of sixteen?!"

"Right? And it looks like the Latin guy, Hiro, is doing that many too. Oh my God you should see this guy. He's like the Japanese version of Vince."

239

"Ooh baby."

"Yeah. Hot as fuck." A snort of laughter from Baltimore. "Oops. Anyway, off track. Best case scenario. Low pressure, relatively small commitment. Not even in two of the acts."

"Is that all Vince would be doing?"

"No. He and Michelle will take a duet in the foxtrot and swing act, then they're part of a group in the waltz act."

"Does that bother you?

Kelli sighed. Of course Diana would ask that. Everyone would. All the way through, people were going to be looking at her going 'is she jealous,' and "Oh for fuck's sake, I just now figured out what my problem is."

"Yay! Sister therapy for the win!"

"For real. I'm not afraid of doing this show, I'm afraid of biting someone's head off when they ask me if I'm jealous of Michelle. Everybody in the damn world is going to."

"Oh. Oops. Sorry."

Diana sounded so penitent, Kelli had to reassure her. "You are not the problem, honey. You are never a problem and you shouldn't apologize. I needed that little jolt of annoyance to figure this out." Another laugh from Baltimore. "I better nip that shit in the bud."

"Maybe get your filmmaker buddy to do an interview," Diana suggested. "At the studio where people can hear you. Let the grapevine do the work for you."

"Girl! That is *so smart*. Totally doing that. Thank you. So is Jay excited about high school?"

Diana accepted the change of subject. "Crazy excited. The school has a gymnastics team, so he can keep up with that without us having to drive all over creation." They talked about that for another few minutes before Diana had to get off the phone. Kelli thought for a few seconds before returning to work mode. Scrolled to the video Linda took at practice, thought *do it girl*, and sent it to Alison.

The interview took a few weeks to organize, because everybody was crazy busy. Kelli talked to Vince about it, and he asked if she wanted him there. She said he didn't have to be, but did he think Michelle might join in. That led to a three-way phone call. The two women met up with Tony at Shall We Dance on a Saturday afternoon, when the place was always packed. Dmitri told them to use the office. It was just big enough for Tony to set up a two-shot with Michelle behind the desk and Kelli seated in front of it. He left the door open, knowing there was a reason this was a joint interview, if not what that reason was. The music and conversation in the studio wouldn't interfere with his mic.

"I wondered if you would have time to meet before the group rehearsals begin," he said to Michelle once they were rolling.

"Oh, sure. I'm only doing three numbers. And one of them is with Dmitri so you know what that means."

"Eh, no," he said apologetically, mostly so she would laugh. The camera loved it when Michelle laughed.

"It means I really don't even have to remember it. One day I'll probably get there with Vince, but you know I worked with Dmitri for three solid years. We kind of share a brain, on the dance floor."

Kelli was nodding. "That's the way we are. It came pretty fast because we were dancing only with each other."

The women smiled at each other. "It's a great feeling, isn't it?"

"Tell me about the pro show." Tony knew all about it, but the viewers needed background.

Michelle nodded, understanding. "Alison really got technical with this one. It's four acts, each one based on a ballroom style. Each act has four dances, and each one uses that ballroom style in a different genre. So for example in Act One, which is foxtrot and swing, Vince and I are doing a foxtrot-quickstep duet. Then there's a group foxtrot. There's a jazz number based on foxtrot, and there's a hip-hop number set to a modern cover of a classic big-band swing song. The cast for that is three of our Latin guys with the b-boy choreographer. They're using some jitterbug and jive."

"Cannot wait to see that on the stage," Kelli said. "I've seen our boys fooling around with it but once Lucas gets his stuff worked in it's gonna kill."

"I understand every act has a duet, a group, an urban-dance number, and a jazz or contemporary number. A challenge for the cast. We will see you, Kelli, in two of the groups."

"Yes and I'm so excited. It feels like I've been out of this forever. Oh! And I'll finally get to dance with Ricky again!" Ricky Castillo and his professional partner were in several numbers. "I've seen the things he and Anya have done with the Cabaret and I'm so thrilled they're in this cast."

"Oh, me too," Michelle said excitedly.

Tony got her back on track. "And your other number, the one with Dmitri?"

"That's in Act Four, the waltz act. Vince and I are dancing again in the group. Dmitri and I are doing a contemporary number set to this gorgeous pop waltz."

"Will we see so many lifts now?"

Michelle shook her head. "There are some lifts, but we aren't going to that adagio place anymore. None of the overhead stuff. I probably could have talked Dmitri into it, but Patrick would have had words for me. I'm already working every trick in the book with Vince."

"And Vince dances with Kelli in the cha-cha and rumba group, and in the tango group."

"Yes! It's so cool! It is so, so good to see them dancing together again." Another smile across the desk.

Tony smiled, knowing her sincerity would come through. "You and Vince used show dances to, I quote, get in the groove for your upcoming debut in Rising Star Smooth. How did it work?"

"It *totally* worked." Michelle was excited again. "Give that man a thing to perform and he will not stop. I literally had to throw him out of the studio a few times. Like, your wife is waiting for you, and my husband is waiting for me. Gee Tee Eff Oh." Kelli laughed. "When we took the routines back to the studio after the show dances, all the tension was gone. He opened up. His foot speed is better. He travels more, he's not afraid to move through me. More body flight. He *feels* it. We haven't done much tweaking yet because of this show, but in September we'll go through each of the routines with the boss. I'll be honest, I would have agreed to go into Embassy if Dmitri said we should. He still says California Star."

"The full year of preparation."

"He knows Vince wants to be as close to perfect as possible. I don't want to get too cocky, because the only other partner I've had was Dmitri, so what do I actually know. But it feels really, really good."

"Vince says the same thing," Kelli put in. "He knew it was going to be a challenge but, for the record, he said he would never have even considered it with any other partner."

"Aww!" Michelle gave her a grateful face. "That's only because you didn't want to."

"I didn't and I don't! Four dances, at that level, out in a pack of other pros? Forget it!" She was grinning; Michelle was making a 'seriously' face. "You know, we did some group events back in the day but I don't really see doing that again. We'll do show-dance events so we can pick our music." They hadn't even really talked about it yet, but it felt right as soon as she said it. "Make it about us."

"And be the only ones on the floor," Tony suggested. Both women giggled. "In the spotlight," he added, smiling.

"Exactly." Kelli deliberately made it sound smug.

After all the weeks of rehearsal, the entire gigantic cast of 'Face the Music' felt like a family. Most of them had known each other for so long already; they'd seen each other meet, get together, get married, evolve. Kelli was in a tizzy of excitement, dread, and overemotional hugginess, but at least she wasn't alone.

The full-cast run-through at Shall We Dance was one thing. The tech rehearsal at Chrome was another thing. It was unlike most Underground Cabaret shows, where a performer went on and did their one routine, and then they were done. This time, costume changes were expected to cause trouble. Stage managers (and newlyweds) Rory and Dana marked up the cue sheet, talked to tech and wardrobe, and said "Maybe we need to bring Red and Mary and Lucas out to the wing." Red

244

and Mary were only in the one number, a tango duet opening Act 3, so they didn't have any costume changes. Lucas (the urban dance co-choreographer) was in one number per act. Setting up screens so he could do his changes in the wing, parking Red and Mary out there during changes, and having the other guys do shirt-only changes in the wing served to reduce the body count in the green room.

Even with all of that, dress rehearsal was a hot mess. Kelli wasn't in Act 1, so she parked herself in the wing behind the tech panel. Vince and Michelle opened the show with their duet set to Nat King Cole's 'Let's Face the Music and Dance.' The first transition, to a three-couple foxtrot group, went smoothly. A music clip helped cover the brief delay before the third number; Mike and Paula had to change for their jazz duet. The fourth number went on without delay.

Act 2 was a scramble. Hiro had three costume changes. The Latin group number was four couples, which included Anya, who also had to change for the urban number. Kelli got a pretty good look at Hiro changing from Latin pants to jeans. She wasn't too married to enjoy it.

Then it was Act 3, which she was kind of living for. The tango group closed the act, so she parked in the wing again to watch the first three numbers. Mike and Paula had a change, from a contemporary duet to the four-couple group. Kelli tried to really focus in on the experience, knowing that once they were performing for real she wouldn't have the bandwidth to absorb the impact of passing from Vince to Sam to Hiro to Mike. And finally being paired with Vince again, for their featured phrase. He really had changed since 'Gaucho.' Even though they weren't in character for this number, his intensity was breathtaking. Getting a deep, open-

245

mouthed kiss as soon as they were offstage felt like a drink of water on a hot day.

And they had a few minutes to come down from that, thank God, because Vince wasn't in the first number of Act 4. From there on out the only speed-change was Michelle, getting from her group-waltz ballgown into costume for her contemporary duet with Dmitri. Kelli watched it on the green-room monitor. "You know," she said to Vince, "this show is amazing. Completely amazing. Can you believe this is the same place we did our little thing all those years ago?" Back when the dance pole was right there on stage, with plain wood underfoot instead of the marley laid down for them now.

Vince stood beside her, arm around her waist, letting her lean on him. "Feels like we're really part of something, doesn't it?"

"For real." She glanced up at him. "How confusing was it to do that waltz group?" The choreography had (unlike his opening duet with Michelle) nothing in common with any of his competition routines.

He huffed out a laugh. "If it was only me and Michelle I'd've been like, let's just do our routine please. With six of us it wasn't too bad."

"Considering you were in, what, ten numbers in 'Gaucho?'"

"Mm-hmm." Michelle and Dmitri came back into the green room. Mike and Paula were already out in the wing, ready to go on for their closing duet. They were doing a Viennese waltz interpretation of 'A Thousand Years.' Vince watched the first minute in silence. "I'm glad they brought that back."

"It's way different." The first time the number was on the Chrome stage, it was a theater-arts routine full of lifts; Mike and Paula performed it less than a month after they all lost Ray. "But yeah. I'm not surprised Alison asked for it, and I'm glad they decided to do it."

"How about you," he murmured into her hair. "Glad you did it?"

She turned her head to make eye contact, and also to facilitate a kiss. "So glad. Mind you, I will be glad when we are *done*." He laughed, kissed her again, patted her hip. Kelli caught his hand and squeezed it. "And then you and Michelle get serious."

CHAPTER 18

Most of their friends (the ones who weren't actually in it) saw 'Face the Music' onstage. A week after they closed, Kelli sent a copy of the official DVD to her sister Diana. The expected call came when she was out on the patio with Carlos and Celia, enjoying a quiet Saturday morning. She picked up the buzzing phone and said "Hey girl."

"Hey yourself. That was a hell of a show."

"Right?!"

"Tell me about the opening number."

Kelli was so ready to do that. "You better be glad I sent that video because that was supposed to be Vince and Michelle's show dance but they're changing it so you'll never see this one again. What they're doing now is, oh my God. Never mind. About this one. What did you think of the costumes?"

"I immediately thought, is it World War II? Was that what I was supposed to think?"

"They were aiming for that. The dress Michelle has on, that was her costume for the last show dance she did with Dmitri. And what Vince has on, that was Dmitri's costume."

"You mean based on that?"

"No, I mean the actual thing. They're almost exactly the same size. The designer, our friend Kenji? He made a couple of adjustments. Anyway yes, that last show dance was 'I'll Be Seeing You,' and they made it look like a uniform because the idea was Dmitri was going off to war and might not come back, right? Oh lord, everybody was bawling." A laugh from

Baltimore. "True story. You can find it online, you'll see. So their music for this is from 1964 but the song is from the Thirties and they were like, this works."

"It really does. That was like a whole movie in three minutes."

"Yes! What did you think of the transition to the next number?"

"Loved it. I loved the whole show, seriously. Jay's already watched it twice. Mama's like, when you bringing that over again. It was so good to see you and Vince doing your thing."

Kelli sighed happily, wiggling her toes, admiring the fresh pedicure. "It was so good to *be* doing our thing! Even only being in those two numbers, it was so much fun. I'm fitting in my 2015 stuff again. My ankles look like ankles again." Another laugh from Baltimore. "You know what I mean."

"Oh, I do. So what's next?"

"Well, Vince is in high gear getting ready for the big debut in November. But he's also like, what are *we* doing next. He's all, aside from the show dance we're just running shit now, so let's you and me work up something new. Taking it easy though. Starting with a number we did before."

"I'm so, so glad. I know you missed that so much. It's like those years when Jay was little and I couldn't deal, then he went off to school and I had a minute to breathe and think and start doing my thing again."

"Exactly like that."

"And the home situation's still good?"

"So good. Esmeralda is literally the best. She's out today doing something, so me and the rug rats have the place to ourselves. I'll fill up their pool in a little bit, we'll all go splash in the sun."

"Oh, shut up. It's pouring rain here." Kelli stifled a laugh but Diana heard her anyway. "You're a California girl for real now, huh."

"Here to stay. We'll find a minute to come back East, though. It's time everybody got to meet the monsters face to face." Kelli wouldn't say so out loud, but that was another reason she was glad to be looking like herself again. A family visit wouldn't be all about that. "Tell me how it's going with your baller."

"Ooh child. Steve was like, you know you don't have to, and I was like, my brain is turning to mush. It'd been so long I wasn't even sure I'd *get* the job. But they were like, can you type? Do bookkeeping? Answer phones? Keep a calendar? Okay then." She started talking about her part-time gig as a personal assistant for a pro athlete. Kelli listened, smiling at the sunny day on the other side of the screen.

September 2017

Kelli was talking as she went through the door of Tony and Elena's apartment. "Oh my goodness look how cute Gio is!!"

The two-and-a-half-year-old was a great combination of Elena and Tony, who gave the toddler an indulgent look and said, "I confess we both hope he will be taller than me." There was some nonsense about that while they all crowded into the kitchen. It was roughly two years since Vince and Kelli had last been there for dinner.

"Wow," Vince said, finally noticing the editing suite after a few minutes to catch up. "Are those new screens or were they always that big?"

"New," Tony said. "I needed to upgrade for the documentary last year." The one that resulted in a prize at Cannes.

"We saw that, finally," Kelli said. "Amazing. When we watched the Emmys this year I was squinting at the screen going, I wonder if any of those women are really men. Or, like, vice versa." The subject of Tony's 2016 project was a man who'd been in a twelve-year relationship with a top Hollywood producer who was closeted, cross-dressing to attend red-carpet events with him.

Elena nodded, grinning. "When Mateo saw it he said you know, I was nervous about doing the geisha thing for our wedding, but now I feel like I didn't fully commit."

"He looked beautiful, though," Kelli said, accepting a glass of wine. "And Sam's face when he made his big entrance? Oh my lord. I'm so glad they finally did that."

"Me too. I'm so glad you could come over tonight!"

"Thank God for Esme." They clinked glasses. Then Kelli and Vince took Gio out of the prep area so their hosts could get dinner on the table.

After the meal there was some more catching-up chat, this time mostly dance-related. Elena and Tony were hoping to win the Open Professional Rhythm event at the California Star Ball, the same weekend Vince and Michelle would debut. "I think I'm more nervous than he is," Kelli confessed. "Have you talked to Kenji lately?"

"Eh." Tony exchanged a glance with Elena. "Last week."

Vince exchanged a glance with Kelli. "I haven't had a private conversation with him for months. Should I be concerned?"

"Maybe they should see that interview," Elena said softly, laying a hand on Tony's arm. She looked at

Vince. "I kind of doubt there's anything you can or should do, but it might be helpful for you to see this. Just in case." Gio was half-asleep, so she went to get him ready for bed while Kelli and Vince cleared the table.

Tony went to his desk to cue up his interview with Kenji. Not too much later, they were all seated. "Whether or not I will use this, I don't know," he said. "It might depend on how things go in November."

"Let's see it," Kelli said, holding Vince's hand. Tony clicked the start button.

Kenji sat, apparently relaxed, in the assembly room at his home business. A rack of ballgowns could be seen off to one side; a wall of cubbyholes filled with bolts of fabric was behind him. "You must be looking forward to finishing this," he said.

"We come to the end soon," Tony said offscreen. "I have enough to make two films, or three. The editing will kill me. But now, to business. Michelle and Vince debut in two months. They have performed together regularly this year. Your thoughts?"

Kenji sighed. "It hasn't been as bad as I feared. Last year, when they started, I thought I would have to say something. It was too much, too fast, too intense. And it wasn't that there was anything improper. I would swear that Vince has never touched her outside of a dance scenario, certainly never kissed her. He is completely professional. It was just so much time."

"This spring, the first performance. Who did the choreography?"

"They did, together, with Dmitri. The theme of that show was 'Casino,' you remember. So they chose 'Gimme Shelter,' because of that movie, and they chose tango because Vince had so much experience

252

with tango show dances already. You saw that one a couple of times."

"It was very straightforward, I thought."

"Yes, there wasn't much storytelling in that number. It wasn't personal. So that was something I could appreciate wholeheartedly. All of their studio performances, too. Even this summer with 'Face the Music.' That number of theirs, Michelle thought at first it would be their competition show dance. And it would be a great show dance. The blend of foxtrot, quickstep, and Broadway style, set to that well-known song, it's a sure winner. But I guess that made it too safe. Which of course meant that I liked it."

Tony's voice had a smile in it. "The whole show, it was good. Then Michelle had the other duet, the waltz, with Dmitri. How did you feel about that?"

"I wished she were still dancing with him. And I feel so small about that. Because my problem, it's all mine. I have zero basis to feel any resentment, any jealousy. I have a feeling I'll find myself traveling with them every time they compete out of town, the way I did before. I'm afraid I'll disappear if I don't."

On the couch, Kelli heard a quick intake of breath and squeezed Vince's hand.

Offscreen, Tony said, "You think Michelle would forget you?"

After a pause, Kenji said, "Not exactly. She is very single-minded on campaign. She has to be. Loss of focus could mean much worse things than not placing, not winning. It could mean injury. She's been lucky so far. The worst injury she's had is a sprained knee. That was when she gave up pole. But that has to be worked around, because the ligament will never be quite the same. She's had to adapt her movement. Has to always

253

be conscious of it. Michelle is forty years old now. I believe that she and Vince will be the champions if they can get there within two or three years the way she and Dmitri did, as long as she doesn't get injured again. Anyway, it's not that she would forget me, it's that I need to make it easy for her to remember. Which means I need to be there." He took another moment. "And what annoys me about this – about myself – is that I would go anyway. It's good for the business for me to join the vendors."

Tony looked across at Elena; he could sympathize. It was good for his business, too, to accompany Elena and Mateo to out-of-town events. But he understood the necessity of not distracting the competitors. He had to consciously avoid asking for her attention. His invisible self said to Kenji, "So then, the show dance."

Kenji sighed again. "It was Vince's suggestion. After 'Face the Music,' he turned around and said, it's too predictable. Not so much the construction of it, the choreography, but the music. He said, what got you here, what got *us* here, and she said burlesque. So they're dancing to 'Show Me How You Burlesque,' and I hate it." Vince flinched. Kelli squished closer to him as Kenji went on. "I have not allowed myself to think that before, much less say it. It's foxtrot and quickstep again, with jazz, but it's so fast, and all the tricks frankly terrify me."

"You worry she'll be injured again."

"I know she wouldn't do these things if she weren't confident she can execute them safely. Vince can and will do things Dmitri wouldn't. He's so much younger and he's never been injured. So I say nothing, even though I'm afraid they're overconfident."

"What will she wear?"

"Not a ballgown. I've already designed the costume. She loves it. Vince likes it. It's basically a high-necked boy-cut leotard with a mesh back. Full mobility, nothing to get caught or tangled, because of all these lifts and tricks."

They could all hear and see Kenji's ambivalence about such a bare costume. Offscreen Tony said, "Safer for her."

"Yes." There was a pause. "My issues are so trivial, so shallow, so unjustified. Vince is two years younger than Michelle, which means he's eight years younger than I am. He is an outstanding dancer. He still has that thing we talked about two years ago. She deserves the best partner she can have, and I know that's Vince. I'm afraid because I am the calm center, and she thrives in chaos."

The video stopped. Vince blew out a slow breath. "Wow. I had no idea."

Kelli was slightly appalled. She'd been talking to Michelle all along and there was never a hint of this. "What're you gonna do?"

"What *can* I do?" He really couldn't think of anything. It was too late to change the show dance now. And talking to Kenji felt pointless, because what could he say? Promise not to drop Michelle? Shit happened, and they all knew it. "Should I even mention it to her? I mean, I'm assuming Kenji is not having this conversation with Michelle." He looked from Kelli to Elena and back.

"This is going to sound cold," Elena said slowly, "but like he says, it's his problem. He would feel the same way no matter who her partner was."

Tony made a slight movement, one that signaled disagreement. "It's different from us." That surprised

255

everybody because he generally didn't allude to any conflict he and Elena might have over the Mateo situation. "I may have the same concerns about safety, I may have the same resentment about time. But." He shrugged helplessly. "I can't help but feel that for Kenji, it's about." He hesitated.

"It's about sex," Kelli said bluntly. "Like we talked about way back. Vince is a sexy guy, everybody thinks so, and Kenji doesn't feel that way about himself. Nothing any of us can say or do will fix that. And, you know, there's something else I'd like to say to your camera."

Tony was surprised, but he said, "Now?"

"I'm not super camera-ready but if you want to take the time." She glanced at Vince, who made a 'no time like the present' gesture. She leaned over to kiss his cheek. "It's not your fault, baby. He said so himself." They conferred for a few minutes, then Tony got the camera set up while Kelli took a bathroom break. When she returned to the living room, Vince was sitting with Elena at the kitchen table. Kelli took a seat on the couch. "Let's go."

Tony started the camera. "We've spoken previously about your husband's partnership with Michelle Matsumoto. As their debut event draws near, how are you feeling?"

"I'm happy for him," she said. "For *them*. He is so, so good. Michelle was phenomenal with Dmitri but I honestly think she's even better with Vince. Because, you know, he's loco." Tony laughed. "He'll do anything. They're gonna do their thing, and the whole ballroom world is going to go" - she made a confused Scooby Doo sound - "what just happened. There are a few people out there who know Michelle is working with a new partner. But you know those ballroom people, they don't look outside to the other circuits. They won't know Vince Connor from the Salsa Challenge or the Tango Championships. They are going to get a hell of a surprise."

"When did you last see them dance?"

"Last weekend. Obviously I saw them doing their stuff for the pro show, and I saw every one of the prep-phase show dances. But I knew they were changing some stuff after 'Face the Music,' so I said tell me when it's done and I'll come in to watch. It's bananas how good they are."

"The year of preparation was a good strategy, then."

"Oh my lord, yes. They were patient, and they found their groove. There is no doubt in my mind that this is what Vince was born to do."

"When will the two of you dance again?"

"Very soon. We're dancing in 'Milonga.' He says he wants to do November and December too, I have no idea what yet, but when the Cabaret posted 'Mamboscope' for November it was like, okay, gotta do that."

Tony was grinning. "So he's doing four ballroom routines and a show dance with Michelle, and three show dances with you."

"Yeah." Kelli was grinning too. "I win." Tony cracked up. Kelli could see Elena had her hand over her mouth. Vince was shaking his head, laughing silently. "But seriously. I honestly hope that this works for all of us. All four of us. It is not easy to do what Vince and Michelle are trying to do, and it's not easy to be on the sidelines like me and Kenji. But what I've been thinking is, it's the same in any sport. Isn't it? If they were playing mixed doubles tennis, or, I don't know. Golf? I hate sports." Tony stifled the laugh this time. "It's time, and money, and time, and proximity to the teammate, and time, and risk, and time. It's tough, and I think the only reason I'm okay with it is I have safe spaces to say, this is tough. I have people making it okay for me to have moments where I'm not okay. I hope all four of us get that, because I want them to fucking *win*." She knew Tony would bleep that, but there were times when no other word would do.

They didn't talk much on the way home. When Vince parked, he didn't immediately get out of the car. Kelli turned her head. "You okay?"

He was gazing at her. "I love you so much. I literally could not do this without you. You're my Patrick."

Kelli gulped, instantly tearing up. "Your number-one fan," she said shakily.

"I remember the night we met. Going up to dance with you at Monsoon. Then having dinner, and going home from that thinking I am not going to do better. She is perfect. Now all I have to do is be perfect for her." He smiled a little. "Not for a minute have I second-guessed that."

"Jesus, Vince." She was fully crying now.

He was wet-eyed too. "If we win, that trophy will be as much for you as it is for me."

"When. *When* you win." She sniffed, swallowed, heaved a breath. "Let's go in, mi amor. Hopefully the monsters didn't give Esme a bad time tonight."

He reached over, touched her face, leaned in for a kiss. "Mi corazón. Siempre mi amor."

November 2017

Vince was pacing. Kelli watched him go up and down the row of tables, spectacular in his tuxedo. She and Michelle had fought him and won on the issue of makeup. His skin tone didn't call for tanner, but a little eyeliner went a long way. His expertly-cut black hair was swept back, controlled with gel and spray. The style allowed his sideburns and eyebrows - grown more emphatic as he approached forty - to define his face. Michelle was standing beside Kelli's chair, shoes off, absent-mindedly working her feet against the carpet. "Your husband looks amazing," she said after a minute. Kelli stifled a laugh. "I mean," Michelle leaned down so she wouldn't be overheard, "the rest of these guys hardly even look like men with him in the room." Kelli laughed out loud. She couldn't deny it.

Some of the other Smooth competitors were taller than Vince, and none of them were unpleasant-looking. But he had that Thing. It was the same thing that, combined with world-class talent, had made Hiro Miyazaki a multi-year champion in International Latin, and Ricky Castillo a repeat World Salsa Champion. It was not a thing that had come to the American Smooth dance floor very often. Even Dmitri, a charismatic competitor, had not conveyed such total physical confidence.

Michelle was still leaning close. She turned her head toward Kelli. "I hardly have to ask about your sex life, do I?" Kelli started giggling all over again. "Wish I could say the same."

"Oh no! What's the matter?"

"Kenji hates our show dance. He thinks I don't know." Michelle's husband was sitting with Dmitri at the next table. "He thinks I'm going to break myself into a million pieces."

Kelli knew that Kenji had a tendency to withdraw when he was unhappy about something. He didn't fight, he didn't complain, he just disappeared into his work. Kelli suspected that when Michelle got home from a rehearsal, she didn't go searching for her husband. If she was like Vince, all she wanted was something to eat, a shower, and bed. Although Vince was still invariably happy to find Kelli in his bed, and let her know it. It sounded like Kenji was disappearing there too. *Ugh*, she thought, *this is awkward*, and offered, "Well, it is pretty fast and furious."

"It feels like a pole-dance routine," Michelle said, finally sitting down, arranging the skirt of her ballgown so she could hook one ankle over the other knee and stretch. "It's a full-body workout. I love it."

"I was a little nervous about it myself the first few times. I know Mike coached Vince on all those tricks, but they're still new." Kelli combined a deep breath with a shoulder roll. "I shouldn't worry. He's Mr. Do It Right Or Not At All. If he wasn't getting that shit, he would take it out, right? Save it for next time?"

"Exactly right. He's hitting them every time in practice." Kelli was reassured. Then Michelle said, "I'm not at my best right now."

"What do you mean?" Kelli studied her friend. "You don't mean your dancing." She would not have thought that this would come up now, but evidently it was time to Talk.

"No, it's … I shouldn't talk about this here." But she didn't stand up, and she looked troubled. Kelli leaned in close, so they could hear each other but no one else could hear. "I'm pushing back. I'm pushing him away. I'm so annoyed that this is an issue. It's not fair, I wish I could stop, but goddammit."

"Sweetie, have you guys gone to a counselor?"

Michelle pressed her hands to her temples. "Maybe we should."

"You should if you're planning to take this show dance to Ohio. That's a long time to let something fester." The Ohio Star Ball was nearly a year in the future. Kelli knew that Vince and Michelle intended to go. They had an excellent chance of winning the Rising Star division by then, as well as the show dance. After that, they would compete in the Open Professional division, shooting for the World Championship. "Seriously, honey, the only reason this is working for me is Vince sticks to that calendar so we have time together. Well, and he fucks me blind about once a week." Michelle sputtered, laughing behind her hand. Kelli put a hand on her shoulder. "I know poor Kenji has already been through all this once, he probably hoped you'd never do it again, but you are doing it. And it's going to take years. You guys could be in real trouble if you don't sort this out."

"I know." Michelle sat back, switched legs, and stretched the other side. Both women were ignoring the event currently on the dance floor. "I'd better get up on my feet again so I don't congeal. Where's Vince?"

Kelli tuned in. "Still doing laps. And there's only one more event before your Rising Star. I'll walk with you."

CHAPTER 19

Vince pretended not to be watching Kenji, who was sitting beside Dmitri. He'd been trying to maintain the professionalism that was keeping their friendship from imploding. But Kenji should be walking with his wife; he should have been sitting with her. That they weren't even at the same table seemed ominous.

He couldn't hear what Dmitri said, or Kenji's reply. But Kenji stood and looked down the row of tables, catching sight of Michelle and Kelli. Vince had joined them; they were all returning to the Shall We Dance tables. When they got there, Vince picked up his water bottle and took a swig. Then he checked the state of his patent-leather shoes (still perfectly shiny), looked out over the dance floor, and finally nodded to Kenji. He didn't say anything, kept his face blank, as if all his concentration was on the coming event. Kenji stepped close to Michelle, who was sitting down again and leaning over, reaching for her shoes, and knelt in front of her. "I'll get those for you." He took one foot and slid it into the shoe, fastened the diamanté buckle, and lightly caressed her calf. He glanced up to see that she was smiling at him. He smiled back before addressing the second shoe. "You look beautiful," he said, looking up at her again.

"Thanks, honey." Michelle let Kenji pull her to her feet, and leaned close. He kissed her lightly.

"Time to go." Kenji offered his arm. Vince was hugging Kelli and giving her a not-at-all-light kiss before heading for the on-deck area. Kenji walked with Michelle. Before he left, he tugged Michelle close, whispered, "I love you," and kissed her again properly.

262

"Oh," she said when he let her go. "I love you too." She was smiling. He ran his thumb under her lower lip, where the scarlet lacquer was slightly smudged. She patted his chest. "See you in a few."

Vince said "Everything okay?" after Kenji was out of earshot.

"I think so." Michelle sounded surprised. "You ready for this?"

"Fuck no." She laughed. The other couples waiting to be called to the floor looked over at them, smiling in reaction.

There were fourteen couples in the Rising Star Smooth event. Vince and Michelle made the final. In the second round, Kelli moved to sit beside Dmitri. They watched with concentration, trying to identify any weaknesses in their dancers' performance or technique compared to the other couples on the floor. After this event, there would be two months to correct or refine the routines before the next competition. Dmitri shook his head slightly. Kenji said, "There's not much wrong, is there?"

"No." Waltz, tango, and foxtrot had been perfectly executed. The style was up to date, and the choreography was distinctive. Vince's musicality was a serious advantage in Smooth. Kelli knew that at least two other leaders in the final had switched from International Standard, and their connection to the music was nowhere near as good. Now the finalists were dancing the Viennese waltz. It had evolved so much from when Michelle was competing with Dmitri, becoming a blend of styles, with only the strong, fast 1-2-3 rhythm to tell the audience which dance it was. The DJ had chosen a modern pop track. Vince knew exactly what to do with it. When Michelle was suddenly blocked by another competitor, he simply moved in and scooped her away, breaking from their routine to turn a potential collision into a spontaneous moment of near-flight. Kelli squealed with delight. She heard Dmitri say "Excellent."

"He kept her foot on the floor." Kenji was smiling too. Michelle had followed Vince's improvisation to a clear space on the floor. They'd gone back into choreography. "Are they going to place tonight?"

Dmitri half-shrugged, unwilling to commit. After a moment he said, "He will be better than me," as if to himself. Kelli glanced over; Dmitri was smiling.

Kenji said, "Only you could say that and sound pleased about it. Where is Patrick tonight?"

"His niece is married tomorrow. Tonight, the rehearsal." Dmitri stood to applaud, looking satisfied, as the emcee confirmed the end of the round. Michelle and Vince started off the floor, both smiling. Vince said something to Michelle and she laughed. She was looking for Kenji. He took a step away from the table and extended a hand.

She took it, moving close and folding her arm so that both their hands came to her breast. "Did you see that? I thought I was going to crash for sure, and then swoop! I didn't even know what direction we were going for a second there."

"It was great. If the other dancer hadn't looked so startled, it would have seemed the whole thing was planned. You'll see, on the video." He leaned in for a kiss. "How long till the show dance?"

"Like, no time, I have to change." The emcee was announcing a short break for general dancing.

"I'll help." He turned his head to locate Vince, who was letting go of Kelli and turning toward the changing room. "Vince, do you need anything for the change?"

"No, I'm good, thanks. See you back here in a few." Vince smiled over his shoulder and kept moving. Kenji and Michelle followed along.

Dmitri looked around at his tables; nearly every seat was vacant. Everyone knew that his attention was all on the new competitors, so his colleagues and students had been occupying themselves. He'd been aware of their applause and cheers while Vince and Michelle were on the floor. Now most of them were out there dancing, taking advantage of the music. He turned to Kelli. "Shall we dance?"

"I would be honored," she said, and placed her hand in his. They stayed on the floor until the emcee warned that the general-dancing break was ending, calling the show-dance competitors to the on-deck area. Kelli looked that way, shielding her eyes from the glare of the lights. "Is Michelle in her fight robe?"

"She says the costume is a surprise. You have seen it?"

"Yeah, just last week. You haven't?"

"Somehow it is never dress rehearsal when I am there." Dmitri sounded indulgent. They headed back to the table.

Kelli realized that the risers behind them were now packed full of people she knew, from the Underground Cabaret as well as the studio, plus friends and co-workers. "Wow, I think everybody I know in L.A. is here. This is nuts!" She waved, grinning, then making an 'eek!' face as the emcee called the first couple in the show dance event. She sat down next to Dmitri, still holding his hand and not even realizing it.

He glanced over at Kenji, who was just now joining them, and who looked considerably happier than he had earlier. "Is all well?"

"Everything's good," said Kenji softly, as music started for the first couple. "I wish they weren't dancing last, though."

Kelli murmured, "Me too. I'm all amped up." They had to wait through three more performances before it was finally time for Vince and Michelle. When they were announced, the ballroom lights went down to almost full dark. Dmitri had used the same tactic in his last show dance with Michelle; it gave the couple time to get into position on the floor. Now a spotlight came on, revealing Michelle in a sleek black costume: cap-sleeved leotard, fishnets, and lace-up mesh dance boots. All the pins were out of her hair; it fell to just above her shoulders, carelessly tousled. Vince was in black Latin pants. His fresh white shirt was buttoned only halfway up over a white tank top, with the sleeves rolled up and pinned. He'd changed from his patent-leather smooth shoes to matte-black jazz shoes. They looked like they had come to play. Someone in the audience wolf-whistled. Then the music started, Christina Aguilera's unmistakable voice filling the ballroom as the lights came up.

In the first few bars, Michelle and Vince did a complicated series of lifts and tricks, ending the lyric 'and you can't keep a good girl down' with Michelle perched on his shoulder. Then he flipped her down and they went into sixteen counts of jazz. From there it was straight into a foxtrot sequence that broke out into quickstep. Half of the spectators were clapping along in time to the music. The routine was nonstop action, with lifts and tricks scattered throughout foxtrot, quickstep, and jazz sequences racing around the floor.

It seemed Michelle's legs were constantly in the air, but Vince was flying almost as much as she was. There was hardly time for the crowd to react to one stunt before there was another. When they hit their final Fosse-esque pose after 'show me how you burlesque,' the applause was thunderous. They took several bows before exiting the floor at the back corner.

"Well," Kenji said to Dmitri, "that could hardly be more different from the last one you did."

Dmitri's final competitive show dance with Michelle had been a heart-wrenching adagio. He said, "No one will remember that now."

"Oh sure they will," Kelli protested. "That was a wonderful dance. Everybody was bawling." Dmitri made a sound that might have been a laugh. "Man oh man. I see them in rehearsal and they never just mark it through, but wow!" She fanned herself. "That looked really solid. Like, titanium. Don't you think so, Kenji?"

"Yes I do," he said. "She's never looked stronger. And Vince was sensational."

"They'd better win." Kelli wasn't sure if the awards were being given out immediately. The emcee hadn't called for more general dancing, though there was some music playing. The crowd was restive. Some of the gang on the risers started chanting 'Shall We Dance,' and Dmitri was visibly trying not to laugh. It wasn't all that long before the emcee announced the final awards of the evening, and called up the seven couples from the last round of the American Smooth competition. Vince and Michelle appeared again; she was back in her fight robe and he was in a long-sleeved gray thermal. "I'll bet that white shirt is soaked," Kelli said. "Damn, I'm glad I wasn't doing that. That was some crazy shit." Dmitri snorted and Kenji laughed.

They waited, nervous, applauding each couple as the places were announced. When the fourth-place couple was called and it wasn't Vince and Michelle, things got loud on the risers again. Then it was "Placing second in all dances, Vince Connor and Michelle Matsumoto!" The risers went nuts.

Kelli and Kenji looked at each other. "I suppose they couldn't place them first. Not their first time out," he said grudgingly. She laughed, still applauding as the winners were announced. As soon as the official photos were taken and the Smooth finalists left the floor, the emcee called the show-dance competitors. Vince and Michelle stepped back onto the floor with the others. The 'Shall We Dance' chant started again. Vince was cracking up. When he and Michelle were announced as the show-dance winners, it was pandemonium. They barely made it back to the table for hugs from Kelli, Kenji, and Dmitri before being swarmed by their friends.

It was some time before things settled down. Michelle said, "I need to get these fishnets off, stat. Kenji, can you give me a hand?"

"Always," he said. "Always happy to help you take your clothes off." It was so out of character for him to say something like that in public that her eyebrows went up, but she couldn't help laughing. He put his arm around her and they headed for the changing room for the last time.

Vince sat down and blew out a breath. "Fuck me, what a night. How'd I do, boss?" The awards didn't really mean anything unless his coach was satisfied.

"Excellent," said Dmitri. "Better than me."

"Um, that's impossible. But if you're saying we don't need to change a bunch of shit before Cal Open, you know, yay." He leaned back against Kelli, who was standing behind him, and looked up. "Hey gorgeous. Shall we go see if the video is ready?"

"Sure." She leaned down to kiss him. "You were incredible. Awesome. Smoking hot. In the tango, there was this girl across the floor like -" she mimed leaning on her hand in a swoon. Vince laughed, rolling out of the chair to stand up. They went across the floor, holding hands, to the video vendor's table. After they collected their disc, they spotted Kenji and Michelle working their way along the edge of the ballroom, heading for the doors. "Kenji had some kind of breakthrough," Kelli said. "In the nick of time, too."

"Glad to hear it. Michelle always puts on the happy face, but I could tell something was up."

"She needs to get laid," Kelli said in his ear. He laughed. "I think that might happen tonight. Oh, are we not going home?" Vince had turned toward the elevators for the hotel, instead of the garage. He didn't say anything as they stepped into a car. "You better have some overnight stuff for me."

"You can wear one of my shirts to breakfast. Ma said not to come home, she'd keep us up all night chattering, and she thought you might like to be up all night some other way." His garment bag was slung over his shoulder and his other arm was around her waist.

"Well, that depends. Are you going to be up all night?" Kelli had her mouth on his throat and a hand on his body. "Conditions are promising."

June 2018

Dmitri and Michelle prepared a routine for the Cabaret's show celebrating California. So did Vince and Kelli. All four of them were, like more than half of

269

the cast, involved with a low-budget independent film about tango that would start filming the following month. Vince and Michelle were also still on campaign. They were no longer the subjects of Tony's documentary, however.

"It's so weird to be doing this without the camera," Vince said one day after a rehearsal at Shall We Dance. "Tony checked in last month. Said well done at the Emerald Ball. Asked if we were going to Ohio in Open Professional."

"What did you tell him?"

"Told him we hadn't decided yet. What do you think?" They were sitting side by side in the office, across from the empty chair that – during regular studio hours, and when he wasn't out on the dance floor – was generally occupied by Dmitri. His new manager had her own office in the recently-acquired adjacent space.

Michelle gazed back at Vince. She and Dmitri had discussed this very question the day before. "The boss says if we don't move ourselves up pretty soon people are going to push back." It was the same reason they'd done their show dance only once – at the Emerald Ball – since their debut the previous November. They wanted to take that same show dance to the Ohio Star Ball. Too many wins would look greedy; they had to leave room for other people to do well. And they'd been placing first or second in the Rising Star multi-dance event at every competition. They had three more on their schedule before Ohio. "I'm game if you are. The worst that can happen is we don't place." Michelle was confident they would make the final. "How are you going to feel if that happens?"

"As long as we still win the show dance," Vince said, knowing it would make her laugh. "Look, I want two championships, same as the boss. If we could knock out the first one next year, instead of the year after?" He gazed back at Michelle. "Pretty sure your husband would be happy if we got it done as fast as possible."

Michelle grimaced. "He's feeling a lot better about it now than he did when we started, or even right before Cal Star last fall. But yeah. The faster we can wrap it up the happier he's going to be."

"Are you going to be happy to call it at two?" He knew his tone and face said 'because I hope so.'

Michelle sat back and blew out a breath, studying him for a minute. Then another minute, during which she seemed to be thinking hard. Vince raised his eyebrows, inviting an answer. "Oh. Yes. Really," she added. "Because that's four for me, which is ridiculous. At my age? With two partners? Hello, luckiest girl in the world here."

"So if we win it twice, you're going to retire from competition?"

"Yes." It sounded both confident and untroubled. "I haven't got a clue what I'll do after that, but I'm not going to cling to it just because I don't know what comes next."

"There's always the Cabaret." Vince was smiling now.

"You're going back into tango, aren't you."

He didn't answer directly. "Well, I think that the student showcases might need to move to a different venue. Alison said that May did really well, but that was the Andrew Lloyd Webber tribute so it got a lot of the regular Cabaret audience. April, not so much."

"If we find a new venue for the showcases, or if we just stop staging those, actual *shows* might get back on the schedule at Chrome. The whole calendar might get shuffled." Michelle was still involved with managing the Underground Cabaret. It kept evolving.

"It might."

"I should talk to Alison after 'Democracy.' I know her head is exploding right now." That year's pro show was already in rehearsal. "But we have jumped the track."

Vince laughed under his breath. "Yeah, we have. But I guess we basically made the decision. We're entering Open Professional at the Ohio Star Ball, where we may or may not get our asses handed to us." She snorted out a laugh. "We'll do the current show dance there. And after that, we'll make a new show dance. Do you want to re-work the routines a little before Ohio?"

"We should. When can we do that?" Michelle already had her phone in hand, looking at their calendar.

"We'll have five weeks between Chicago and Ohio. That's enough time, right?"

"Plenty of time. And speaking of time, let's get out of here." Michelle stood up. There was more than a month before she and Vince were traveling again; they had nothing to change; they were basically only running what they already had. "I'll see you next week."

"Yeah. Say hi to Matsumoto-san for me." She patted his shoulder and went out. Vince sat there for another minute, sending a text to Tony. Then he sent one to Kelli to let her know he was on his way home. He added: *Got a little anniversary present for you Mrs. Connor*

She replied right away: *Oh yeah? How big of a box is it in?*

He laughed. *It won't fit in a box.* That would keep her guessing.

All Vince told Kelli was that the present was at the dance studio. She honestly had no idea what kind of scheme he was running. If he hadn't been up to his ass in tango choreography (for the movie) for the past three months, and up to his neck in ballroom for the past eighteen, she would think it might be something to do with dancing. But they'd done that routine at 'On the Edge,' they were doing all kinds of stuff together for the movie, they'd be dancing again at this year's edition of 'Milonga,' and he swore there would be something for 'Under the Mistletoe' in December. She'd assured him that she did not feel neglected. Now she said, "No hints?" as they made their way up to West Hollywood.

"No hints." He was looking awfully smug over there in the driver's seat. *Awfully sexy, too*, she thought. He had to be one of the best-looking thirty-nine-year-olds on planet Earth. He parked the car, they got out, and they walked up to the studio. Vince opened the door and held it for Kelli.

"SURPRISE!"

She shrieked a little, and then started laughing. "Holy hell I just about peed my pants! You are all so sneaky!"

"Go put your dance shoes on," Vince said. "You're performing tonight."

"I am not."

"Yes you are." He pulled her close and kissed her. "Happy fifth anniversary, baby. I love you. Sorry we couldn't do this on the actual day."

"I love you too, and I don't care. I got a different present on that day." A present called 'great sex.' "Did you sneak a pair of my shoes in here when I wasn't looking?"

"Yes I did." Kelli kissed him again, but she was shaking her head when she went over to the office. She knew that was where he'd have stashed things.

While Kelli put her shoes on, someone started some music. Someone else opened the champagne. The studio was full of their friends. It was so much like their wedding party that she felt she'd gone back in time. *Good present, honey*, she thought as she left the office. "Do I get some champagne before this performance?"

"You might want to keep your wits about you."

"Lord have mercy." She was laughing as he led her to the middle of the floor. They stood there together, talking and laughing with Vicky and Elliott and a dozen others, until the music got really quiet. "Oh you did not." Vince started dancing. It was 'Bring Me Sunshine,' of course. He was singing along. "You won't be able to keep that up when it kicks in," she said. Trying to keep it light so she wouldn't cry. Crying was not called for here. She had the best man in the world, and the best friends in the world, and she was the luckiest woman in the world.

She still thought so at the end of that song, even though she was out of breath. Vince didn't leave the floor, because the next song was 'You Are My Sunshine,' and apparently they were doing a little foxtrot. They weren't the only ones now; lots of other people were dancing. When the next song started – Ella Fitzgerald's cover of 'Sunshine of Your Love' – the floor was crowded. By the end of that one, Kelli and Vince were kissing too much to get a lot of dancing done.

Half an hour later, everyone in the place had worked their way over for hugs, kisses, and congratulations. Vince was talking to Elliott over in the corner; Kelli took Alicia into the new space to find a couple of chairs. "He did good," she said, leaning over to stretch her hamstrings.

"Yes he did," Alicia said. "E says he is setting the bar unacceptably high." Kelli laughed, still face-to-knees. Alicia patted her on the back. "You're having another great year. Just like old times."

Kelli sat up. "For real! Only, what the fuck, a fucking movie?!" They both cackled. Then she changed the subject. "So you're really buying that house?"

"We're not going to find a better place in this market. The fact that it's in your neighborhood is a bonus."

"Your commute is gonna suck," Kelli warned. "Or, crazy idea. Maybe we could carpool. Take turns." She was the HR manager now. The firm offered her one day a week to work from home, but she liked being able to keep it separate. Having someone to share the drive with would be great.

Alicia turned and stared at her, thinking. "You know, that might work. Actually," she hesitated. Kelli made a 'say it' face. "I was wondering what the odds were of Esmeralda being willing to add a kid to the corral."

"Huh!" Kelli thought about it. It definitely made no sense for Alicia or Elliott to bring Elizabeth all the way up from Westchester to West L.A. for daycare. "Let's ask!" She dug in her pocket – all of her clothes had pockets now, thanks to knowing a few designers – and pulled out her phone. Sent a text. Looked at her friend. "She will insist that you don't have to pay her."

"Well, too bad." Kelli's phone pinged. She read the text and turned it around. Alicia said, "Aww. Can I?" Kelli handed the phone over. *Hi Esme this is Alicia*

275

you are an angel. But no we absolutely will pay you and don't argue or we will get the men involved

A few seconds later Esmeralda's reply landed, a crying-laughing emoji. "Okay, that's handled." Kelli was actually thrilled. Moving out of WeHo had been such a huge change; they'd seen so much less of all their friends. Having more of their own people in walking distance again was going to be an unmixed blessing. "Let's go find those guys of ours." She put the phone away and stood, pulling Alicia up off her chair and into a hug. "So glad."

"Me too." Alicia patted her. "Time to dance some more, movie star."

Kelli was still snickering about that ten minutes later, when she was in Vince's arms again. "We're going to fucking *own* 'Milonga' this year," she mumbled after a while, face pressed against his neck. She felt him laugh.

"You don't think you'll be sick of tango by then?" Principal photography was in July; they were both committed for multiple days. The thought of being in a movie was pretty mind-blowing.

Kelli eased back enough to make eye contact. "Sick of dancing tango with you? Mr. Movie Choreographer Gonna Be A Champion? That's a no." He was blushing a little; she was delighted.

Vince cleared his throat. He and Michelle had won Rising Star the previous month, but "Don't jinx us." She made a dismissive sound. "We may not be able to get back to Argentina for a while." They were dancing tango again, to another song that wasn't really a tango.

"When we go, it'll be like our honeymoon all over again. Which means we're not taking the kids." He laughed out loud. Kelli was grinning. "Just you and me, mi amor."

"Forever, mi corazón." He kissed her again.

THE END

The show that brings Kelli back to the Chrome stage was conceived for the novel titled 'FACE THE MUSIC.' With a cast of eighteen dancers, I was able to involve a lot of my characters! Here is the show I've imagined.

Act 1 – Foxtrot & Swing

A: Duet – Let's Face the Music and Dance – Nat King Cole; performed by Vince & Michelle

B: Group – Dance Me to the End of Love – Madeleine Peyroux; performed by Mike & Paula, Dmitri & Alison, Hiro & Vicky

C: Jazz – Strange Face of Love – Tito & Tarantula; performed by Mike & Paula

D: Urban – Gettin' in the Mood – Brian Setzer Orchestra; performed by Lucas, Hiro, Sam & Mateo

Act 2 – Cha-Cha & Rumba

A: Jazz – Ain't No Other Man – Christina Aguilera; performed by Ann, Bonnie & Hiro

B: Group - Pa' Bailar (Siempre Quiero Más) – Bajofondo + Julieta Venegas; performed by Hiro & Vicky, Vince & Kelli, Sam & Mateo, Ricky & Anya

C: Urban – Is You Is Or Is You Ain't My Baby – Dinah Washington (Verve Remixed); performed by Lucas, Hiro & Anya

D: Duet – Sway – Michael Bublé; performed by Sam & Mateo

Act 3 – Tango

A: Duet – Diferente – Gotan Project; performed by Red & Mary

B: Urban – I've Seen that Face Before – Grace Jones; performed by Lucas, Ricky & Anya

C: Contemporary – Oblivion – Quintango; performed by Mike & Paula

D: Group – Santa Maria – Gotan Project; performed by Vince & Kelli, Sam & Mateo, Hiro & Vicky, Mike & Paula

Act 4 – Waltz

A: Urban – Misty Blue – Dorothy Moore (Chilled Jazz); performed by Lucas, Ann, Alison & Bonnie

B: Group – Still Crazy After All These Years – Ray Charles; performed by Mike & Paula, Vince & Michelle, Hiro & Vicky

C: Contemporary – Please Forgive Me – Melissa Etheridge; performed by Dmitri & Michelle

D: Duet – A Thousand Years – Christina Perri; performed by Mike & Paula

Author's note:

The House of Blues nightclub on the Sunset Strip closed in 2015. It was an iconic music venue. The pro/am variety show on New Year's Eve, 2011 as described in this book is entirely fictitious.

*****

About the Author

Alexandra Caluen lives in a small purple house with her husband, a bottle of Laphroaig, a lot of books, and nine pairs of ballroom shoes. She works in patent law and has enough hair for three people.

Find out more about this story universe at:

www.thelastories.com